Also by Mitch Davies

A Wind In Montana

The Inn of Fallen Leaves

This novel is a work of fiction. The characters and events are creations of the author's imagination. Any similarities between the fictitious characters and events to persons living or dead and events past, present or future are purely coincidental.

Library of Congress Control Number:  2010912984

ISBN 978-0-9843907-8-6

Published in the United States by Pensmith

A tribute to
Robert Louis Stevenson's tale of the South
Pacific,
The Ebb-Tide.

*Stolen Breeze*


By


Mitch Davies

# Prologue

After a day of filthy work at the marina, Ben Beck stopped at the fish-and-chips shop he'd become addicted to. With a six-pack in one grimy hand and an order of halibut and fries with an extra piece of fish in the other, he was all set for his favorite dinner. He'd frequented the shop almost every night since he discovered it on his way to the run-down motel located within walking distance of his new job. The greasy fish smell that filled his room made him smile and told him he was as close to a home as he could get right now.

He turned on the black and white television set and popped open a can of beer. On the end of the bed he spread the pile of brochures for a local amusement park—he'd taken them from the stand in the motel lobby. He pulled the contents of his meal from the bag and placed the gray cardboard cartons on the brochures. The first bite of fish burned his mouth, forcing him to juggle the meat lightly on his tongue while huffing, mouth wide open, to remove the heat. His urgent attempt to cool his burning tongue created a loud panting noise that prevented him from hearing the doorknob turn. The sudden change in air temperature caused him to turn toward the open door.

A tall, dark-haired man stood blocking the opening.

Ben forgot about the tongue-burning fish in his mouth and stared at the odd but familiar-looking man. When he realized who stared back at him, he spat the fish out onto the brown, grunge-stained carpet. "Oh shit. Carl?"

Carl stepped into the room as another man rolled around the wall into the room and side stepped to Carl's left.

"Duane?" Ben asked.

Duane pointed a gun at Ben as Carl slowly reached for the edge of the door and closed it. Both men wore dark, baggy clothing.

"How did you guys find me here?"

"We never lost you, Ben. We just couldn't approach you until the FBI agents decided to leave."

"FBI agents?"

"Don't worry, they're gone now." Carl smiled his big white smile, looking more like the happy, confident man Ben remembered. "You took something from me, Ben."

"I didn't mean to knock him overboard. I didn't even know I'd hit him," Ben explained.

"Not Rudy . . . fuck him. He can soak in the cold watery hell you sunk him in. That prick was blackmailing me anyway." The smile still glowed. "Where's Miss Malloy?"

"That I truly don't know. I left her outside the airport in Tahiti."

Carl said, "Duane told me you spent her last night onboard in her cabin. He also told me the two of you got a little greedy. You stole all my money, then you took the little bit Duane and Rudy had stashed as well. Not very nice, Ben. The two of you have really pissed me off."

"I gave her Rudy's, Duane's and my money. I don't know anything about *your* money."

Carl stepped back and leaned against the door. He tilted his head forward and stared at the floor, working the muscles in his lips. When he finally looked up again he said, "I need them both back, Ben. You got one chance. Tell me now; help me out. You know I'm going to find her anyway, so if you help me, you keep on living."

"What?" At the sound of the threat, Ben began to think about how he was going to get out of the room.

"Normally Rudy would do this sort of thing, but thanks to you he's not available. And, with the kind of heat you've placed on me, none of my other contacts are taking my calls. You've forced me to do this myself. Where is she, Ben?" Carl's voice stayed calm.

"Carl, I don't . . . " In mid-sentence Ben swiped backhand at the food that lay in front of him, sending it in the direction of Duane, who was holding the gun. The large fish chunks flew off level with the bed and landed on the floor, but the fries got airborne and shot toward Duane. He stood his ground, letting two or three of them hit him in the chest, but otherwise didn't react to the attempted distraction.

Ben rolled across the bed away from them and landed on the floor. He listened to see which direction they had moved.

"Get up, you idiot," Carl demanded.

Ben looked around for something else to throw, but found nothing. Slowly he stood to see Carl and Duane standing in the same place. He moved nearer the table bolted to the wall next to the bed. His hand shot out and grabbed the phone, and he threw it at Duane. The phone's cord stopped it halfway to the target; the receiver continued on its trajectory, missed its mark, and landed with a thud. It scraped along the floor as the outstretched cord drew in its coils.

Carl and Duane stared at Ben. "This is ridiculous. Are you done?" Carl asked.

"No." Ben turned his back and sat down on the bed. As soon as his haunches touched the mattress, he grabbed the square, brown glass ashtray, turned, and sent it spinning at Duane's head. Duane saw it coming and turned to his left, but too late. A corner of the ashtray struck the cartilage near the back of his right ear, cutting through it. His own momentum, the impact of the ashtray, and the immediate burning sensation caused him to hit the wall and drop to his knees. Ben followed the ashtray over the bed. As Duane reached up to protect his ear with his empty hand, Ben hit him in the jaw, crashing his head hard into the wall. Duane fell unconscious to the floor. Ben reached for the gun as Carl landed on his back, and together they landed on top of Duane. Ignoring Carl's grasping hands, Ben concentrated on getting a firm grip on the pistol. When he felt his hand close tight around its grip, he tensed his shoulders and neck, and then labored to stand under the tall man's weight. Carl's fingers dug into Ben's shoulder; his other arm stretched across Ben's face, twisting his head back and to the side. Ben pushed back hard toward the wall, slamming Carl into the thermostat box. He heard Carl's breath jet from his lungs with a deep grunt. He took a quick step away from the wall, braced his leg, and slammed back again. When he heard Carl gasping to refill his lungs, he jabbed back with his elbow and struck him in the soft flesh just below his ribs. Carl slid off his back, landing on his side when he hit the floor. He rolled to look up wild-eyed at Ben, his mouth open but unable to draw in air.

Carl slapped the floor and pulled his knees into his abdomen while making short sucking noises. Ben offered no help.

"You have to believe me, Carl. I don't know where she is, and I don't know anything about your money. There's nothing I can help you with." He opened the door, ran down the metal stairs to the parking lot, and turned toward the street.

When he arrived at the sidewalk, he stopped and looked both ways. The marina and other places he was familiar with were to the left, so he turned right and ran as fast as he could. When his lungs started to burn, he hid in a dark corner at the side of a building.

He realized he had been running with the gun still in his hand. He tucked it into his pants and bent over to catch his breath, but the gun poked at his stomach. He pulled it out and decided to get rid of it, knowing he would never use it. He fumbled to get the clip out, then went to the back of the building and threw the gun in a trash bin. He removed the bullets from the clip, and then threw them and the clip over the fence into an open lot.

He had nowhere to go, so he climbed the fence and rested against the wall. Tall grass and a stack of torn mattresses shielded him from the street. He felt he should keep moving, but he stayed in the parking lot until morning.

# Chapter 1

Ben thought that selling the dehydrated juice of young barley plants was going to be a sure thing. It had to be—the obvious health benefits easily justified the purchase of the product.

He'd made good money in the beginning when he bought the franchise for central and northern Idaho. It hadn't cost a lot, and he signed up about twenty representatives in the first two months to be part of his marketing team. With the money he accumulated from the combined sales of his force, he purchased the franchise for eastern Washington and eventually built his team to thirty-nine members. Earnings were good. At the peak he was making about four thousand dollars a month, a lot more money than he had ever made in all his previous endeavors.

But this was the first opportunity in which he worked for himself. Another year and he would be earning in the six figures, just like the dealer had told him he would.

Throughout his life he had worked for different companies or different government agencies, mostly performing semi-skilled jobs or flat-out unskilled labor—like the ones he worked for a few years on the ski slopes.

Yet being his own man proved by far to be the best work ever. It was the eighties. The decade he felt was when he'd make it big, and the dehydrated juice of young barley plants was the ride he'd been waiting for.

Then his representatives saturated the market. They sold jars of dehydrated barley juice to every relative and friend they had. Strangers were a hard sell, but the relatives and friends were glad to help in the beginning and even said they felt they were getting the benefits the product promised. Over time they forgot to call for additional supplies. The representatives grew tired of preying on their families, and they couldn't stand the rejection of strangers. The orders stopped coming in. Then Ben's savings were gone, and he needed a job.

While he worked for others, he kept looking for the product that would have him working on his own again. This time, with the experience of previous franchise ownership, he asked a few more questions and for references to consult. As a result he did not get into the worm-farming franchises or into selling partial ownerships in jojoba bean oil cooperatives.

Even after he got the job working on the new hotel, he had tried to keep an eye on the franchise world. But he began to enjoy the construction work and the sense of accomplishment he was receiving at the site. He knew the job wouldn't last forever, so he satisfied his entrepreneurial spirit by reserving the intent to work for himself again after the job was completed.

When the construction job started, he was twenty-six years old and one of the oldest laborers on the project, so they gave him leadership responsibilities very quickly. The younger men listened to his instructions, assuming he had years of experience to back them up. In truth Ben had never worked in construction before. He applied common sense, listened to his boss, and followed instructions. As time went on, he gained the experience he had already been credited with. He learned to operate light machinery, and then he learned the signals for communicating with the crane operators. All the supervisors knew that if he didn't posses a certain skill already, he would surely pick it up after a short period of training. He became a fill-in guy for a wide range of jobs. For the last year of the project, he became a supervisor himself and managed his own pool of laborers. He found the work gratifying and the pay good. He took pride in knowing his hourly wage had increased a number of times in reward for his hard work, allowing him to entertain himself liberally while managing to build his savings account.

Three months after the construction ended on the very elaborate Grand Luxe Hotel and Resort, Benjamin Andrew Beck sat in his second-story apartment above the only horse and saddle shop left on Sherman Avenue. He looked out at downtown Coeur d'Alene. If he pressed the right side of his head against the window, he could see the thirty-one stories of the flashy hotel he had helped construct for the past two years.

On his first day of unemployment, Ben sat and looked out the window with the commitment to take his time and find the best possible opportunity. This time he wanted to find a franchise with real earning potential. On the thirtieth day, he lowered his standards a little and trimmed down the earning level he thought he required. On the ninetieth day he got desperate and decided that almost any job — didn't have to be a franchise — would be acceptable.

His life ran on the vapors remaining in his savings account. The franchise world had changed, and no other projects like the hotel would start up in the near future. Faced with these facts, he realized his definition of an acceptable opportunity had to be blown wide open. Sitting around doing nothing had to stop. If he didn't find something soon he would have to go beg for the job his friend had offered him a month earlier. A job he had turned down.

He sat in his bottom-sagging armchair with his feet resting on the radiator that ran along the wall under the window. Beneath his open bathrobe he wore only his pajama bottoms. Today he had slept late, and when he did get out of bed, he chose not to go downstairs to retrieve the paper from the hooks under the mailbox. For weeks the want ads had been offering the same old jobs he knew he couldn't bring himself to apply for.

Across the street, he could see people leaving the grill. To catch up to his normal routine, he forced his clothes over his limbs, then forced himself out the door and across the street to get lunch in the nearly empty bar, victorious once again over the inertia, to start a day of no hope.

Bells jingled on the opening door. He walked down the length of the tall wooden bar with its line of green vinyl stools fixed on tarnished chrome posts. Murals painted by the employees during the weekend the mountain erupted covered the back and side walls. They'd been stuck inside the bar with nothing to do but paint and drink free booze. Within the mural, prominent members of society were depicted performing a number of ludicrous acts. Those acts of an erotic nature had been repainted after the employees could safely leave the building and sober up. None of them could remember painting the erotica in the first place.

At the end of the bar stood a clear, one-gallon glass jar filled up a third of the way with quarters and the rest of the way with water. Submerged in the middle sat a solitary shot glass on the quarters.

Ben reached into his pocket, pulled out a quarter, and held it over a slot cut into the jar's lid.

"You better come and watch this," Ben said to the bartender who stood at the other end of the bar.

"Is the shot glass empty?" the bartender asked.

"Yes."

"Then fire away."

Ben hunched over to look at the shot glass, and then adjusted his aim of the quarter in the slot so he held it directly over the glass. With the point of his tongue poking from one corner of his open mouth, he let the quarter drop. The coin swooped to one side, then fluttered back and settled on the other coins soaking outside of the still-empty shot glass.

"Shit!" Ben slammed the bar top.

"Thank you. Please try again," the bartender said in a mechanical voice.

Ben walked back halfway down the bar and sat on one of the stools. Seconds later a glass of beer landed on the coaster and the bartender asked, "Burger?"

Ben nodded.

The bartender turned to a plastic tub filled with ground meat and pulled off a sizable handful, slapped it back and forth in his hands to form a patty, then flopped it onto the grill beside the tub. He cooked and delivered the burger, which Ben immediately lifted and bit into. He chewed, oblivious to life around him, his eyes closed, his cheeks stuffed. Taste and texture filled his mouth, the cheese soft, the meat juicy, the pickles and mustard tart.

"Everything all right there?" the bartender asked after waiting until Ben had a full mouth.

"Woo pwick," Ben mumbled around his food.

"Tim came in for lunch today. He asked about you," the bartender said. He walked down the bar to get a towel.

"I hate to say it, but I have to go see him about that job," Ben said.

"You two still not talking?"

"Yeah, I kind of toasted the bridge on that one. I hope I didn't burn it."

Tim Leweski held the title of Ben's Best Friend. He had offered Ben a job working at his father's car dealership a few weeks earlier, and Ben hadn't talked to him since. When Ben had politely declined and thanked Tim for the offer, Tim had implied that in Ben's current state of ambition, he probably wouldn't find a better one.

The putdown made Ben try harder to get a job on his own for the next several weeks. The distain he had felt then, returned as he ate his burger, but this time he thought he'd better swallow his pride and accept the job. As he neared completion of the sandwich, the bartender returned.

"You want a refill on the burger?"

"Yeah, why not?"

Ben ate the second burger, then wasted another quarter on the shot glass in the jar on his way out. On the street he looked toward the new hotel and admired his work. *I know how to do that,* he thought.

Back across the street, he looked into his landlord's store window to see if anything had changed. Nothing had and never did. He grabbed the paper and climbed his stairs. With the paper spread on the table he scanned the want ads for something he knew he wouldn't find. *The thrill of the hunt,* he would tell himself. He began to think of his hometown as an employment desert.

***

A few days later, Ben sat with his friend Tim Leweski in a booth near the back of the bar. In the mural above them, the ex-mayor rode a donkey that looked like the local newspaper's editor. Ben told Tim about his recent job-hunting efforts, all of which had resulted in no opportunities at all. "I've been thinking about the job you offered me. It's really a good job. So I decided I would like to come work for you and your dad, if the job's still available."

At twenty-eight, Ben knew he should be working to establish a normal life for himself. However, to him, normal also meant dull and predictable, and in his hometown he had no alternative.

Tim said, "Ben, I've been thinking about this since we talked. You put a lot of effort into finding another job after I offered that one to you, so I don't think you're really interested in the job with us.

"And I want you as my friend, not my employee. If you come to work for us, our relationship would be different. We'd know too much about what each other did all day—and dad and I would have to keep secrets from you, because some things you can't let your employees in on." Tim could see Ben losing a little steam. "I can't give you a job now. I can help you out if you need money, like a loan, but I can't hire you."

Ben slumped a little as if giving up. "I understand."

"Sorry, I hate seeing you sit around in that apartment with no prospects. What do you think you'll do?"

Ben stared at Tim for a few seconds, then shrugged. They continued their lunch in an uneasy quiet. Tim suggested various approaches to find a job, and Ben nodded in agreement at each idea. He didn't express the fact he had already tried everything Tim suggested.

When they paid their bill, they stopped at the glass jar filled with quarters and water, and each took out a quarter. They called the bartender over to witness their attempts, but he just asked if the shot glass was empty. He knew it was; if someone had been successful, he would have had to pay off with a free beer, but asking was part of the routine.

They got the go-ahead, and Ben lined up his quarter. He bent down to watch it drop and let it go. It flipped once, then a soft dive to the side, and it came to rest beside the glass wall of the jar.

"Not even close," Tim remarked as he placed his quarter above the slot. He pinched the edge of the quarter between his finger and thumb and let the bottom arch of the coin down into the slot. He took a look at the shot glass, and moved his other hand over the quarter with his index finger extended two inches over the coin. He looked at Ben and smirked, then snapped his finger down hard onto the coin, driving it straight through the water. They heard a muffled clink as the quarter landed in the shot glass.

"All right! A slam dunk. Gimme my beer!" Tim shouted with the spirit of a champion.

The bartender shook his head, then twisted the top off of a bottle and placed it in front of Tim.

"Enjoy your beer. I have to go." Ben shook Tim's hand and left.

When he stepped back out onto the street, his eyes returned to the Grand Luxe Hotel and Resort. He thought of the various stages during the construction and how he'd been involved in every one of them. He hadn't set foot in the place since he picked up his last paycheck. He'd be in that building right now if there had been more work. Instead, he did what he did every day—he crossed the street, stopped to look in the display window of his landlord's store, grabbed the paper from under his mailbox, and went upstairs to his apartment. He tossed the paper onto the kitchen table and went to change out of his pants into a pair of gym shorts. When he returned to the kitchen, he opened a beer, sat down at the table, and opened the paper to the want ads.

He spotted a few ads for domestics, a few for ranch workers, and a long list offering the opportunity to own your own business—none of which garnered his interest. Then his eyes settled on one that flipped his curiosity switch.

Sailors Wanted. Crew for
South Pacific. No Exp. Nec.
*691-5111 EXT. 3101*

Ben circled the ad and reread it a few times before scanning the rest of the section.

The thought of sailing to the South Pacific played with his imagination for the rest of the day. Sun, beaches, something new to do every day instead of sitting in an apartment hoping for a break in a fruitless routine. Finally he called the number. The receptionist greeted him by saying, "Thanks for calling the Grand Luxe. How may I help you?" Ben asked for the extension number in the ad. Once connected, he talked to a gentleman who set up an appointment for the next day.

Palm trees swaying in a light breeze and sandy beaches with scattered seashells projected in his mind all through the night as he tried to sleep. They tempted and excited him as they tore at the fact that he loved his hometown, a hometown that now offered no opportunity to create a reasonable life. Then he realized that for him, a reasonable life wouldn't do. He wanted a great one, one it appeared he would have to pursue elsewhere.

\*\*\*

The next afternoon, the concierge at the Grand Luxe escorted Ben to the penthouse elevator and used a key to send him to the top of the hotel. When the doors of the elevator opened, Ben found himself in a marble foyer facing a set of creamy white double doors flanked by antique white end tables topped with fresh flower arrangements. Ben spotted a rose-colored button mounted in an ornate fixture, also creamy white, and wondered if he was seeing things. *A knock won't do for people who stay in the penthouse? They have to have a doorbell?* He pressed the button, expecting to hear a chime from within, then stood waiting in silence.

Once inside, he sat in an overstuffed white armchair that reminded him of the one back in his apartment. He sunk as deep as he did when he settled into his own broken-down recliner. Across from him, Carl Claymont crossed his ankle over his knee and smiled. Carl's torso rose high above the back of the sofa. To Ben he looked fit, about fifty. Neat golden hair, clothes with crisp lines, tapered shirt with an open collar, sharp pleats and a straight seam in his trousers. Everything balanced and even. The most symmetrical human being Ben had ever seen.

After providing Ben with the soda water he had offered, Carl poured himself an amber-colored drink and sat across a thick, glass coffee table from Ben. He drank half of the amber liquid in one tip of the glass and continued to smile. "So you think you might be interested in sailing in the South Pacific?" Carl asked, his eyes holding steady on Ben's.

"I imagine everyone has had that idea at some time in their lives," Ben responded.

"Yes sir, I imagine they have. But you have an opportunity to actually do it. Here's the deal, son. I have a rather substantial sailboat moored down in Huntington Beach. It's been doing absolutely nothing for about a year, so I've decided to send it down to the South Pacific and make it a tour boat for tourists. Except they're going to be high-rolling tourists. I want to do that for about a year, then get the boat to Auckland and sell it. I'm eager to get started with the project. I have a captain, but I need a crew."

Ben thought about this for a moment. "And you came to the eastern side of the mountains, to a lake town, to find sailors?"

"Yes, but not really. I came to see this hotel. I invested in it a few years back, and now that it's been completed, I wanted to come and see it. I've been having one hell-of-a-time finding a crew down south. So when I got here to Coeur d'Alene, I thought I'd place an ad. I know this isn't the most nautical of towns and that I face low odds of finding sailors with qualifications, so that's why I said 'No Experience Necessary.' What I need is a person to be the handyman, deckhand, grunt worker, waiter, and host—a person to take care of the incidental things that come up on a tourist boat. The captain will teach that person whatever sailing knowledge they need to know, and it ain't much."

"I think I can do all of those things. I can fix things and I can sure do grunt work; I worked putting up this hotel for two years. Deckhand sounds like something I can learn. Waiter and host are jobs I've never done, but I'm willing to give it a try."

Carl pursed his lips and nodded his head for a moment. "You're a strong-looking guy; I think you'd have no problems with the physical stuff. And you talk sense, you're polite, don't appear to be an anti-social type, so you probably wouldn't piss off any of the customers. As long as you can take orders from the captain, you could fit right in."

"I had no problems with my supervisors on my last job. But I wonder though, why can't you get a crew down south?"

"They're all sailors. They want real pay, not what I'm offering."

Ben smiled. "You're not offering real pay? What are you offering?"

"I pay all expenses, you sail for a year, and when I sell the boat in Auckland, you get a cut."

"How much of a cut?"

"Maybe five percent. Boat's worth about a mil, give or take."

Ben did the math quickly then opened his eyes wide. "Sounds good. Let me think about it," he said.

"Well, I haven't offered it to you." Carl stopped to watch Ben raise his eyebrows a little. "It turns out, this town of yours has more than a few people interested in getting out of here to go sail in the South Pacific. I should have looked inland for a crew a long time ago."

Feeling a slight drop in confidence at this news, Ben asked, "When will you know who you want to take?"

"Couple days, and then I hope to be on the road to L.A. I want the crew to be driving with me. Why don't you call me tomorrow?"

That night, Ben's thoughts of palm trees and sandy beaches returned. But this time they slipped out of view as he saw himself laboring as a lumberjack or loading asses as a lift operator at the ski hill. The anticipated depression he knew he would slip into if he worked either of those jobs caused him to get less sleep than he had the night before. In the morning, he paced the floor and frequently placed his head against the window so he could strain his eyes to see the hotel. When he remembered he hadn't gone for the paper, he ran down the stairs to get it so he'd have a diversion to take his mind off placing his phone call to Carl. When he brought the paper back up to the apartment, he went straight to the want ads and saw that Carl's ad had disappeared. This caused a minor panic as he envisioned his boat sailing without him. He picked up the phone and placed the call.

When he hung up he felt relief. He felt new, he felt ready, and he felt a tropical sun shining down on his ready-to-be-tanned skin. He saw a white sand beach behind his own feet as he lay in a hammock in the shade of a palm tree. Carl had told him he'd made the cut! They would leave the next morning.

# Chapter 2

The next day, Ben made arrangements with his landlord to keep the apartment available for another month. If he didn't hear from Ben in thirty days, Ben asked him to put his things in storage and consider him vacated. After packing a few items, Ben waited inside the store for Carl, so they could begin the trip to Los Angeles to start his new life.

At about noon a large black truck with an extended cabin and an enclosed cargo space pulled up. Carl stepped out and stood looking up and down Sherman Avenue. Ben didn't rush out to meet him; he continued to watch from inside the store as two more people climbed out of the vehicle. From the rear driver's side, a young man with dark hair and a two-day beard slipped out and stood on the street while lighting a cigarette. His T-shirt, stretched and worn, hung outside of his loose and baggy jeans. From the front passenger door a blond woman with straight stringy hair, still damp from a recent shower, emerged. Her meticulously-applied makeup seemed more important than well-groomed hair. Her lashes were covered with thick, black lining. Above each eye, a thinly-drawn, straight black eyebrow slanted upward.

Precisely penciled purple lips contrasted with her creamy cheeks, which had a slight brushing of pink. She had strong, shapely shoulders and limbs, a thin waist, and large, well-proportioned breasts. She wore brown leather sandals, a silver anklet that barely stood out against her white skin, black spandex shorts and a low-cut, hot pink sports bra with black trim. It took little work to show off her freckled valley of cleavage as she leaned back against the door of the vehicle. Then she whipped her head and hair forward while bending at the waist to begin combing it with her fingers.

Ben stood and watched for a moment to get a first impression—and to stall an extra minute for a last chance to decide whether he really wanted to join the crew. He did, and turned to say so long to his landlord, who sat behind the counter on an old shiny brown saddle he'd mounted on a stump as a chair and conversation piece.

On the street, Ben called out to Carl, who turned, walked to the back of the vehicle and opened the tailgate.

"Ben, good to see you again. We're all ready to go, so throw your stuff in," Carl greeted him.

The young man and the woman turned to take a look at Ben. He felt their eyes following him as he stowed his bag.

"These are your two traveling companions. That's Rudy Fletcher over there, and this is Purrette."

Rudy waved with his cigarette hand, ending his wave by flicking off the ash with his thumb. When Ben nodded to Purrette, she continued to stare silently without reaction.

"It's nice to meet you," Ben said.

"You, too," Purrette responded vacantly, while climbing back into the vehicle.

"Well, let's get out of here," Carl said, "Ben, you know a drive-through on the way out of town where we can get some coffee?"

"There's a coffee shop near the exit."

"That'll do."

As they made their way out of town, Carl explained how he would pay all of the group's expenses from this point forward. If they used their own money for anything, he would reimburse them. He then pointed out that this rule applied everywhere except Las Vegas, where they would only get back money they spent on food.

They stopped at the coffee shop and Carl went inside. Ben turned to Rudy, who sat with his head resting on the window, looking down at the surface of the parking lot. Matted hair covered the back of his head, and he gave off the dead stale smell of an ashtray. His eyelids had bright red lines scattered through the blue-gray skin. A line of thin lashes poked out from the edges. They fluttered up and down, making Ben unsure whether Rudy fought to keep them open or shut.

"So, Rudy, you're going to crew on Carl's boat too, are you?" Ben asked.

Rudy remained silent. Purrette stared out of the windshield. She displayed no interest toward the men in the back seat. Ben wondered if Rudy had heard him so he approached him again. "Rudy?"

"I doubt it," Rudy responded.

"You doubt it? Then why are you riding with him to L.A.?"

"I want a ride to Las Vegas. I told him I'd think about it until we got to Vegas."

"Oh." Ben paused, and then asked Purrette, "What about you, Purrette, are you part of the crew?" The thought of a woman being part of the crew hadn't occurred to Ben, but it seemed like it might be a pretty good idea. As hard as Purrette seemed to him, she emitted a seductive appeal.

"No," she answered without turning.

"Then how come you're riding with Carl to L.A.?"

Purrette paused, then said, "I do a lot of riding with Carl."

"I see. Well, do you know anything about Carl's boat?"

"It's a ship. Once a boat gets to be a certain size, it stops being a boat, and it starts being a ship. Carl tells me his boat is a ship. That's all I know."

"Have you ever been on Carl's ship?"

"Yeah, a few times."

"What's it like?"

Purrette pursed her lips and began nodding her head without looking at Ben. "It's nice. You'll like it."

Ben became concerned with this newly-gathered information. Carl had indicated he had interviewed a number of people with an interest in signing up for the crew. Yet here sat Rudy, who showed no enthusiasm at all, and Purrette, an acquaintance of Carl's who appeared to be along for the ride only. Ben sat as the one person committed to the project, and now fifteen minutes down the road he wondered if he had blindly committed to an endeavor that others clearly viewed as flawed.

About an hour later, after the energy from the breakfast sandwiches and coffee kicked in, Ben's traveling companions showed a little personality.

"I figure we'll stick to the two-lane highways most of the way, that way we take a more direct line to Vegas. It may take longer, but what the hell?" Carl said.

"Fine with me," said Ben. "Best bet is ninety-five south to eighty-four. You may want to re-think the two-lane idea and consider going over to fifteen. If we don't make that switch at eighty-four, we're pretty much stuck until eighty, and then you go east to ninety-three south. It's going to be long and slow."

"Ben, you're a regular road map. It's okay if it's slow, though. How long do you think it will take?"

"Twenty-four hours if we drive straight through."

"Shit." Carl, Purrette, and Rudy spoke with one voice.

"About fifteen if we take the interstate," Ben said.

"I think we'll stick to the two-lane. It's a good thing we brought some entertainment. Ben, why don't you reach in the back there and pull up that television so you and Rudy can watch some movies, you know, kill some time?" Carl asked, "We'll switch drivers at the end of each movie."

"I've never seen a television in a truck before. You guys must drive a lot, or really like movies, if you've got a television that works in a truck."

Ben looked behind his seat into the cargo area and spotted the portable television. It was awkward to move, and it barely fit in the space between the top of the seat and the roof of the vehicle. He had to support its weight with just his arms and back, and when the cord snagged behind one of the suitcases, his efforts to spring it free caused a muscle in his back to cramp. He wrangled the set over the seat, and then did his best to stretch the muscle in the already limited space. He hunched over the set, stretching his arms out between the front seats, as the cramping muscle tried to pull his shoulder blade down to his belt.

Rudy watched him contort his body. "What did you say your name was again?"

Ben groaned while Rudy's question sunk in, then answered, "Ben Beck."

Rudy nodded and said in a contemplative voice. "Ben Beck. B. B. I'll bet your friends call you B. B., right?"

With his arms still stretched into the front seat, Ben turned his head to look at Rudy and answered, "Black And Blue, actually, they call me Black And Blue. BAB for short. My middle name is Andrew."

"Black And Blue? Why?"

Ben pulled his arms back and sat up straight in his seat. He crossed his left arm over his chest to keep his back from cramping again. "When I was younger, I used to fight a lot, and I really liked to beat the shit out of people. When I finished with them, they were black-and-blue. It matched my initials and one of my smart-ass friends started calling me BAB."

Carl and Purrette both turned to look at Ben from the front seat while Rudy sat frozen, watching Ben's face for a sign indicating a joke. In Ben's look of sincerity, Rudy could see a dark desire, a longing to break through years of restraint.

***

A few years earlier, Ben sat at the bar in Post Falls drinking beer after eating a steak dinner. The hazy room glowed in the weak yellow light emitted by a pair of bare bulbs inside a brewery's promotional lampshade. Rough-cut planks on the top portion of the walls contrasted the dark, shining, wooden lower wall panels. Spots on the rough wood appeared brown and smooth where years of leaning customers had polished them to a shine.

He worked in the bush every day, counting the marked trees to make sure the lumber companies hadn't cut more than their quotas. At the end of each long day, he reported his count back to the district office, and then tried to make it to the bar before the kitchen closed. The long summer days allowed him to stay in the bush till late evening and made it a close race each night to get his meal.

Most nights, he enjoyed the quiet of the nearly vacant bar. Tonight the pinball machine had captured the attention of two sturdy young men from the college in Spokane. They came to enjoy the lower legal drinking age of the Idaho border town. They'd been playing and drinking since Ben's arrival, making sure they talked loud enough for everyone present to know how expertly they played the game. They wore tight white T-shirts and blue jeans. They whooped and smiled exaggerated smiles while high-fiving a particularly high score. As time passed and they consumed more beer, the skill of their play diminished, and they began to hammer at the machine, often tilting the game. Each time they tilted, they accused the bartender of setting the tilt weight too loose and demanded their quarters back.

Ben received a fresh glass of beer from the bartender just as the larger of the two pinball players let a ball slip through the flippers and, in disgust, smashed his beer glass down on the small table near the game. Beer shot up into the air and splashed the wall and floor. The young man hip-checked the machine and the lights went out as the game tilted again.

"What kind of bullshit game is this?" he asked, turning to the bartender.

Ben turned toward him. "Hey, you want to keep it down over there?" he said.

"Why don't you mind your own business?" he told Ben, then turned to the bartender and asked for his quarter back.

"It is my business," Ben responded in a low voice. "I've been listening to your noise all night, and I think it would be nice if you quieted down a little."

The young man cocked his head to the side, smiled with his mouth closed, and scratched his eyebrow. He walked over and stood in front of Ben.

"We'll play our game and make as much of our noise as we want. And I don't want to hear from you again." He stared directly at Ben for a second or two longer, then turned and began to walk back to the game.

"You won't hear from me again as long as I don't hear from you. How's that?"

The young man stopped, turned, and came back in front of Ben. His friend joined him.

"Listen, asshole, you shut your face, or we're going to have to take you outside." Neither of the young men were smiling.

Ben looked from one face to the other. He said, "Okay. I'll meet you out there as soon as I finish my beer."

"Finish your beer?" He paused for a second. "You say you want to go, but you're also stalling. That's not going to work, buddy. You go ahead and drink your beer. We're still going to meet you outside even if we have to drag you out when you finish that beer."

"You won't have to drag me out. I'll come out gladly. You see, I like to fight."

The big one pulled his head back a little, and the other one looked at his friend to determine how to react.

Ben smiled at the big one. "I haven't been in a fight for a while, but I'm getting that old rush again. I like no-rules fighting. I just want to finish the beer and let the rush build. I'll be out there. Count on it."

He reached back, grabbed his beer without taking his eyes off of the two men, and drank half of it.

The big one huffed off and said to his friend, "Grab your stuff. We'll take care of this guy outside, and then get the hell out of this dump."

After watching them leave, Ben turned around, took another drink from his beer, and put it on the bar. He got up and removed his jacket and shirt so that he stood in a sleeveless undershirt. He removed his watch and placed it in the pocket of his jacket. Then he finished his beer.

"Watch my jacket, will you?" he asked the bartender.

"Can I put it in the back? I want to come out and watch."

Ben nodded and left for the parking lot.

Outside he saw the two men standing near their car. When they saw him, they spread apart and stepped out to meet him. As Ben approached, the big one made a jerky step to one side, then bounced back. He threw a wide arcing haymaker that Ben easily side-stepped. Ben threw a punch at the man's head, but it also missed. They both spun and stood facing each other. Ben felt his face heat up and his heart thump up in his throat. He stood still, watching. As soon as the other man moved, Ben stepped in quickly and shot a punch at his face, catching him on the cheek and snapping his head back. The small man shuffled closer, but Ben stopped him with a look. The big man shook his head. Ben hit him again, this time in the jaw. He followed with a punch to the stomach. The big one fell to his knees holding his gut.

The smaller man came to his friend's aid, rushing Ben from the side, trying to tackle him. Ben moved forward to get out of the way, but the small man's fist caught him on the meaty part of his shoulder, sending zingers down his arm. Ben waited for the smaller one to rush again and he did. This time Ben sidestepped the rush completely and popped the man in the side of the head as he slashed by, sending him off balance to the ground.

The big one managed to stand again while Ben dealt with his friend; in a daze and totally defenseless, he stood bewildered. Preoccupied with the other man, Ben hadn't registered the big one's confused state when he turned and saw him standing behind him. He reacted as if it were an attack. He ducked low then rose, using the power of his legs, and delivered a blow to the big one's jaw. The punch spun the man on the spot. He looked skyward and crumpled softly to lie still in the gravel.

The smaller man, seeing the way his friend had fallen, ignored Ben and ran straight to the prone man. "Ricky . . . Ricky!" he yelled. "Shit, he's turning blue."

The bartender stepped closer and looked down at the man, then turned and ran into the bar and called an ambulance.

Ben stood ready, breathing heavily, waiting to continue if the smaller man tried another attack. His deep breathing and state of alert prolonged the rush of the fight that filled his consciousness.

Assault charges were laid against Ben. He spent the night and the next day in jail, and he lost his job. The man named Ricky lay in a coma with a broken jaw. The bartender explained to the police what had happened, and later that day the charges were dropped.

Three days later, Ricky woke up with considerable memory loss and slurred speech. Ben went home and found a construction job and never learned if Ricky fully recovered.

***

Rudy finally spoke. "So I guess I better not piss you off."

"That was a long time ago," Ben said, and then smiled. "I don't beat the shit out of people like I used to."

"Well, BAB, you called the friend that gave you the nickname a smart-ass. Is it okay to call you BAB?"

"No."

"Well then, Ben, even though you say you're semi-retired from beating the shit out of people, I'm still going to try not to piss you off," Rudy said, smiling.

Purrette's gaze shifted to Rudy momentarily. Then she turned and looked out at the highway where Carl had already returned his focus. They drove in silence for a few miles until Carl told Rudy about the box of movies in the back. Rudy shuffled around in the cargo area while Purrette plugged the television cable into the cigarette lighter. Finally Rudy discovered the box of movies.

"What do you want to watch, Ben? 'Wet, Luscious, Lips,' 'Jail Bait Lover,' 'Loose and Available,' 'Deeper Yet,' or 'Tina Touches and Tickles'?" Rudy asked.

"Sounds like it's my turn to drive," Ben said.

After switching drivers and solving the puzzle of how to make the television work, Ben faced the highway with the wheel in his hands. Purrette stared out at the graying blacktop. From the backseat the sounds of exaggerated sexual gratification were heard on the raspy television speakers.

Carl watched as a large-breasted woman prepared to reach some exalted level of orgasm, apparently a level no woman had ever reached before. Prior to her climax, Carl exclaimed loud enough for the others to hear, "Will you look at the way she can arch her back!"

No one responded. Ben glanced at Purrette to see how she reacted to the men in back watching the sexual exploitation of a woman. She waited a few seconds before turning to look at him but said nothing. Then she turned back to look out the windshield.

"So, do you work for Carl?" Ben asked Purrette.

"Yes."

"Doing what?"

Purrette appeared to be searching for the right words. She finally answered, "I'm his assistant."

"What do you assist him with?"

"Carl entertains a lot of high-profile people and I assist him."

"I see."

"What's that supposed to mean?"

"Well, if you aren't going to provide much of an answer, then it means whatever I want it to mean."

From the backseat, Carl again asked a question without expecting an answer. "How in the hell did she tie a knot in that?"

Ben looked over his shoulder to see Carl mesmerized in the glow of the television. He turned back to find Purrette looking at him intently. "I go to meetings and parties with Carl. He thinks having a good-looking woman for an assistant is a good idea. I smile, I laugh and generally act like a bimbo, but what I really do is watch. Carl likes to hear about the things I see at these parties," she said.

"And what do you see?"

"Reactions. I see how people react to the things Carl says, and I tell him about it."

"How come you weren't at my meeting with Carl when I came to the hotel?"

"I was. I watched from the bedroom door."

Ben stared at Purrette, but turned his attention to the radio when he heard a new tune start to play. He turned the volume up and said, "I haven't heard this song in three years, and the time before that it was five."

"You remember the amount of time that goes by before you hear a song again?" she asked, staring at him.

"*This* song I do."

She nodded, and then stared at the radio.

"So . . . " Ben started to say something, but Purrette held up her hand to stop him from talking.

He watched the highway until the song finished, then turned back to Purrette.

"So, what did you tell him about my reaction to this opportunity?"

"I didn't tell him anything, I told him I couldn't read you. And the song's okay."

"Yeah, I like it. And could you read me?"

"Easily."

"So what was your take?"

"You played it cool, you showed interest, and you wanted to believe he offered you the best deal on earth. I knew you would accept it if he offered it to you. The thing is, this is a good deal if it works out the way he has it planned."

"Do you get a cut when the boat is sold?"

"No, I've already been paid. I'm working off my earnings now."

"Why did you tell him you couldn't read me?"

She waited a long time before she answered. "It was too easy. I figured he read you, too."

The next driver change had Ben in the front passenger seat with Carl behind the wheel again. Purrette sat in the back beside Rudy, who fell asleep shortly after starting another movie. Ben could hear the movie continue to run, and wondered if Purrette had also fallen asleep or if she watched it alone. He took a quick glance over his shoulder and saw her glued to the action on the screen.

Carl commented periodically about certain things they passed along the road, but long silent spells, in which they could hear only the murmur of the video coming from the backseat, filled most of the time. One such silent spell broke to a loud slapping sound.

"Keep your fucking hands to yourself, asshole!" Purrette said as Carl and Ben turned to see what had happened.

Rudy sat rubbing his face and laughing. Purrette's eyes squinted at Rudy, and her muscles tensed to strike him again.

"I was just trying to help you, you horny bitch," Rudy said mockingly, "but I guess you'd rather do it yourself."

She struck at him again but landed her punch on the arm he had raised to protect his head. The punch still had enough force to bounce his head off of the window.

"Prick."

"Your nipples are hard," he taunted before his head was bounced off the window by another blow from Purrette.

Carl looked at Ben and said, "I guess we can't let them get too near to each other." He pulled off onto the shoulder so that Ben could get in the back. When Purrette was out of the car, she stood looking into the backseat at Rudy. Then she lunged at him and tried to drag him across the seat and out the door.

"Come out here, you pervert. I'll bet little pussy-ass pantywaist shits like you get beat up by women all the time. I'll even bet you like it, you fucking little weasel prick," she said. Rudy's seat belt saved him as he fought off her grasping hands.

Ben wrapped his arms around her from behind, pinning her upper arms to her side, then spun her away from the door and walked her a few paces away from the vehicle. She strained against his arms trying to break free; at one point he thought she would. He could feel the strength in the hardened muscles of her arms and back.

"Slow down, slow down. I think you got him," Ben said, feeling Purrette relax. He loosened his grip and let her go, but watched her in case she turned to launch another attack. He stayed between her and the open back door as she made her way back to the truck and into the front seat, where she sat looking out the windows as if nothing had happened.

"Okay, enough blowing off steam. Let's get rolling," Carl's voice ordered.

Ben closed Purrette's door and climbed into the backseat beside Rudy, who sat staring out the window at the road.

"Looks like you better not piss off Purrette either," Ben said to the non-reacting Rudy.

For the rest of the trip to Las Vegas, Carl and Ben made sure that Purrette and Rudy stayed apart. During the time when Ben and Purrette sat in the back together, he noticed with amazement that she watched the movies with enjoyment, not just killing-time interest. He tended to gaze out the window rather than witness the lewd activities on the small screen. From time to time she slapped his shoulder and said, "You've got to watch this." He would turn to see what she wanted to bring to his attention, but couldn't watch for long. She never noticed whether he had responded to her alert.

He hadn't noticed that the fields going by had slowly turned into desert, and he hadn't noticed the silence of the television. When he realized that the movie had ended, he turned and found Purrette staring at him. He gave a quick nod.

"You don't like sex?" she asked.

"I don't like watching other people have sex."

"I know *you* like sex, Purrette," Rudy said, turning to look into the backseat.

Purrette ignored Rudy and asked Ben, "Why, you gay?"

"No."

"It's just sex."

"Yeah, but they're not doing it for themselves."

"Purrette wasn't doing it *for* herself, she was doing it *to* herself," Rudy said from the front, causing Purrette to punch his headrest.

"You're a scumbag, Rudy," she said calmly.

"That's not what you said last night," he taunted.

Ben looked at Purrette. She lowered her eyes and turned away in her seat.

"Yes, sir, she liked it last night." Rudy nodded at Ben with a wide smile on his face.

Ben turned back to watch the desert. *These are the people I work with,* he thought, *porno-watching wackos. Give it to Vegas and then decide again; that won't be too late to turn back.*

## Chapter 3

The direct two-lane route took more time than either Carl or Ben had anticipated, so the Las Vegas skyline didn't come into view until dusk on the second day of their drive. They took the Sahara off-ramp to the Strip and found their motel.

Carl pulled up in front of the lobby. Built on a long thin lot next to Caesar's Palace, The Pleasure Inn was a two-year-old dwarf of a motel.

"What is this place?" Ben asked.

"Oh, I like to send business this guy's way. He's got balls."

"How so?"

"Caesar's wanted to buy the land from the guy, but they wouldn't meet his price, so he built this place. Been running it at a profit since it opened. If Caesar's wants to buy it now, it's going to cost them a few million more than the original asking price."

Carl jumped out of the truck and went back to access the cargo area. He told everyone to bail out and grab his or her bag. When they all stood on the sidewalk, he told them of a late evening meeting he had scheduled and that the room had been reserved in Ben's name. He also told them to charge anything they wanted to the room. Then he left.

The clean, mirror-paneled lobby had polished black marble countertops on the front desk. The furnishings consisted of sofas the color of light coral and sand, and chairs beside which stood vivid green plants. A small lobby by Vegas standards, but it served the purpose of checking in and checking out.

Ben shook his head when he learned that Carl had booked only one room for the three of them, and when he asked for additional rooms, the desk clerk informed him that The Pleasure Inn was sold out for the next four months. He took three room keys and led the way to find their room. They arrived to discover the room could comfortably sleep three. They found two double beds, a small sofa, a television bolted onto a built-in chest of drawers, and a small refrigerator.

Ben flipped on the television. Rudy opened the small refrigerator hoping for a mini-bar, but found only a small blue plastic tray of ice cubes. He slammed the door and stood to see what Ben had found on the tube.

"We gotta get some beer," Rudy said.

"I think I need a shower, some decent food, and some sleep before I need a beer," Ben responded.

"Your priorities are fucked up, man," Rudy said as he turned to look at Purrette. "Whoa, I think my priorities have changed."

Ben turned to see Purrette lying topless on one of the beds. The unexpected sight of her firm, bare breasts caused him to stop and gawk. He didn't blink until Rudy interrupted his view by jumping onto the bed and standing over her, forcing Ben to move to one side so that he could see around Rudy. When he had regained sight of her, he ventured to tear his eyes away from her breasts to look at her expressionless face staring back at him.

He looked into the eyes that had stared vacantly out through the windshield for over a day, but these eyes stared at him with intent. *Well?* they asked without blinking. He felt a warmth surge in his chest, and he noticed his heart beating faster against his ribcage as he held the stare. Then, as he looked at her eyes, the image of those eyes watching trance-like as the action of the porn movies unfolded popped into his mind. He turned away to look at the television.

Rudy unbuttoned his shirt as he muttered about Purrette's intentions and how he would help her fulfill them. He threw his shirt to the floor, then got down on his knees at her feet. He reached up and grabbed either side of her shorts and slid them down her thighs to her calves and finally over her feet. By this time Ben's eyes had returned to see the removal of the rest of her clothes, and they gravitated to the thin strip of dark hair. When he looked at her face again, she continued to stare at him. This time her eyes asked, *Why not?*

Rudy stood and began to unbutton his pants in a hurry. Ben, not believing his own eyes, turned and focused on the television again to try to gather his thoughts. He wanted a shower, he wanted to sleep, and he thought he wanted Purrette. But he knew that couldn't happen as his travel mates prepared to entertain themselves carnally.

He turned back to see the struggling Rudy trying to get his last pant leg over his ankle and said, "Well, it looks like you two want to be alone, so I'll just go out and find something to do . . . I guess."

"Ben," Rudy said as he knelt between Purrette's legs, "I think she wants you to stay. I think she wants us both."

Ben's eyes flicked back to Purrette. She watched him with the same intent, and her eyes said *Stay*, then shyly turned away.

"Ah, well, thanks . . . but I don't think so. I'll catch up with you guys later." He felt so out-of-place that he hurried for the door stiff-legged, as if another body propelled him forward. He was out the door and on the Strip before he realized he hadn't picked up a room key. Before he could turn to go back, the traffic light said to walk, so he walked and found himself moving toward the MGM.

Inside the casino he roamed around aimlessly. The multi-colored lights, the noise of coins crashing into metal trays, the busy patterned carpets, the commotion of people, and the lack of sleep placed him in a state of confusion. He couldn't decide what to do. He wandered through the casino, not certain if he had walked in circles, passing everything over and over. He turned a corner by a series of slot machines. There, he thought he recognized a young man with a wispy comb-over, dark tan, loose-fitting white shirt unbuttoned too far, gold chain with a gold razor blade, and tight polyester denim pants with bright white stitching. *There can't be more than one guy who looks like this in Vegas,* he thought.

As he passed the man, he spotted a large projection screen showing a horse race in progress. He stopped to watch, and at the end of the race, walked toward the screen to find the sports book all but empty. Cigarette smoke rose slowly from one of the desks. This looked like an opportunity to sit and rest for a while.

Sitting in a row of theater-style seats, he watched another race and decided that he needed a drink and something to eat. A strolling cocktail waitress headed toward him. He admired the high cut of the gold and red outfit that displayed her well-rounded hips and the low-cut front, which fortified her cleavage. Flesh-toned hose made her legs shimmer. Over these she wore black fishnet stockings. Her mane of streaked hair fanned out away from her face, held in place by some glitter-laced spray. He asked her for a beer.

"Have you got a ticket?" she asked.

"A ticket? Okay, where do I buy a ticket?"

"Not a drink ticket, a tote ticket. If you have a bet on a race then the beer is free." She paused to see if the idea registered with Ben, but he continued to sit there with a blank look on his face. "If I see your ticket, I bring you a beer for nothing. If I don't see it, it will cost you four dollars."

"Where do I bet?"

She pointed to the wagering windows. Ben stood. "I'll have a ticket when you get back."

When he returned to his seat, he stared up at the big screen, but didn't comprehend the action. His lack of sleep began to affect his ability to concentrate. He was bewildered when the waitress placed the beer down in front of him, and he reached for his wallet to pay for the beer.

"How much did you say it cost, four bucks?"

"Yeah, but now I see you've got a ticket. It's free, remember?"

"Yeah right, then this is for you." He placed a five on her tray. "Can I get food in here? I'm too tired to walk anywhere."

"You want like a sandwich or something?"

"Sure. Can you do that?"

"Yeah, I'll be right back."

"Do I have to get another ticket?"

"Not yet. I'll be right back."

Ben took a long draught of the beer. The refreshing chill tingled throughout his chest. He looked up at the race on the screen with no idea which horse he had wagered on. He took another draught, and his throat felt good as the golden liquid ran down and chilled him again. His eyes grew heavy as he stared at the screen. The cocktail waitress woke him when she placed a sandwich in front of him and told him he couldn't sleep there.

"Sorry," he said. "Maybe the food will get me going. How much do I owe you?"

"It's okay. I took the sandwich from the staff tray in the kitchen, but if you want to stay here you have to stay awake. The management doesn't want customers to think this place will put people to sleep. You want some coffee?"

"No, thanks."

"Maybe you should go get some sleep."

"Yeah, I'd like to, but I can't go back to my room."

"Why?"

"My roomies are coupling." Ben bit into the sandwich.

"Well, you probably need to get another tote if you want another beer. I don't want them to think I'm treating you special."

"What, you think they watch you that closely?" Ben asked, then continued when the waitress nodded. "No problem. I'll bet again, but can you tell me if I won the last race? I think I saw number six come in up there."

The waitress looked at his ticket, then up at the screen. "No, wrong track. You bet on a night race at the Meadowlands; that screen is showing the races at Santa Anita."

"Great, I don't even know what time zone I'm betting in. Maybe you better not bring me another beer. I'll finish the sandwich and clear out."

When he finished the food, he sat for a minute intending to finish his beer and leave, but the food made him sleepy and his head began to bob. He jerked himself awake a few times, but eventually his chin ended up on his chest. It stayed there for a few minutes until a security guard yanked him out of his seat and started dragging him in the direction of the big screen. Ben scanned about trying to determine why he was moving and what propelled him. Everything blurred as he continued toward the screen. When he looked to see who held his arms, he saw the back of a large head hustling him past the wagering windows. He snapped his arm out of the big man's grasp and stopped, only to have another security guard grab his upper arms from the rear and pull them together behind his back. The man in front then grabbed his shirt, and together the two men accelerated him through a door under the screen. He still hadn't completely regained his memory of the situation and he began to get angry and resentful of the two men pushing him to who knows where.

"Hey, what's going on?" he yelled.

"You're outta here, buddy. Go home and sleep it off."

They threw him at an exit door, and he barely managed to get an arm out to protect himself. Even so, he still slammed into the door hard with one shoulder. His head made contact and, an instant later, stung him into alertness, triggering an angry response. He kept his shoulder against the door and turned his head to see the two security guards coming at him again. He gave them his left arm; when the first guard had a grip on it, he swung an uppercut from below his waist with his right fist, straight up into the man's chin. The staggered guard backed into his wide-eyed, angry, snorting partner, who brushed him aside to get to Ben. As the crazed second guard lunged at him, Ben stepped back. The guard missed while slamming into the door then turned toward Ben and pushed off the door to get at Ben. The heel of Ben's hand hit him square in the forehead, driving his head back to make hard contact with the door. The man glared, stunned and motionless.

Behind him, Ben heard steps approaching and turned to see more guards rushing down the hall. He grabbed the stunned guard and wheeled him around, flinging him at the approaching guards, then he popped open the door and ran. Once outside, he turned down a long driveway past a row of garbage bins, then turned left when he got to the end of the driveway. He sprinted past the back of the jai alai court to a side street. Another left back toward the Strip, and he found traffic at a dead stop while a mob of jaywalking weekend gamblers zigzagged between vehicles on their way from one casino to another. He joined a group walking down the middle of the Strip between rows of cars trying to turn left and didn't worry about being followed.

The walk down the Strip helped settle him. He took pleasure in the long-missed adrenaline rush that he had sought so often in the past.

Eventually, he turned and walked back in the direction of his motel. There, in the lobby, he asked the clerk for another key to his room, explaining that he had knocked on the door and his roommates hadn't answered. He provided identification and the clerk gave him a key. He expected to find his roommates, or at least signs of their existence, but instead found his bag sitting alone in the corner and both of the beds made up. In the bathroom, none of the towels had been used. The room was as fresh as it had been when they first arrived.

\*\*\*

A white sedan waited outside the open-air baggage claim area of John Wayne Airport. Leaning against the passenger side, with his feet on the corner of the curb, stood a tall slender man in white slacks and a white sleeveless T-shirt. He had short black hair, cut to show crisp straight lines against his brown skin. His deep brown eyes seemed to make their surrounding whites glow. He had slender lips that reflected the upturn of his eyes as he smiled at everything around him.

The airport security people had thanked him for waiting with the car's engine turned off and left him alone. When he heard his name called from behind, he turned away from the terminal, moved to the back of the car, and opened the trunk. "Rudy, you look like hell, man. You ever think of getting any sleep and maybe taking a shower from time to time?"

"I just finished a long drive, my brother, so why don't you shut the fuck up. How you doing anyway, Duane?"

"Doin' good, doin' good," answered Duane. "But seriously, man, you got to do something about yourself. You look like you're hurtin' for some rest. And what the hell you comin' from the parking lot for, man?"

"I returned a car. Is the boat still in place?"

"Still there. Should be ready to go in a few days. When's Carl going to show up?"

"Tomorrow night, if he doesn't get involved in anything in Vegas."

"Good. I'm getting antsy. I want to get going. What's this new guy like?"

Rudy updated Duane about the long drive from Idaho and about how Ben seemed to be a reasonable guy, yet hard to read. Maybe too nice a guy, might take some getting used to. He also pointed out that Ben didn't know shit about sailing.

Duane pulled up in front of the Sandler Suites Hotel and retrieved Rudy's bag from the trunk of the car.

"Okay, man. You get some sleep and we'll see you in Catalina in a couple of days," Duane said as he shook Rudy's hand.

"Yeah, see you then."

***

Ben had waited most of the morning for Carl to show up. Eventually hunger got the best of him, so he left to find a coffee shop and have breakfast. Carl could wait for him for a change. When he got back to the motel, he still found no sign of Carl. He had checked out, so he sat in the lobby and watched the parking lot. Around mid-afternoon, when he began to feel he'd been left for good, the black truck driven by the man with golden hair pulled up to the lobby door.

Ben had been wondering what Carl's reaction would be when he told him that Purrette and Rudy had disappeared. But when he saw Purrette sitting in the front seat, he decided that, with this group, anything could happen, and none of them would find it strange. When he looked in the back, there was no sign of Rudy.

Carl got out and helped load Ben's bag, and Ben asked him how he managed to hook up with Purrette.

"I called her last night. I needed to take her somewhere. Why?"

"Nothing. It's just that I thought I was going to have to tell you that she and Rudy disappeared. I went out and when I came back they were gone, and there were no messages."

"Did you get my message?"

"No."

"Fucking motel clerks. I left a message saying I would be here sometime in the afternoon. I didn't want you waiting around." Carl's voice sounded sincere.

"Yeah. Well, I didn't get it. Rudy appears to have split, unless you know otherwise."

"I figured he might. Purrette said he left just after you took off last night. Well, he knows where we're headed and I told him where the ship is moored, so maybe he'll catch up later. What happened to your hand?" Carl asked when Ben lifted his bag into the back of the vehicle.

"Minor scrape. How did your meetings go?"

"I think we have some customers. I invited some people out to Catalina in a couple of days to take a look at the yacht. They're planning a trip to the South Pacific in a couple of months and if they like the ship, they may book a week with us while they're down there. So you have your first port of call."

"If we don't have Rudy, won't we be short-handed?"

"Naw. You and the captain can make it to Catalina on your own if you have to. Then we'll see."

"Okay, if you say so."

"I say so. Let's get going. We'll be in Huntington Beach tonight."

From the backseat Ben said hello to Purrette, who sat and looked out the windshield without acknowledging the greeting. Ben wouldn't allow himself to be ignored. He greeted her again, causing her to turn her head to look at him. Her eyes were full of confusion. She couldn't hold the look for long, and turned her stare back out the windshield.

Ben found he had no words to say to her. The look she had given him contained accusations and a request for mercy. He had seen her naked. He had seen her about to engage in sexual activity with a man she had earlier wanted to beat on. What kind of a relationship could now occur between them? Certainly not a relationship of the normal man-woman kind, and a normal co-worker relationship would be out of the question. A person doesn't normally see his co-workers when they're naked and suggesting a threesome.

Sitting mostly in silence, he contemplated his relationship with these people all the way to California. Carl periodically initiated a conversation related to some topic or another. Each time they talked, Purrette monitored the pavement and ignored them.

As it was getting dark, they pulled into the outskirts of Huntington Beach. They found a gravel road that led to a small marina. No buildings existed, just a small parking area with room for about six cars. Ben put himself on the alert when he saw a white sedan parked in the area. Why the alert, he wasn't sure; he didn't know what to expect. His anxiety eased a little when he reminded himself that he didn't have anything worth stealing.

The door of the white sedan opened as they approached, and a tall African-American man stepped out to greet them. Carl hit the brakes hard. When the car came to a stop, he jumped out and excitedly greeted the man from the white sedan. As Ben exited the backseat, he stretched his stiff muscles, feeling like an old dog getting back on his feet after a long nap on a cold concrete slab. He heard Carl's voice as he spoke to the new man. "Duane, it's good to see you. You're looking to be in pretty good shape; you been working out? I'm sure you've got everything under control, as usual. Come and meet your crew."

Ben relaxed his stretched back and arms, then cut his yawn short when he heard Carl's remarks. When he shook his head to clear it and looked forward, he found the two men walking toward him.

"Ben, this is Duane Hawes. Duane is our captain, and he's also part owner of the *Aurawind*," Carl said.

"Hey, Ben."

"Hello, Mr. Hawes, or . . . uh, Captain."

"Call me Duane, Ben. Rank is for the navy and cruise ships," Duane said with a slight chuckle. "You look a little tired. Was it a tough drive?"

"Not too bad. It's amazing how sitting looking out a window can beat you up though," Ben said, returning the stare that Duane had fixed on him while they shook hands.

"Well, we have a fairly light day tomorrow, busy but light, then you're going to get a chance to get all those muscles working again."

"Good, I'm ready to go."

"Ben," Carl said, "I'm going to be leaving you with Duane. I want him to take you out and get you some sailing gear tomorrow. We'll probably meet up again in the evening. Why don't you get your stuff and take it over to Duane's car?"

"You bet."

Carl and Duane strolled away from Ben to get some distance between them.

"What?" Carl asked.

"What do you mean?"

"The look. What's with the look you gave him?"

"What look?"

"Duane, you were challenging him."

"Where did you find this guy? Something doesn't feel right."

"Christ, you just met him. Give the guy half-a-chance. He'll be fine."

"Yeah, well, we'll see."

Ben retrieved his belongings and stood next to the passenger-side door waiting for Purrette to look at him. He stood silently as she stared out the front windshield. Realizing she wasn't going to acknowledge his presence, he leaned over the front of the vehicle so that only the thin slice of glass separated their faces. They made eye contact. Ben raised his eyebrows and passed his hand in front of her eyes three times. Purrette's eyes followed his hand, then she nodded slowly, three times, before resuming her distant stare. Satisfied that he had said good-bye and wondering if she welcomed his departure, Ben turned with his gear and moved toward the white sedan.

After Carl and Purrette had driven away and any hint of the sun was gone, Duane walked to his car and locked it, confusing Ben. They would need to load his gear in the trunk and take that car to go anywhere.

Duane saw the look on his face. Instead of clarifying the situation, he began to walk toward the water. When he had almost disappeared into the dark, he called back, "Come on, grab your stuff. We're sleeping onboard."

When Ben caught up to him, he could see Duane trying to turn over the small tender, tied with a long line to a gray log, which lay high on the beach near a line of trees. They would use the tender to get out to their ship. Ben stood watching Duane struggle for a minute, not knowing what he should do. Duane suddenly stopped bending over the small craft, stood upright, turned to Ben and said impatiently, "Would you mind taking the other end and helping me get this thing in the water?"

"Oh, sorry," Ben said, dropping his bag and hurrying over to help with the tender. "You're going to have to tell me what to do. I don't know a thing about what goes on around boats."

"Well, the first thing you do is use common sense. If you see someone that needs a little help, you help him."

"Sorry. I didn't know if maybe it was a point of honor for the captain to handle the boat by himself. Like I said, you're going to have to tell me everything you want me to do."

Duane pointed toward the water and said, "Let's head west."

# Chapter 4

Unsure of himself as he climbed the ladder in the dark, Ben could hear the water lap against the side of the ninety-foot ship. The tender they'd ridden in gave a light thud as it bounced against the larger hull, rising in the water without the load of their weight. In the moving darkness, he could see highlights reflected off the rails, the lamp fixtures, the polished wood of the deck, and the white canopy that covered the pilothouse. He saw Duane disappear down a chute, and a few seconds later a dim yellow light fought its way out of the main companionway.

Duane's voice came from below. "Come on down, but leave your bag up top."

Ben stepped wide-legged, unsure of his footing, toward the entrance and down the stairs. Once below, he found himself in the main salon. He detected a light oily scent as he scanned the room in the low light that glowed from the small hallway next to the stairs. White textured panels like picture frames, each with a light fixture of polished brass mounted in the middle, broke the teakwood panels of the walls. The wall behind the stairs he had used consisted of bookshelves that were fronted by thin brass rails to hold the books in place. In the middle of the room, a horseshoe-shaped white leather sofa with brocade cushions encircled an oval teakwood table with a raised edge on its top. Across from the salon was a tight but open galley containing all the features of a full kitchen. Its teakwood cabinets were mounted with sturdy locking hardware of the same polished brass used in the light fixtures. The full-sized sink, cooktop and oven sat in a white acrylic countertop.

He could hear Duane rustling around somewhere behind him, down the narrow hallway.

"There's sandwich-making material in the refrigerator. Beer too, and there's bread in the cabinet beside the microwave. Help yourself if you're hungry," Duane called from the hall.

Ben built himself a sandwich and cracked open a beer. Stepping out of the galley, he found a dining area with a lengthy oval teakwood table and eight chairs. The white leather seats matched the sofa. He sat on one to eat his sandwich and continued to look at his surroundings. The same teakwood and white paneling from the salon surrounded the dining room table. He saw stars through the skylights on both sides of the room, and he could imagine the warm, natural light the skylights would provide during the day.

He finished his sandwich and beer, and then waited for Duane, not knowing what he should do. When he couldn't wait any longer, he decided to search for Duane. He heard paper being shuffled down the hall and found Duane looking over a number of charts.

"Is it okay to look around?" he asked.

"Yeah, but I'm trying to conserve battery power so I don't want to turn on any lights up top. Give me a few minutes, and I'll show you to your berth. I'll give you a complete tour in the morning when we have some light."

"Great. What I've seen so far is better than I imagined. This ship is incredible."

"As it says in the brochure, 'She's well appointed'."

Later, they walked along the deck toward the front of the ship. Duane stopped at a hatch and lifted the lid, then slid open the wooden door underneath. "This is the hatch to the crew quarters. There are two small berths and a head in here. Let me go down first and get you some light."

After handing his bag down to Duane, Ben descended into a small, wedge-shaped room with curved sides. He felt no surprise to see that everything in the room was made of teakwood. The wall panels, the built-in desk along the small front wall, the chairs, the storage drawers underneath the two bunks, and the ladder that he had come down. The floor gleamed of recently varnished teakwood with imbedded white strips of friction inlay. Behind the ladder, a low, thin hallway led to two small doors, one leading to the head on the left and the other to some additional storage space on the right.

"So this is going to be home for the next year," Ben said.

"If you last that long."

Ben sensed skepticism in Duane's tone. "I told Carl I'd work it for a year, so I'll be staying for a year. What makes you think I won't last?"

Ben watched Duane as the other man formulated his answer.

"Carl said you've never sailed before, and it isn't easy," Duane said.

"Carl told me that and said I don't need to know about sailing. I'm the grunt work guy, I do everything I'm told to do, and any sailing knowledge I need will be taught by you."

"Well, Carl doesn't sail much. But he does have one thing right—you do everything you're told and things will go nice and smooth."

"Good, but like I told you before, right now I don't know a thing about what I'm expected to do. Assume I need to be told everything, but rest assured that I will learn what needs to be done and I will eventually be doing things without being told."

"Okay," Duane said flatly, causing Ben to wonder if he meant it. "Tomorrow we have to go shopping. I'm going to be getting you up pretty early." He climbed the ladder and left.

Ben could hear his footsteps above returning to the back of the ship. He stood on the first step of the ladder and slid the wooden door closed. Duane's steps suddenly stopped above and returned to the hatch. "You may want to leave the hatch open," Duane said.

"Thanks," Ben called back, but made no move to do as suggested. The footsteps above moved away again.

In the middle of the night, Ben awoke soaked in sweat. His pillow wet, his bottom sheet damp, his top sheet and blanket thrown on the floor. He sucked in hard at the room's hot, thick air, but didn't seem to be getting enough oxygen. Spinning his legs off the bed, he sat up and felt rivulets of sweat run down behind his ears, tickling him. He stepped over to the ladder and up onto the first rung, then slid the hatch door open. A rush of cool, sweet air quenched the thirst of his lungs. He climbed up another two rungs so that his upper body poked out into the night air. He stood leaning back against the hatch opening, staring out at a sliver of moon still high in the sky. The light breeze cooled and dried his skin. The stars rained down to a dark horizon, dark except for the tiny lights reflecting off the crests of the waves. The night was silent, but for the waves sounding against the hull of the gently rocking ship, and the groan of stretched line straining against the pressure from forces trying the set the ship free.

He stayed in the hatch opening, unable to take his eyes off of the ocean rhythm he could barely see but could vividly feel. When he finally returned to his berth, the room was cool enough for sleep.

***

Before sunrise, they returned in the tender to the spot from which they had taken it the night before. They drove to the main harbor in town and purchased tokens for the public showers. By the time they had finished, the new dawn began to illuminate the harbor. A small outdoor café provided them with a big breakfast. They sat in white plastic chairs at a white plastic table with a collapsed marine-blue umbrella stuck in the middle. Ben watched the gulls coasting on the currents, swooping down and landing just outside the white plastic PVC fence with laced-on marine-blue vinyl fabric that separated the café from the sidewalk. The birds stood stoically watching from the corners of their eyes until a crust got tossed over the fence, then they rushed pell-mell with their wings slightly raised and their beaks open, screaming and stabbing at each other to get the small morsel of food. The winner of the battle flew off with the prize, while the losers all turned away in a huffy manner as if they hadn't wanted the food to begin with.

If he hadn't been so hungry, Ben would have tossed them all of his bread, but the sandwich of the night before had only made his stomach rumble for more. After consuming every morsel on his plate, he and Duane lingered over coffee. They looked out over the harbor with not much to say.

"We going to be eating a lot of sandwiches when we go to sea?" Ben asked to make conversation.

"Pretty much. Is that a problem?"

"No, I like sandwiches."

"Then you should be happy."

Ben turned from the harbor to look at Duane. He kept his eyes on him and waited for Duane to turn so they could make eye contact. He could tell Duane felt his stare, and he noted how long it took Duane to get uncomfortable enough to turn to him. When Duane did turn, he returned Ben's stare without word or reaction.

"You got a bug or something up your ass about me?" Ben said, "You sure don't seem to be trying to get along."

"Listen, all I know about you is that you've never sailed. I need a sailor. Based on that, I wouldn't have hired you. Carl hired you because he wants to get the ship out to sea, and he figured if he waited for me to hire a crew, we would have been waiting forever. Now, I have to live with you. That's the bug up my ass. I would have preferred to hire someone myself, but Carl decided to do things his way, again."

"Then I guess you'll just have to try and make the best of it, won't you?"

Duane smiled a sarcastic smile and said, "I guess."

First they went to the barbershop. Duane ordered his own hair cut short but told the barber to tidy up Ben's, leaving it a bit long. Ben wondered about Duane providing the haircut instructions and shot him a questioning look, which Duane ignored. He wanted to point out that he could order his own haircut, but then remained silent. After the haircuts, they went to buy clothing. Duane picked up the tab on several white, off-white and navy-blue shorts, slacks and shirts. They purchased deck shoes and rain gear next, and then they went to a scuba store for snorkels and fins. Ben noticed that Duane purchased based on the quality of the items without paying much attention to the cost.

Around mid-afternoon they were back in another restaurant for a late lunch. Duane got up from his seat to use the phone. Alone, Ben stared out the window and watched the sun circling westward, about to slip behind a bank of clouds. Duane returned to the table when the clouds hazed the sunlight.

"Drink up. We're setting sail," Duane said, as he reached down and picked up his wineglass, finishing what remained. He pulled cash out of his wallet and threw it on the table. He turned and walked out without a word, leaving Ben sitting alone.

Onboard, Ben waited near the main companionway while Duane made preparations below. He didn't know what he should be doing and wanted to stay within earshot in case Duane had an order for him. Duane appeared from the hatch with a chart rolled up in his hand and went into the pilothouse. He spread the chart on a small table and started the engine. Ben felt the rumbling in his feet. He looked at Duane, who was flipping switches, testing the running lights, and checking other gauges that Ben could make out, but didn't understand. Duane signaled for Ben to come to him.

"Take that boathook and catch the line up front. Pull us forward and take up slack until you get the mooring float. Let me know when you've got it, and when I signal you, release us from the clip then toss the float clear," he ordered.

Ben fumbled getting the hook out of its rack. Then it took him several tries to catch the line that connected the vessel to the float. Once he had it in hand, he easily pulled in the required slack, and then signaled to Duane. He released the clip and tossed the float as far away from the ship as possible. As he walked back toward Duane, the ship suddenly powered forward. Ben stumbled sideways for a few steps, battling to maintain his balance, then lost his footing completely, and went down on the deck. He rolled over, then came to a stop at the base of the pilothouse lying on his back, looking up to see Duane's face smiling down at him. Embarrassed, he jumped to his feet and walked around to Duane.

"Sorry," Duane greeted him. "I'm not quite used to this throttle yet. You okay?"

"Yeah. You get your jollies?"

"No. Sorry. This engine has some pep. I didn't realize I'd revved it up so high when I shifted it into forward. It will be a lot easier when you get your sea legs, and when I get used to this throttle. Really man, I'm sorry."

"Yeah," Ben said, not quite believing the explanation. "How long does it take to get to Catalina?"

"Around seven hours, maybe a little more," Duane said distractedly as he returned his attention to the dials in front of him. "Once we clear that buoy out there, we'll set some sail and cut the engines."

Duane made for the buoy he had pointed out. The engine thrummed, its exhaust periodically filling the air. Not long after they passed the buoy, Ben felt the wind strengthen. The ship rode higher on the waves and plunged deeper into the following valleys. Duane told him the mainsail needed unfurling and pointed to the straps that held it in place along the boom, and then he pointed to the tackle that would raise it. Ben struggled trying to identify exactly which objects Duane was referring to. He told Ben he would help get it started, but would have to get back to the wheel quickly. He cautioned Ben about how the sail would react when he lifted it. Once the sail was partially hoisted, the wind would start to fill the canvas and begin to lift the sail itself. If it rose too fast, the line could burn Ben's hands, so he showed him how to hold it to control the ascent. They went down and started removing the straps. Once Ben had the hang of it, Duane left him to finish the work on his own.

With the sail now free, Ben nervously moved to the line and took hold of it the way he thought he'd been shown. He pulled down and saw the sail start to rise. When he had hoisted it barely a yard, the wind began to fill the sail and gently assisted him in raising it the rest of the way. Ben looked up to see Duane nodding his approval in the pilothouse, and then Ben signaled to find out what to do with the rope. He thought that if he let it go the sail would just come down, and he would have to raise it again. Duane pointed to the cleat attached to the mast and indicated that Ben should wind the line around it. As he wound, he noticed that the engine's thrum had disappeared, that the deck had become still.

"Good work," Duane called to him. "Stand by to jibe. The boom's going to swing over your way. Come back here, and I'll show you how to use the winch."

Duane instructed Ben to wrap two or three turns of the line around the winch, then showed him where the winch handle was stored. Ben inserted the handle and was shown how to use his free hand to pay out the line behind him while cranking on the handle. After delivering the instructions, Duane moved to the wheel and started his turn to starboard. Ben felt a mild panic when the mainsail went slack as their turn took them directly with the wind, and he stopped cranking, thinking he'd done something wrong.

"Don't stop, don't stop. Keep cranking," Duane called anxiously. His words got Ben cranking again so they could complete the jibe. The sail filled with the wind again, and Duane said, "Good. Cleat the line and put the handle back."

Ben pulled the handle and replaced it, but didn't know what was required to cleat the line. Duane watched the compass, adjusting their course, while Ben, reluctant to interrupt his concentration, coiled the line and laid it on the deck. When Duane finished setting the course, he looked at the sail and attempted a slight adjustment to its setting, but the mainsheet played out too much. He looked back, saw the line feeding off of the winch with the coils lying on the deck, and moved quickly to grab the loose line so he could snug it up against the winch. He looked sharply at Ben. "I thought I told you to cleat this."

"You did. I don't know what that is."

"You managed to cleat the main halyard. Why didn't you cleat this?" Duane said, but continued before allowing Ben to answer. "Get over here and hold this. I have to take the wheel."

Feeling like a landlubber, Ben took the line from Duane. Once Duane returned to the wheel, Ben spoke to his back. "First of all, I don't know what a halyard is, so if I did cleat it, I didn't know it. Secondly, I don't know what cleating is, so I don't know when I cleated this halyard thing. Maybe you could tell me."

Duane looked at the gauges before turning to Ben.

"Get the winch handle. You have to crank it in again."

After Ben retrieved the handle, Duane said, "The halyard is the line you used to hoist the sail. The cleat is the two-ended hook you wound the line around when you finished hoisting it. There's another one back there behind you to use for the mainsheet after you finish cranking in. The mainsheet is the name of the line you're using right now. Crank."

The mix of anger and embarrassment created by the condescending tone of Duane's words made Ben crave a physical release of his anger at Duane's expense. He controlled his craving and instead began to crank the winch and continued to crank until Duane told him to stop. Then he wound the line around the cleat, the way it was supposed to be done. His anger subsided as he told himself that he hadn't done what was expected of him, therefore Duane had every right to address him angrily.

With the autopilot holding the course for Catalina, Duane took Ben forward to show him how to raise a jib.

"We'll make better time with more sail," he said, "Now, remember I told you that the line you used to hoist the mainsail was called the halyard? Well, this one is called the jib halyard."

Together, they raised the additional sail. Duane took the time to teach and explain the name and purpose of each piece of equipment so the confusion that occurred during the jibe could be eliminated. Ben felt much better and appreciated the instruction he had received. He checked the halyard he had just wound onto the cleat, confirming for himself that it remained tight. He knew he would remember most of what he had been told despite his nervousness at learning something so new. Not having the least bit of understanding of what Duane had demonstrated made learning a little more difficult than he preferred. Ben would have liked more time and more light during his first sailing lesson. The second half of the sailing had been done in the dark.

The seven-hour sail passed quickly as Duane pointed out various aspects of the ship. When they saw the lights of Avalon Harbor, he instructed Ben about the process of docking the ship. Ben had lowered and secured the sails as Duane started the engine and turned into the harbor under power. They cruised to a mooring where Ben fished in the float and attached a line. The engines died. In the silent calm that followed, Ben could hear the noise of a bus traveling on the waterfront street of the harbor. The clear sound of its tires and its gear changes seemed amplified by the still and quiet peace of the water at night.

# Chapter 5

Ben's thigh muscles burned during the climb up the steep stairway leading to a large white house perched high on the hill overlooking Avalon harbor. The burning made him forget how good he felt about his new clothing and his new station in life. He had just made his maiden voyage as a sailor, and now he felt like one, familiar with the life of the sea. An out-of-shape sailor, he thought.

He and Duane entered the grounds through the gate in a white picket fence, and a sign pointed them in the direction of another stairway at the side of the house. This one led up to a large cone-roofed, gazebo possessing a view of the harbor and casino in front, the cove to the left, the city to the right, and the hills behind. A strong breeze blew in from the water and up the hill, so the bartender kept a cocktail glass on the napkins stacked on the bar. People, some in jackets, some in golf shirts and shorts, milled about near the bar and buffet table, while a three-piece band played in tones low enough to allow the pockets of conversation to hum along uninterrupted.

Duane told Ben to wait near the door while he searched for Carl. Waiting would be easier with a beer to drink, so Ben moved to the bar and placed an order. He hadn't been back to his spot by the door long enough to take a drink when Carl greeted him.

"Ben, you made it. How was your first sail?" Carl asked, placing his hand on Ben's shoulder and stepping in front of him. He bent down close to Ben's face and in a low voice said, "Ben, I guess Duane didn't get a chance to tell you, but there's no alcohol around clients. Make sure you get rid of that." Then Carl stepped back a pace, all smiles.

"No, he didn't tell me. In fact, he didn't have much to say to me at all," Ben said, inviting a question.

"Really, is there a problem?"

Ben could see Duane approaching with an expression of displeasure. "I'd say so, but why don't we ask Duane?"

Carl turned to look at Duane as he approached. Carl's own look of displeasure caused Duane to hesitate for an instant.

"Carl," Duane said with a nod, "I was just looking for you."

"Ben says you two have a problem. What is it?"

Duane looked at Ben with burning eyes. He appeared to be unwilling to start the discussion, so Ben turned to Carl and said, "He indicated he'd rather not be sailing with me. He said he wouldn't have hired me, that he needed a person with some experience. You told me I wouldn't need any sailing experience. So I'm a little confused about what it is I'm doing here. If I'm going to be a cause for concern, then let me know and I'll clear out now."

Carl listened intently to Ben. He stood silently for a number of seconds before he turned to Duane and said, "Ben is part of your crew, Duane. Are we clear?"

"I would like someone with more experience," Duane responded. He waited for Carl to speak again, but Carl just continued to stare at him. When he realized Carl wasn't about to speak, he said, "We're clear."

Ben saw ripples in Duane's jaw muscles.

"I want to bring some people over to meet you. All smiles, right?" Carl waited until they both nodded, then left.

Duane gave Ben a confused and angry look, and then said, "Lose the beer."

"Carl already told me that. Thanks for giving me the heads-up."

"I didn't get a chance to tell you."

"Right, you couldn't have filled the silence during the cart ride over here with any warnings. You couldn't have said something during the silent climb up the hill."

"You didn't have to shoot your mouth off about my preference in choosing a crew member."

"Fuck you. I wanted to give you and Carl another chance to decide whether you wanted me to stay before we really got into this little adventure. I don't want to spend a year with you reminding me that you wished you had a better crew. If Carl had second thoughts, then he better get them out now. I'm sure you still want to get rid of me, so you better get with Carl later and get it settled. I'd like to know as soon as possible so I don't end up treading water while you two make up your minds."

Carl returned with a man not much older than Ben and a pretty woman with long black hair.

"Duane, Ben, this is Mark Labrio. He and his wife are considering a booking on the *Aurawind* in a month or so."

Labrio's eyes smiled out from a well-tanned face, his delicate features straight, thin eyebrows, thin lips, and a thin nose with mere slits for nostrils. He shook hands with both men.

Ben turned to the woman and said, "Hello, Mrs. Labrio."

The woman furled her brow slightly before responding, "I'm not Mrs. Labrio."

Chuckling, Mark Labrio said, "I couldn't find my wife when Carl asked me to come and meet his crew. She's around here somewhere."

"This is my assistant, Miss Malloy, Lindsay Malloy," Carl said to Ben's questioning face.

Miss Malloy's feathered black hair hung down to her strongly muscled shoulders. She wore a low-cut dress, its length mid-thigh, and its hold on her hips tight. Ben registered Carl's words *my assistant* as he looked at her legs and spotted the silver anklet. He raised his eyes to her face and saw eyebrows penciled in. A name would have escaped his mouth except he heard Carl's voice again.

"This is the third member of the sailing crew, Rudy Fletcher. Our cook won't join the crew until we're in the South Pacific."

Ben watched in confusion as Labrio shook the hand of a well-dressed, well-groomed Rudy. Before Ben had a chance to react, Carl whisked Labrio away, saying he would have another opportunity to talk with the crew the next morning when he visited the ship.

In a stilted voice, Duane turned to Rudy and introduced himself as the captain of the *Aurawind*, which caused Rudy to screw up his face in confusion as he shook Duane's hand. Ben looked back and forth from Rudy to Miss Malloy, trying to choose which mystery to solve first. Finally, Rudy asked, "Seen a ghost, Ben?"

Ben ignored Rudy and turned back to Miss Malloy. "Purrette?" he asked.

"Not while I'm working," she answered.

"What?"

"It's Lindsay Malloy, when I'm working." She cocked her head to emphasize the point.

"Okay, Lindsay."

"Call me Miss Malloy. Carl likes the way it rolls off the tongue, so he has everyone call me Miss Malloy. He also thinks it sounds more businesslike."

"Jesus Christ," Ben muttered.

"She looks pretty good with her clothes on, doesn't she, BAB?" Rudy interrupted.

Ben slowly turned to stare at Rudy and said, "What's it been, two, three days, and you pick up as if we've never been apart. I thought you ditched us in Vegas."

"I just couldn't shake the fond memories of our drive together, so I decided to join you. Carl told me how to get ahold of him."

"Great. I'm glad to see you with your clothes on, too. Looks like you scrubbed up a little as well. It's amazing what a shave and a haircut does for a man."

"Sleep too. I felt a little strung-out a few days ago." Rudy's voice had a round, rich tone that Ben hadn't heard during the trip from Coeur d'Alene. He also had a smile that he hadn't shared before. "Now that I've met the potential client, I guess I can get out of here. I found this dance club downtown that gets pretty dirty. I'd ask you to come along, but I think you're a little too proper for this place. I'll see you onboard." Rudy slapped Ben on the back and left without saying a word to Duane or Miss Malloy, both of whom stood quietly waiting to talk to Ben.

"Since it seems to be the compliment of the day, let me tell you that you look pretty good with your clothes on, too," Miss Malloy said.

"Thanks. Duane bought them for me." Ben turned a smile on in Duane's direction.

Duane's naturally smiling eyes conflicted with his heavy brow and pursed lips. "I'm going to talk to Carl. One of the water taxis can take you out to the ship. Do you think you can make your way back on your own?" he said to Ben, who nodded that he could.

Looking at Miss Malloy, Ben felt relief for the opportunity to try and make sense of the way these people acted. "You're not supposed to be drinking martinis, or didn't Carl tell you that?"

"It's not a real drink. I just want to look like everyone else."

Ben reached over and took the toothpick out of her glass and ate the olive. The gin constricted his throat the way it always did. He raised his eyebrows. "We come up here and meet a guy for twenty seconds, and then we're free to go? Why couldn't we just meet the guy in the morning on the ship?"

Miss Malloy gave him a contemplative stare over the edge of her glass as she sipped her drink. She swallowed. Then with her mouth closed, she licked her top teeth before saying, "There were actually two reasons for you to come here for a twenty-second introduction. The first, to meet the client. Carl wanted to see how they reacted to meeting you and Duane and Rudy. That's why I'm here, to watch. Remember? Carl wants me to watch how people react.

"The second, to see how Duane fixed you up. Carl wanted to see you for himself. My guess is he'll be happy at how you turned out. After all, he told Duane what kind of clothes to buy and that he wanted your hair to cover the tops of your ears."

"What?"

"Carl knows what he's doing. He talked to you before you met the client. He wouldn't have brought the client over if he didn't like the way you looked, but he was pretty sure you'd look fine. You're part of the living brochure tonight, Ben. The people we want sailing with you are not expecting a crew full of creepy sailors. You had to have the look, and Carl could see that look in you when he first met you. He just completed the look with the clothes and the haircut. You've got a rugged look. The type of guy you want sailing your ship, the type of guy you want on your side. The clients will feel that.

"You see, Mr. Labrio is a sailor. He sails near the shore, but he'd like to put out to sea and do some real sailing. Problem is he doesn't have time to sail to the South Pacific, and by the looks of him, he probably doesn't have the nerve either. Still, he wants to sail in the South Pacific just so he can list it on his sailing resume. Get it? We have everything in place. They fly down and sail with us for a week, then talk about their exotic sailing adventure like the man-of-the-world sailor he wishes he could be. You and Duane and Rudy make them feel confident that they can pull it off."

Ben nodded while her words sunk in. He felt pride and embarrassment. Proud of being the rugged, good-looking type that people would want on their side. Embarrassed for being window dressing, a prop used to close the deal. "I see," he said. "I guess I get it. But what's up with you? Your hair is black. Who are you, Miss Malloy or Purrette?"

She looked at him hard while obviously thinking inwardly. He didn't feel she was searching to provide him with an answer, but to answer the question for herself. For the first time that evening, he saw the zombie that had watched the highway relentlessly during the long drive.

Her smile straightened, her eyes hooded over and drifted toward the floor where they stayed for a long time. Ben watched, confused, wondering what made her tick. Slowly, she closed her eyes, and while they appeared to be moving under her eyelids, she lifted her drink to her mouth and drank it all. She swallowed, lifted her head, opened her eyes and said, "I'm working."

"Okay," he said with concern, but when he saw the smile return to her face he felt relief and changed subjects. "Can I ask you about Duane? He seems a bit hard-boiled. Is he always this hard to get to know?"

"Duane?" she asked pulling her head back. "Duane likes everybody. You're not getting along with him?"

"I'm trying, but he's not having it."

"Well, you two better get it worked out soon. You're headed out on a long sail in a day or two."

***

Carl made eye contact with Duane, then jerked his head to the side, calling him over. "What seems to be the problem, Duane? Is Ben that hard to work with?" Carl asked.

"No, he picked things up just fine on the way over here. I meant to tell him that, but I forgot. If I had, he might not have brought it up to you, but like I told you the other night, I have a bad feeling about this guy. He's smart enough to learn everything we show him. Maybe he's smart enough to figure out the things that we *don't* show him. He wants things right and he watches everything."

"Hmm. Then be real careful what you show him. You're going to be spending more time with him than anybody else. You better be on your toes. Try not to make him think too much. Try and get along with him so he thinks everything is right."

"Yeah, I guess I better give him a little vote of confidence. Is Rudy sailing with us?"

"Not yet. I wanted him to go with you so he could lay low for a while, but I need him for something. He'll catch up with you at your next port of call."

\*\*\*

Ben lay awake in his berth. He had listened to Duane's footsteps up top for some time and wanted to go see the ship for the first time in daylight. He delayed entering Duane's world for as long as he could, but when he heard a new set of footsteps walking on deck, he decided he'd better go topside. He pulled on a pair of shorts, a T-shirt, and his deck shoes, and then climbed up out of the hatch. His view filled with infinite masts and ropes and chrome and marine-blue sail covers as he emerged. Yachts lined up in rows, facing out to sea. He could tell that Catalina was a popular sailing destination.

For most California sailors, it was the nearest non-mainland location they could sail to and feel they were not just hugging the coast.

Ben had seen the other ships in the dark. But now the details and abundance of sailing equipment flooded his eyes, stunning him with the sheer numbers of streamlined, elegant sailing craft displaying an exorbitant expenditure of rich people's money. The dollars invested in each of these yachts exceeded his imagination. Considering how hard he had worked to save the amount he had to tide him over for the last three months, he knew he would be ill parting with the lofty sums required to buy something of this value. The thought of that much disposable cash ricocheted in his mind.

He shook his head, performing a reality check, then looked at his own ship, the ship on which he had slept for the past two nights.

Both nights, in the dark, he could see the glossiness of the deck, and he could tell that the lifeline stanchions gleamed, but he had not expected the immaculate whole of what he saw in the bright daylight. The shining decks, the crisp sail covers, the new awning over the pilothouse. He looked at the other ships tied up in the row of moorings and felt proud that the *Aurawind* looked so much better than the vessels surrounding her.

Remembering he had come up to investigate the new footsteps, he turned and walked toward the stern. As he came to the pilothouse, he noticed, for the first time, the upper salon located behind the area where he had worked the winch the previous evening. Fixed vinyl-covered seating, a large table, and at the aft end, a small bar sitting on top of a half-size refrigerator. The salon allowed guests to sit and watch the sailing activity performed in the pilothouse, while enjoying their drinks and meals. Beside the small bar, the salon opened out onto a flat deck, providing the guests with a relaxing and protected area to take in the sun and scenery.

A stack of brand-new beach towels sat on one of the vinyl benches. Still no newcomer in sight. He turned and went down the companionway. Once below, he met Miss Malloy pulling various items from paper sacks erupting with celery stalks, snack bags, and foil-wrapped bottles.

"Good morning. Is it Purrette or Miss Malloy?" he asked lightheartedly.

She halted her turn toward the refrigerator and faced him, while placing on the counter the squat jar of caviar she had just pulled from one of the bags.

"The only time we'll see each other from now on is when we're working. Forget about Purrette."

"I can try."

Miss Malloy kept her eyes locked with his for a few seconds, then sighed and said, "I think I'll get you to put the rest of these things away, and when you're done, put one of these bottles on ice in the bucket and bring it to me up top, okay? The Labrios will be here in a half hour, and I have to do some setup."

"Sure. Anything else I can do?"

"I'll let you know when you bring me the champagne."

In the paper sacks, Ben found a number of cheeses, exotic-looking crackers, onions, olives, strawberries, melons and croissants. Another bag held basic supplies such as salt, pepper, sugar and a variety of dried herbs. He washed the champagne flutes that he found in a box on the counter, then placed them and the ice bucket on a tray. Finally he placed a bottle of the champagne in the bucket, surrounded it with ice, and took the tray to Miss Malloy.

"Would you like me to put out the cheese and crackers?" he asked from the bar area of the upper salon as she spread a marine-blue-and-white-striped tablecloth.

"Sure, good idea. Can you dice an onion? I mean finely diced?"

"I'll give it a try."

"Okay, but maybe just do half of it. As fine as you can get it. You're going to have to go change before they get here, so make it quick."

He sprinted away in a crazy scamper, waving his arms wildly as if in a panic, attempting to make her laugh. When he disappeared down below, she rolled her eyes and continued setting the table.

After getting himself ready, Ben returned to the upper salon to help again. When he came around the pilothouse and first looked into the salon area, he saw Miss Malloy peeling off the yellow golf shirt she was wearing. She shook her hair and threw her head back, stopping him in his tracks. The string bikini top barely covered her well-shaped breasts, the weight of the tanned, curved flesh threatening to break the thin string that rose up her chest and around her neck. The slight suggestive covering tweaked his imagination with more pleasure than when he had seen her breasts fully exposed. She wore tight-fitting short shorts and on her ankle, the anklet.

He wanted to say something casual to break the silence they had entered. When he managed to tear his eyes away from her body to meet her eyes, he remained speechless. Then they heard Duane's footsteps coming up from below. Miss Malloy smiled as Ben muttered, "Somebody put my eyes back in my head."

"Ben, when the boat arrives, be ready to drop some bumpers over the side," Duane ordered. "You may not need them, but have them ready."

"Okay, but you have to tell me what a bumper is, what it looks like, and where I can find them."

Duane pointed to a locker in the pilothouse and told him what to look for, then said, "And be sure to tie them to a cleat before you throw them over the side."

"Thanks, you did need to tell me that," he said in all seriousness.

When the Labrios' boat arrived, it pulled up to the ladder. Ben dropped a bumper at the forward end of the boat, but a stern bumper wasn't required. It did, however, cause a problem when Mark Labrio tripped on the line that attached the bumper to the cleat. When he fell to his hands and knees, Duane shot a look at Ben as they helped Mr. Labrio to his feet.

Laughing with some embarrassment while brushing off his slacks, he said, "No harm done. This deck doesn't appear to have a speck of dirt on it. You do a great job of keeping it clean."

"It's freshly varnished," offered Duane. "I'm sure Carl told you about the major refit the *Aurawind* received recently."

"Yes, I'm looking forward to seeing all the new gadgets."

By the time Mrs. Labrio made it to the top of the ladder, Ben had cleared the line from the bumper out of the way. She wore a neckerchief over her blond hair, designer sunglasses, a light sweater, and white slacks. A soft, short, stocky build compared to Mr. Labrio's thin, gaunt form. Nonetheless, she looked elegant and athletic in her movements. Carl came up the ladder next, dressed in gray slacks and a long-sleeved white shirt with a thin dark tie. He looked around as if unfamiliar with his surroundings. Rudy followed, wearing a more marine look and a smirk, while nodding his head as if very impressed by what he saw. Ben observed these reactions while feeling a sense of proprietorship, having lived onboard for the past few days.

"Duane, let's go up to the front of the boat so you can start with a description of the sails," Carl suggested.

"If you boys are going to talk boats, I'm going to just look around on my own, if that's okay," Mrs. Labrio said.

"Of course it's okay, Janice," Carl said. He turned to Ben, who stood off to one side. "Ben, this is Janice Labrio. Why don't you take her and find Miss Malloy?"

Ben turned to the upper salon with Janice. Once the group of men had moved out of hearing range, she said, "When they start talking about masts and sails and sheets and the rest of that crap, I like to set myself adrift. The only sheets-to-the-wind I'm interested in are the ones I get after a few highballs. Tell me you have a bar somewhere nearby."

He smiled the guilty smile of one who knows he can supply the desired vice. "We have some champagne on ice, but I'm sure I can find something stronger if you'd like."

"Champagne will do."

In the upper salon, Ben popped the cork on the champagne, accidentally letting it fly out into the water. Foam rushed out the opening of the bottle, and Janice clicked her tongue, shaming him. He poured into her glass and foam rose up and over the top of the flute.

"I hope you're a better sailor than you are a bartender," she said, then downed the glass of champagne. She handed him back the glass and nodded to have him fill it again, which he did. "Aren't you going to join me?"

Carl's rule about drinking in the presence of clients now created a dilemma for him. "I would, but I'd better go get Miss Malloy."

"Don't worry, she'll find us. Sit, have a drink," she said as she dropped down onto one of the vinyl benches.

A stronger wave of the dilemma crashed onto him. "Actually, champagne isn't my beverage of choice, and when I'm onboard, I don't drink anything stronger than soda," he said apologetically.

She looked at him as if to say, *So, make an exception.* The look tempted him to the point of pouring himself a glass. Miss Malloy, returning from below wearing a loose fitting, coverall windbreaker, greeted them and also poured herself some champagne. She then sat beside Janice and started to rehash some of the events of the previous evening. After a short anecdote that drew a chuckle from Janice, she suggested that Ben offer Mr. Labrio a glass of champagne to get him through the tour. Ben departed, but returned shortly to retrieve the champagne for Mark Labrio. He spent the rest of the time during the Labrios' visit filling glasses and restocking snack plates.

When the group, including Janice, went below to look at the cabins and all the ship's amenities, he wanted to join them, but knew he would be in the way. While they toured the master cabin, he took the opportunity to get another bottle of champagne from the kitchen and place it in the refrigerator up top. The group returned, and Janice made everyone aware of her thirst, so the second bottle came in handy. When it stood inverted in the ice bucket, Mark decided they should depart. During the good-byes, Janice looked at Ben with the look of someone who had had too much, but needed more, and said, "You have the darkest green eyes. At first I thought they were brown, but they're green."

Once they had left, Miss Malloy took off her windbreaker and lay out in one of the deck chairs. Duane joined her while Ben removed the empty bottles and the scavenged platters of fruit and cheese. He overheard Duane say that the Labrios would likely join them in Tahiti in a few weeks' time, and that Mark had been very interested in the ship, the equipment in the pilothouse, and how she handled. When Ben finished the cleanup, Duane grabbed some of their things and told Ben to join them as they took the tender to shore. When they arrived, Duane gave Ben some money and told him to find himself something to eat before taking a water taxi back out to the ship. He intended to keep the tender because he might not be coming back onboard that night.

Alone, Ben found a Greek restaurant and had a meal with a few bottles of beer. Before he left, he ordered gyros for later. Then he returned to the *Aurawind*.

He put the sandwiches in the kitchen, opened a beer, and set out to take a closer look at the ship. In the abbreviated tour the previous night, he wasn't able to linger during his inspection. The teakwood motif continued into the stern cabins. The master cabin, with its elaborately curved woodwork and queen-size bed, made a bigger impression on him than the lower salon had made on the first night. He stuck his head into one of the smaller cabins on the port side. Realizing he had entered Duane's cabin, he quickly pulled out, but something he saw on the small desk caught his eye. A picture of the *Aurawind*, with all of its vital statistics, beckoned to be picked up and read. The document listed the length of ninety feet, the beam—which he assumed was the width—twenty-six feet, the type of diesel engine, the fact that the ship had a steel hull, and a host of other information that read like a real estate sales brochure.

Placing the sheet back in the exact place from which he had taken it, and accepting that he had already invaded Duane's privacy, he decided to nose around a little longer to see if there might be other items of interest in the cabin. He tried to touch as little as possible, and after finding only nautical charts out in open view, he opened one of the small desk drawers. Nothing. When he opened the second one, he stopped short and pulled his hand back as if bitten by a rabid animal. He looked at the handgun for a second, and then looked over his shoulder to see if anyone had spotted him snooping. He closed the desk drawer and hurried out of the cabin.

# Chapter 6

As it turned out, Duane returned to the *Aurawind* that evening shortly after Ben had watched the sun drop behind the mountain. The sound of the tender hitting the steel hull drew him out of the contemplative state he'd settled into after a few beers. Although he knew Duane had arrived, he stayed in his deck chair, enjoying the gentle rocking as long as he could.

"Good news, Ben," Duane said, approaching from behind. "We have visitors again tomorrow and then we set sail for Honolulu."

"Wow. So I'm still part of the crew?"

"Yeah. I did talk to Carl again, and I told him something I meant to tell you earlier. You did pick things up pretty quick, and you'll probably work out just fine. I guess if I had told you so before we went to the party, we might have avoided that whole scene."

"Hmm. I'm glad to hear that." Ben smiled, feeling good. "Honolulu. Wow. How long does it take to sail there?"

"A week or so."

"Is Rudy sailing with us?"

"No. I'm still not sure if Rudy's with us. I just met him, so you probably know more about him than I do. I don't know if he's ever sailed, and Carl won't give me an answer one way or another. He said if Rudy joins us, it would be in Honolulu."

"I don't know a thing about him, except he likes to get on people's nerves—and there's something going on between him and Purrette."

"Something between Rudy and Miss Malloy?" Duane asked with disbelief.

"Yeah, it's freaky. First she tries to knock his head off in the backseat, and then they end up hopping in the sack together in Vegas. If you ask me, she could have done some damage to Rudy."

"In the backseat or in the sack?"

"Both."

Duane smiled then looked at the rigging to spot anything that might be out of place. "Listen, we're going to be busy tomorrow. We have to get provisions to last us a week, and some people the Labrios talked to want to visit us in the afternoon. Then we set sail as soon as we're ready. If you want to go ashore and blow off some steam tonight, feel free to take the tender," Duane offered, then went below to work on his charts.

Ben thought about the chance to see some of the sites of Avalon, but the inertia created by the beer he had consumed anchored him to his deck chair. He also thought that captaining the tender in his slightly numbed state might turn out to be dangerous. It took a few seconds before he realized that Duane had left. Soon after that realization, he revisited the mind-wandering state he'd been enjoying before Duane showed up.

In the glow of the city that arced around him, he craved another beer as he looked out at the open sea toward the mainland. Just as he couldn't get himself to rise and go ashore, he couldn't get himself to rise and go for another beer. Later, when his arm slipped off the armrest and startled him awake, he decided he'd better hit the sack.

Before turning in he would check to see if Duane had other tasks for him to do. He went down the companionway and turned to go to Duane's room, but stopped when he heard a strange whirring noise that he knew was coming from the handgun. Instead of going to Duane's cabin, he called out so he wouldn't startle him. When Duane heard his voice, Ben heard the drawer open and the *thunk* of a weight landing in it.

Duane had no additional tasks for Ben, so Ben turned and went to his own berth where sleep consumed him rather quickly.

***

They split a list of food and objects to acquire, and spent the morning gathering the items they would need during a week at sea. With plenty of storage room onboard, they could have stocked up on a number of luxury items. They realized they really didn't need anything special until they had clients, so they stuck to very basic items to satisfy their needs: dry goods like pasta and rice, canned goods like soup and vegetables, and a few treats like candy bars and ice cream. They would try to catch some fish during the voyage, but sometimes in the deep sea that wasn't practical.

Before going back to the ship Duane checked in with the harbormaster. Ben waited outside near the door, as Duane paid for another evening at the mooring, but explained they may be departing late in the afternoon. Ben thought everything seemed normal until the harbormaster asked about their next port of call and Duane told him Sausalito. Ben moved closer to the door, trying to hear more of the conversation, and came close to being struck in the ear when it opened as Duane came out.

When they returned to the ship, Miss Malloy, in another small bikini top, met them with a stern look on her face. She ordered Ben to ice the champagne, dice the onions, and prepare the snack trays before putting away any of the things he had brought back with him. Once he regained control over the direction his eyes should point, he obeyed without question.

Carl brought the visitors to the ship alone this time. Gordon and Mora Payne toured the *Aurawind* together, both asking questions in knowledgeable sailing terms, and neither inclined to consume any of the champagne during the stroll about the ship. As a result, Ben stayed with the group and learned more about the ship from Duane's answers than he had during any of their teaching sessions. When he asked a question himself, he received a short answer and then an odd smile from Duane. When he looked at Carl, he received a cross look which left little doubt that he should hold his questions until after.

The visitors retired to the upper salon, relaxed, and enjoyed the refreshments. Ben caught Mora Payne looking at him quite often and, when he allowed his eyes to swing in her direction, discovered that she looked straight into them.

As they left the ship and he shook her hand, she looked inquisitively into his eyes and said, "You do have dark green eyes. I couldn't tell from a distance, but up close they are green."

Embarrassed, he responded, "Yes, yes they are."

Miss Malloy, Duane, and Ben took a short break and snacked on the leftover caviar and crackers in the salon. Miss Malloy had stripped off the windbreaker and shorts she had worn during the visit and settled comfortably into a lounge chair. Ben took pleasure in the vision she presented and enjoyed the internal stirrings created by the male reaction to an appealing woman, until he remembered the vision of Rudy standing over her on the bed. He rose to take the ice bucket, empty bottles, and trays down to the galley. Once below, he realized the garbage had to be taken off the ship before they left, so he began to clean up. When he returned topside, he found Duane sitting at the end of Miss Malloy's chair, his hand loosely holding her shin. When Duane heard Ben, he removed his hand, but stayed in his place.

Ben looked for things to do in the salon and opened the mini-fridge to see what needed to be moved. Duane stood up and went about his own preparations for their departure. Miss Malloy left her chair soon after, to join Ben in the salon. She leaned against the table's edge with her arms straight down by her sides, her hands gripping the tabletop beside her hips then leaned slightly forward. She watched Ben from behind in silence. He could feel her behind him. His neck grew warm as he wondered how long she would wait before starting a conversation. He placed the bottles he had retrieved on top of the fridge and stood to look at her. After a brief silent stare, she said, "Seems your dark green eyes are a hit."

"Bizarre, isn't it? No one has ever commented on my eyes."

"It's the first thing I noticed when I got a chance to look at your face more closely."

Miss Malloy looked down at her feet, which she turned and twisted as if inspecting them from all angles.

"So, what do you do now, while we're at sea?" he asked.

"Whatever Carl says I do," she said without looking up.

Her powerful focus on her feet eventually drew his eyes away from her chest, and he found himself watching the lifts and curls her purple painted toes performed. He felt she wanted to say something, but stalled trying to bring on the words.

"What might that be?" he asked.

She looked up and shrugged then said, "I wish I could go to sea for a week with you guys, but I imagine I'll have to visit clients about buying into the yacht."

"Buying in?"

"Oops, wrong term. I mean signing on, booking a sail. There are quite a few with some interest. The problem is getting them to actually commit. But Carl is pretty determined to get them. I'll be going to parties and meetings in their offices. It gets to be a drag." She stepped away from the table and moved close enough to Ben that her sexual gravity pulled him to her. "I wish I could hang out with you for a week. Sailing, sunning . . . "

His heart boomed in his ears, and he could feel his temperature ramping up. His head filled with confusion as the image of this woman about to engage in sex with another man swelled in his mind again. And now the sight of yet another man appearing familiar enough with her to rest his hand on her bare leg churned the desire in which he marinated. Desire he'd felt since he'd held her as he pulled her away from beating on Rudy.

"I wish you could come, too," he finally said.

Close but not touching him, holding his eyes with a stare and a slight smile, she said, "I'll be sure and tell all of the clients' wives about your dark green eyes, and I'll be thinking about them myself."

Shocked to hear her frank words, not knowing exactly how to interpret their meaning—not knowing what he wanted them to mean—he said, "What are you talking about, thinking about my eyes? Don't you and Rudy have a thing?" He stopped and waved his hand in the direction of the lounge chair, then continued. "Do you and Duane have a thing?" He overcame gravity and pulled back from her.

Miss Malloy's eyes widened, then compressed into a squint. "That's history, especially if I start a *thing* with you," she said, "And it's none of your business to know or care who I have a *thing* with."

"While we're talking *things* over, what about Carl?"

Her squint tightened up a level, and he saw the look Purrette had used on Rudy in the truck.

"I don't talk about Carl." She said this meaning Carl in general, not just her relationship with him, and left no doubt he would gather no information related to their boss from her.

"Fine." He stopped and slowly shook his head. "I can't believe we're even talking about this. You hardly talked to me for the two days when we were stuck beside each other in the truck, and we barely talked the other times we've met, yet here we are talking about starting a thing. But I guess—since I saw how much you enjoyed porn, saw you about to have sex, and the first question you asked me was if I liked sex—that relationships with you move along rather quickly."

"I'm not easy and I'm not oversexed, if that's what you're trying to say. And I don't have to explain anything to you."

"You're right, you don't. I'm sorry."

Miss Malloy relaxed. Her shoulders squared and she rose a little taller. "I'm still going to think about your eyes. I guess I better go. See you in Honolulu."

"I wanted to ask you about Honolulu. I heard Duane say we were going to Sausalito. Has there been a change in plans?"

"No one's told me about a change."

Ben nodded as Miss Malloy reached for her windbreaker and shorts.

***

Duane told Ben to expect Carl back onboard for a short meeting, and when he left they could set sail. When Ben asked about Sausalito, Duane insinuated that the harbormaster asked if they were headed toward Sausalito, and he didn't know why it had come up.

In preparation for sailing, Ben went below to make sure he stowed everything away properly. When he finished, he did the same thing on deck.

Ben went below to prepare dinner for Duane and himself. He browned the Italian sausage he had picked up while shopping, and because he liked garlic, he mashed a few cloves and threw them into the pot, reserving one of the crushed cloves for the bread. He knew that half a bottle of champagne was inside the refrigerator, so he poured some of that on the meat and garlic mixture. Steam rose and the pot sizzled as it burned off the alcohol. Next he opened a can of tomato sauce and poured it over the meat. He crushed some dry oregano and basil in the palm of his hand and dumped it into the sauce and followed that with a good pinch of salt and a strong dose of black pepper.

He left the sauce to simmer while he prepared the pasta. Just before the noodles had completed cooking, he added some crushed red chili flakes to the sauce. He cut four toaster-slot-thick slices of French bread, toasted them crispy and brown, rubbed them with the reserved clove of garlic, and buttered them.

The two large servings of the pasta, with the bread stuck in the side of the bowls, sat on the table of the upper salon while Ben retrieved silverware, glasses, and bottled water. When he returned with the utensils, he found Duane with his nose buried in one of the bowls, smiling while taking in the rich aroma.

Carl arrived to find the two diners in the upper salon eating the spaghetti and dipping the garlic toast to get as much of the meat sauce as possible.

Duane smiled at Carl as he chewed. Small shining beads of perspiration stood out on his forehead and under his eyes. His overfilled mouth ground the food with vigor. Neither could speak, their mouths were so occupied, so Carl had to break the silence. "You two look like you're enjoying yourselves too much. You must be breaking the law."

Duane swallowed. "Carl, y'all didn't tell me this boy could cook. Damn, he made some delicious grub." His speech came out fast.

Ben supplied an embarrassed shrug and held his hands out with his palms up.

While they finished their dinner, Carl updated them on the clients who had visited, indicating he may have landed their first booking in Honolulu. Duane shook his head and said, "They won't like it. The water's a bit choppy, it's not very relaxing, and the only places you can sail to are the places everybody sails to."

Carl looked surprised and said, "Really? I'll mention that to them. But I think it's a timing issue. They're interested in sailing in two weeks. You won't be in Tahiti for at least a month. Think about an itinerary that's unique. Of course, they may have their own idea of what they want to do anyway, and they may wait until you're in Tahiti."

"That would be best," Duane concluded, then turned to Ben. "Since you cooked, I'll clean up." He grabbed the empty bowls and the dirty utensils and left.

When Carl and Ben were alone, Carl turned to Ben and said, "So, how have things been since the other night at the party? Any better?"

Ben thought for a few seconds then answered, "I guess. We've been pretty busy, and I know what to do when it comes to putting crackers on plates and pouring champagne, so I haven't had a chance to show any more incompetence to Duane."

"If it's any comfort, he did say you seem to understand what you've been told, and you'll probably catch on pretty quick. So, as far as I'm concerned, you're part of the crew for as long as you want. But here's an offer I'm going to make to you. You gave us an opportunity to cut you loose the other night, so now I'm giving you the chance to cut yourself loose. If you want to leave now—or when you get to Honolulu—just say so. I'll give you enough money to get home."

"Thanks. I definitely don't want to leave right now. I'll think about it and let you know when we get to Honolulu."

"That's fair. I think you're at the beginning of something great. You get to sail the South Pacific for a year, see a number of exotic ports, live onboard a spectacular yacht, and in the end, pocket a significant amount of coin. In a way you're part owner of this ship. A year from now I think the *Aurawind* is going to sell for more than I expected. If that happens, we're all going to get a bigger share. I hope you decide to hang in there with us."

Feeling welcome, wanted and rich, Ben smiled as he said, "I get the feeling I will."

"Good."

"Why isn't Rudy sailing with us? He's helping with the clients, isn't he?"

Carl looked down and nodded his head, then stopped and stared at the deck for a moment before shaking his head slowly. He looked up at Ben and said, "He helped a couple of times, but he's having second thoughts. I don't understand that kid. Maybe he'll come around and we'll have him meet you in Honolulu."

"Do you think it's safe for Duane to sail that far with the meager assistance he's going to get from me?"

Carl continued to hold eye contact, and with a reassuring expression said, "I trust Duane's judgment regarding anything to do with sailing. He wouldn't set out if he thought you presented any danger."

# Chapter 7

The wind blew inland as the *Aurawind* left Avalon under power. Duane and Ben raised the mainsail soon after leaving the bay and struck out on a heading toward the mainland. After a few miles, they changed their heading to a run due south until they cleared the southernmost tip of the island, and later, to go south-southwest to pass by the northern tip of San Clemente Island. The wind came a quarter over the starboard side, so Duane called for Ben to raise the jib. Ben pointed at the jib as a question and waited until Duane nodded, then successfully raised the sail and hauled in the sheet on the port side, the same side as the mainsail, before cleating the line. When he got to the pilothouse, Duane asked him how he knew to sheet on the port side.

"I didn't. I picked a side and figured you'd yell at me if I picked wrong. Why, is the port side the right side?"

"This point of sail is called a broad reach. The wind is coming over the starboard side. If you'd taken the jib to the starboard side, it wouldn't have fully caught the wind. If the wind had been coming from the stern, you could have gone starboard side opposite the mainsail and caught the wind coming from directly behind. So when you raise a foresail, you want to check where the wind is coming from and sheet it to the side that it will best take the wind."

Ben had a serious look on his face as he made mental notes. His automatic recognition of terms such as port, starboard, fore, aft, and stern still needed reinforcement. He checked off what he had just heard. Wind from the starboard side, sail on the port side. He also made a rule to always set sails to take the best advantage of the wind, thinking that one sounded important.

With the sails set, they could stay on their existing course for a great distance if they didn't encounter any traffic. But since they had to cross a major shipping lane, they would surely run across some large ships. Duane kept an eye on the radar screen and periodically raised his eyes to make sightings, knowing that after the sun dropped he would have the other ship's marking lights and tower to aid in positioning. He expressed to Ben his hope to get through the lane before dark, but if they didn't, Ben would have to station himself up front near the jib sheets and be prepared to jibe.

"Once we get out of the lane are we going to park it for the night?" Ben asked.

"What?"

"Park it, pull up for the night while we sleep."

Duane looked at Ben curiously. "We're not on the interstate out here, you know. You don't just pull up at a rest stop and park. You sail all night. The *Aurawind* has an autopilot. Once we get through the shipping lane, I'll explain the nighttime procedures to you. You're going to love it."

"I told you I was clueless."

"You didn't have to," Duane said, smiling.

Duane showed Ben the radar screen and pointed out the bright green blocks that indicated a freighter. "You won't see too many of these in an hour or so," he said. "The closest one looks like it will force us to alter our course so we'd best do it now while you can see, so you'll know what to do later when it's dark." He then explained how he wanted Ben to handle the jib sheet and sent him forward.

Duane changed course to head directly at the freighter's current position, putting them on a more westerly starboard reach. He adjusted the mainsail from the pilothouse and signaled Ben to let out the jib. They stayed on that course until the freighter passed due south of their position then they turned toward the eastbound freighter. By the time they intersected its path, the freighter had left the area. They reset the sails to the positions they'd been in before they tacked and sailed on the south-southwest course again. *Aurawind's* ninety-foot hull cut nicely through the freighter's wake. They barely felt the artificial swells.

Duane called Ben back to the pilothouse so he could explain the maneuver they had just completed. His training philosophy of telling them what they're going to do, making them do it, then telling them what they've done reinforced the hands-on learning process he liked to employ with new sailors.

After the reinforcement, Duane pointed out the position of the other freighters on the radar screen, none of which caused any immediate concern. He told Ben to watch the southwest section of the screen while he made some calculations on the charts—emphasizing that if any new green blocks showed up on the outer circumference of the area, to make sure and get his attention. Flipping on the small light over the chart table adjacent to the wheel, Duane changed chairs to the lower one just to his right. Ben stood and watched the radar screen, wanting to take the recently vacated captain's chair. Long periods of screen-watching followed. Periodically, he looked up in the direction where he thought the freighters should be, to spy only waves and horizon. After sundown in the starlight, he spotted the large ships with their illuminated towers much more easily. Whenever a new green block appeared on the section of the radar screen that his duty compelled him to watch, he would inform Duane, and a new and closer arc on the screen would be defined. If the ship came within that second arc, Duane wanted to be alerted again. In the next hour the second alert happened once, causing a change of course toward the ship then back onto their original course as they had done earlier. In the dark, Ben fumbled with the jib sheet and let it out too far, then managed to haul it in to a point Duane found acceptable for the short time that they sailed on the westerly heading.

Duane explained to Ben how he had let out the sail until it spilled the wind and that, over time, he would begin to feel the spill point.

Now clear of the shipping lane, Duane sat at the chart table to finalize his course calculations. Next, from one of the lockers in the pilothouse, he produced a small box on which he adjusted some dials. The small box had a cable, which he plugged into another small box Ben hadn't noticed, bolted to the pilot wheel's pedestal. Duane then slipped a drive belt over the wheel and connected the drive pulley of the small box to another pulley mounted behind the wheel. With the belt snugly in place, Duane powered on the two small boxes.

Ben watched Duane's actions, assuming that the combination of devices made up the autopilot system, but clueless as to how it all worked. When Duane looked at him, he saw a hopeless smile and a question that required no verbalization.

"The little box up here is the compass box," Duane explained. "The lower one is the drive box. I set the course on the compass box, and it tells the drive box what course to steer. As long as I get the course right, we get to where we want to go."

"And we trust these little boxes?" Ben asked skeptically.

"I do. You will, too. The only problem we could encounter is a major wind change. If we do, the ship may attempt to jibe on its own. Quite a thrill when that happens. You wake up because you just rolled over in bed without intending to, you run up the companionway naked to find sails flapping and the main boom swinging wildly, trying to take your head off. Luckily these trade winds don't make major changes very often."

"That makes me feel better."

"Don't worry, one of us will be up checking every two hours. Let me show you what we will be checking."

Ben moved closer to the green glow that was reflected off of Duane's face. Two masks, one green and one black, hung over the compass as Duane pointed out the compass readings and explained the routine of a night check.

"Tonight I'll be up with you during your checks to see how you do, but tomorrow you'll be on your own, hopefully. I'll do the midnight check. So you set your alarm for oh-two hundred hours. You'll do the check as if you were on your own. But I'll be watching."

"Do I say 'Aye, aye, Captain' now?" Ben asked jokingly.

"You learned all of your sailing from pirate movies, didn't you?"

"Har."

*** 

Nothing changed when Ben opened his eyes after the alarm rang out. He had covered the clock so that its dim glow didn't interfere with the perfect dark. With his eyelids either open or shut, he saw infinite black. He slapped in the direction of the metallic clang and succeeded in silencing the noise on the third swipe. His boxer shorts were found easily and he slipped them on. Later on in the trip he would skip the boxers and roam the deck naked during his checks. If you don't wear clothes at sea, and there's no one there to see you, are you still naked? His tennis shoes almost jumped onto his feet as he stepped into them. With his body halfway out of the hatch, he felt around for his safety vest and slipped it on, then found the safety line and clipped it to the vest. He climbed the rest of the way out of the hatch and stood on deck for a moment to catch his bearings and feel his way into the rhythm of the waves.

Stars densely spattered the sky as he moved forward to check the jib and the jib sheet. The sail's faint phosphorescent glow showed a steady fullness of wind and he heard the slight rustling of air as it crossed the surface of the material. He touched the sheet as he had been told and felt the taut pressure on the rope. He turned to observe the mainsail holding its own volume of wind.

To check the mainsheet he had to move to the pilothouse. Walking along the port side, he slid his safety line along the wire, stopping at each stanchion to transfer his second line to the other side then releasing his first line. He remembered Duane telling him to be sure to attach himself to the safety line at all times, since falling overboard at night with no one around to hear you go in meant a long loneliness at sea. Duane assured him that he himself would be very mindful of staying attached to his line. If he went overboard his only hope would be for Ben to miraculously develop the ability to conduct a sea search. Ben, at least, had the comfort of knowing that the person who would look for him already possessed the required knowledge.

In the pilothouse he tried not to turn and discover where Duane stood watching him. Knowing someone's eyes watched and evaluated him from the dark made him second-guess every one of his actions. He touched the mainsheet, checked the cleats, and turned to confirm the drive belt connection between the autopilot and the wheel. After he completed the physical checks, he finished his tasks by recording the time and compass reading in the logbook. In his search for the pen he knocked the book to the deck, and once he retrieved it had to find the right page by the green glow of the compass. A small reading light was available on the desk area, but Duane had told Ben to try not to use it. If he did, he would be blinded for a few seconds after he had turned it off, and it was better to preserve his night vision.

Coming from his dark bunk, his pupils would be adjusted to pick up the slightest light on deck. If he compromised that vision when he finished his recordings, at a time when he had to make connections and releases on his safety line, he could miss a connection. If he then released his rear safety line, he would be untethered just a few feet above a sea that would gladly accept his body and separate it from the ship. Duane would perform his course check two hours later and, seeing Ben's previous entry, would go back to his berth without any indication that Ben had gone overboard. He would rise four hours later for his next check, but this time, when he didn't see Ben's entry he would get mad and go raise hell with Ben for sleeping through his responsibility. Receiving no reaction from Ben, he would go down into the berth to look for him and then would return topside to find Ben's safety harness was missing. It was then that he would think that Ben had gone into the sea. If that should happen, his first responsibility would be to return to the pilothouse and try to determine when and where Ben had gone in. If it was on his way to the pilothouse before he took his readings then he'd gone in two hours earlier. If it had been while he returned from his reading six hours earlier, then the search grid had to cover a lot more ocean, and the chances of recovery were severely diminished.

Ben chose to accept Duane's advice and make his notations without the aid of the lamp. He took a 360-degree scan of the ocean at night. Though the radar screen showed no other vessels nearby, he couldn't resist the visual check. He saw no sign of Duane.

Returning to his berth, he hooked and unhooked his safety line as he retraced his steps, then went below and set his alarm clock for 0600 hours.

This would be his routine every four hours, every night at sea, for the next year of his life.

*** 

A few nights later, after Duane had cleared him to perform the checks on his own, he arrived on deck to find that clouds had moved in and blocked the stars. He did his checks, made his entry in the logbook, then sat naked in the hatch leading to his berth and stared at a world of total black, wondering at what distance his eyes focused when they had nothing to see. No pin-light of stars, no glow of wave crests, no highlight of wire lines, no glint of masts, no ghosts of sails. Black, dark nothingness. Because he moved at the speed of the wind, he couldn't feel its strength, but he could hear the sound of it moving across the sails. He watched the darkness hoping for something to become visible. To sit and stare at the black dark of the ocean somehow seemed of more interest than to stare at the black dark of his cabin. His hand grasped the safety line still attached to his vest. He caught himself moving his eyes in different directions, right, left, up, down, pulled by the quest for vision. Periodically he looked toward the pilothouse to see the faint green glow of the compass just to prove his eyes still worked. Nights when the stars flickered visibly he could see slight outlines and weak reflections. On those nights he felt confident being alone. But in the black dark voids of the starless nights, he felt the same eeriness he had felt the night of his first watch when he knew Duane observed his movements.

The following morning Duane spent an unusual amount of time working over the charts in his cabin. When he came on deck he looked at the autopilot setting and scratched his head; he seemed confused. Ben watched from the upper salon behind the pilothouse as Duane switched his attention between the chart and the compass. He didn't want to ask why Duane was paying extra attention to the course reading this morning, because he didn't know if he should ever question the captain.

Duane looked forward toward the horizon then turned to look aft and spotted Ben. He summoned Ben to the pilothouse with a wave.

"You sure you wrote the right course down at oh-two hundred this morning?"

"Um." Ben looked down at the log, flipped back a page then flipped it forward again. He hoped Duane didn't see the tremors in his hand. "Whatever I wrote down is what I read. Why? Is something wrong?"

"We're off course."

"Are we lost?"

"No, I can always figure out where we are. What I can't figure out is how we got here."

"Where are we?"

"North of where I expected."

"So what does that mean?"

"I'm not exactly sure. I'll have to set a different course to get back on track, and it may have cost us a few hours of sailing, but we'll have to watch closely for the next few days."

"Is it possible you put in the wrong course?" Ben asked innocently.

Duane gazed at Ben without expression, causing Ben to smile sheepishly.

"A better question would be 'Did you calculate the wrong course?' because I input the course I calculated."

"Why did you ask if I had written down the course correctly?"

"I don't know. Grasping at straws, I guess. Like I said, we'll have to watch closely for the next couple of days. I'll let you know what the new course is so you'll know what to expect on your night check."

A few days later, when they should have spotted land, a similar miscalculation positioned them west of their intended course, and Duane had to make another correction. Ben calmly watched him repeat a series of calculations and review the log recordings in an attempt to find out why they had veered off course again. The recordings indicated they had stayed on the course he had input into the autopilot.

"What do you think happened?" Ben asked.

"Do you know anything about navigation?" Duane responded defensively.

"No."

"Well, then I can't explain it to you," he said dismissively.

"I'm not questioning your ability to navigate, Duane. I just asked a question. You got us this far, wherever that is, and I'm sure you'll get us where we need to go."

"*Wherever that is*," Duane mimicked him, "You think I don't know where we are? You think you could navigate your way to Honolulu?"

"No, that's not what I meant. I don't know where we are, you do. I'm trying to let you know I'm not worried. There has to be an explanation and I know you'll figure it out. So how far off are we?"

"Not that far, but with the trades blowing in this direction, we're going to have to tack to get to Honolulu. It's going to take an extra day or so."

"Okay. No big deal. We aren't in a hurry, are we?"

Instead of approaching the islands with the wind on a southwest heading, they now came in against the wind. The Kauai Channel served up rough sailing and made handling the sails a greater challenge for Ben. They arrived a day late and the extra sailing strained their cool. They accomplished the tacking maneuvers with some difficulties, and Ben noticed Duane's tone had become more forceful and less inviting to discussion as he issued instructions. He brooded over his charts, checking constantly to ensure they stayed on course for the completion of the trip, and Ben learned not to ask questions related to their location.

***

White light beamed from the two levels of the clubhouse. The members of the Honolulu Kai Yacht Club milled about inside. Most of them were upstairs in the lounge while a small group sat at tables on the lawn of the lower level. As Duane maneuvered to tie up alongside the visitor dock, those sitting outside were first to observe the skills of the arriving skipper. Soon members inside moved out onto the balcony to watch as well. Ben dropped bumpers and threw a line to a helpful club member standing on the dock. A few minutes later Duane shut down the engines and all was quiet, except for the din of people mingling and the lapping of the small black waves they had just created slapping against the other ships moored nearby.

Duane called Ben to the pilothouse and explained the series of tasks he performed when arriving at a new harbor. He showed Ben the entry he made in the logbook and then explained the series of lights, indicating the ship was moored and not expecting immediate embarkation. He then asked him to wait onboard while he went to see the commodore. When he returned, he told Ben they would stay where they were for the night, but would move to another mooring for the duration of their time in Honolulu. The commodore had extended full use of the facilities to all crew members of the *Aurawind*, and Duane told Ben to go ashore whenever he felt like it and to ask at the bar for a tour of the clubhouse.

"If anyone asks you where we're heading, tell them we're the startup of a private cruise company waiting to hear from our marketing people about where we're supposed to go to meet our first clients. We may have some people meeting us here. I'll know more tomorrow after I call Carl," Duane said.

Ben hesitated for a second before answering, "Okay."

"Let me know when you go ashore, if you do."

"Will do. How long did you tell them we were going to stay here?"

Duane looked up from the chart he was working on and stared at Ben, wondering at the interruption, then trying to remember what he had told the commodore.

"Ah, three or four days," he finally responded and turned back to the chart.

"You going to go and get a drink?"

Again Duane looked up with a vacant look on his face, held it a moment, then shook his head and looked back down at the chart.

"I can't believe I'm in Hawaii," Ben said as he walked forward to look at the lights of Honolulu's skyline. He looked out at the pink neon saucer-shaped building, the glowing blocks of the high-rise apartments, and the single lights of homes scattered in random patterns against the hills. Cars moved in a steady stream along the busy street across the expanse of grass belonging to the large hotel that shared the enormous parking lot with the yacht club.

Without knowing it he had gotten used to the smell of the sea, but now he noticed the different smells of a harbor. Diesel, garbage, car exhaust, dense vegetation, over-ripe fruit, and cooking food. Smells carried by a soft, warm, humid breeze.

Spotlighted palm trees swayed slightly in the park. At their bases stood smaller plants with strange red flowers. Tourists walked through the park in every direction.

From mountains and evergreens and cold lake water and traveling by car, he had come to the tropics by sea—not by air for a vacation, but by sea to work, to be part of this world. Ben smiled at the sights the beautiful city laid out to welcome him. He went below to the head and readied himself to go ashore for a drink. His stubble stood thick on his chin and cheeks, and his hair barely missed being matted, but he didn't want to take the time to fix himself. Fingers through the hair and a splash of water on his face would have to do. The dock gave under his steps, but when he left it and stepped onto the sidewalk to the clubhouse, his legs felt the shock of solid ground. He walked with a wide stance prepared to brace against the tilt of the deck, but it didn't come. When he entered the lounge at the top of the steps, the patrons all turned to look at his bedraggled frame. He smiled, noticing crisp white shirts, jackets, and creased shorts. The bartender stood suspended, waiting to meet Ben's eyes, and when he did, he gave a quick nod to an empty stool at the bar.

"You just came in on the ship out there?" the bartender asked, pulling on a beer tap with thick, freckled forearms covered with sun-bleached hair.

"Yeah. Name's Ben. Ben Beck."

"I'm Garth. You looking for a drink?" Garth's voice rumbled low.

"Dying for one actually. How 'bout a beer?"

"No. You just landed and you need a Mai Tai. I'll get it in just a second."

Garth delivered the beers he had drawn to a waitress waiting between brass rails at the end of the bar. As he returned, he grabbed a large tumbler and a large plastic jug. He tossed ice into the tumbler, poured the fruit mixture from the jug to the top of the ice, topped the drink with dark rum, and hooked a thick slice of pineapple onto the edge of the glass. He placed a thin square paper napkin in front of Ben onto which he deposited the drink, now frosted with small droplets of moisture.

"Drink's on me, Ben. Welcome to Honolulu." Garth walked down the bar to take another order from the waitress.

Ben ventured to look around, expecting to find numerous eyes staring at him. He met none, so he looked further at his surroundings. Large dark-stained wooden pillars wound in sections with rough, fraying rope. Every wall displayed sailing trophies inside oak-and-glass cases. He turned to his drink, pulled off the pineapple, and sunk his teeth into it. It burst sweet into his mouth, and juice ran out the corners. Never had he tasted fruit with such intense flavor. He took a second bite, then a third, and then found himself gnawing at the remaining flesh attached to the green fibrous skin. Garth interrupted his attention to the fruit, placing a napkin with another slice of pineapple in front of him and kept on moving down the bar. Ben laughed at himself for getting lost in a piece of fruit and picked up the second slice to lose himself again.

Two pineapple rinds sat in front of him as he lifted his drink and pulled liquid into his mouth. He swallowed, then coughed as the rum spiked the back of his throat. Tears formed at the corners of his eyes. He opened them wide and pulled his head back. Involuntarily, he rounded his mouth and blew out a quick breath. He felt eyes watching him and saw Garth looking in his direction. Ben smiled and nodded. "Ooh, that's good!" Garth smiled and turned back to business.

The other patrons were beginning to leave as Ben finished his drink, so Garth had a minute to talk.

"You'll have another," he told Ben.

"How many of those drinks can a normal man handle?"

"One. You a normal man?"

"No."

The second Mai Tai landed on a new napkin.

Ben looked up at Garth and heard a familiar voice from behind him. "Why don't you get me one of those fruity drinks too, barman?"

Ben turned as Rudy took the stool beside him. He stared, but remained silent. Rudy smiled and waited for Ben to speak, but Ben turned back to his drink.

"Not even going to say hello, BAB?"

"Sorry, I hoped to enjoy my drink. Guess that's not going to happen," Ben said, pursing his lips.

"You don't seem like the type that would enjoy a fruity drink. Maybe I have you all wrong."

"I think you do," Ben said, still not looking at Rudy.

"What took you so long to get here? We've been hanging at the hotel for two days."

"I'm crew. You'll have to ask Duane. He's onboard."

Garth approached with another drink. When Rudy saw him, he canceled his order and left. Garth placed the drink down in front of Ben and said, "That guy's with you?"

"I'm embarrassed to say he is. He's kind of like family. You know, you can't pick 'em, but you're stuck with 'em."

Garth smiled. "He's been in here the past couple of nights. I kept wondering why the hell they let him in, but I imagined he'd talked his way in somehow. Is he on your crew?" Ben nodded and Garth continued, "Hmm, I guess he's on the tab then. How many on the crew?"

"Him, me, and we're supposed to be getting a cook. I wonder if that's who's at the hotel with him."

"Well, good luck with that guy. He's no ray of sunshine."

Ben suddenly became tired. A craving for sleep began to creep up on him. Whether from the drinks or the long stressful sail through the strait, he couldn't say, but he resisted giving in to the craving. The thought of going onboard with Rudy back in the picture made him want to fight it off. He stayed and nursed the third drink, keeping Garth company until he closed down the bar.

# Chapter 8

Every Friday night, the yacht club conducted a fun race for the sailors, and fired up their outdoor grill for the members and guests to use while awaiting the race's outcome. Ben purchased beef and ahi steaks at the Asian center, plus a half-pint of ahi poke. He had tasted poke his second day in Honolulu and made sure to eat it every day since. He hadn't convinced any of the others to try it and usually ate the entire half-pint himself.

Ben, Rudy, Duane and Miss Malloy sat at a table next to the grass on the lower level. They could hear the sounds of the moored boats across the lawn. Creaking docks, rippling water, and the occasional chime of a line slapping against an aluminum mast. Each time a racing vessel crossed the finish line, a bell rang out and everyone looked up to see who had silently returned.

On open-grill night, for a minimal charge, the club supplied the grill, use of the plates and cutlery, a baked potato, and a salad. Members and guests brought their own entrée. A waitress brought them a large bowl of salad and a bowl for each person at the table. She placed the bowl in front of Ben, who asked, "Is the salad lady here?"

The waitress scanned the other tables and replied, "Oh, there she is. I'll go see if she has any dressing left." She took off toward the back of the club.

Nel Gayland sat in a white plastic chair smoking a cigarette. Her wiry legs crossed, her ankle resting on her other leg's knee. She drank a clear liquid over ice with a wedge of lime and scanned the outdoor area of the club while the other members of her party devoured their salads. Years of working in a kitchen, providing food for hungry men—who ate to fill their stomachs without noticing how good the food she had prepared for them tasted—had stripped her of the enjoyment of eating with company. The crews on the freighters she worked had no appreciation for her talent. Over time, she had lost the joy she used to feel watching the reaction of people eating her food. On the large ships she had always eaten alone, after the people she was hired to feed had eaten. Then, it didn't matter how well she had prepared the food. It wasn't at its freshest when she ate and eating alone is one of life's loneliest experiences.

Every member of the yacht club knew her, and members invited her to join them on open-grill nights. They knew she would bring a savory dish and her famous salad dressing, a concoction so delicious that other groups clamored for the extras. The members knew good food. They stopped to enjoy her flavors and to appreciate the talent that had prepared their food. But still, she couldn't eat with them.

Nel wasn't actually a member of the yacht club, but the members regarded her as one. She lived on the yacht of a member who lived on the mainland, a member who very seldom came to Honolulu to sail. When the owner did plan a trip, he always scheduled it at a time when Nel would be at sea on one of the freighters on which she cooked. There were long periods of Nel's absence from the club. When she wasn't on a freighter, she quite often signed on to crew for an owner who wanted his yacht sailed from one port to another. The owner didn't have the time, or possibly the nerve, to sail it himself. She had no home other than the yacht she stayed on when she had no cooking or transportation assignment.

Her legs were strong from riding her bicycle all over the city, and her arms were all muscle from the heavy pots and pans she used to cook for the large numbers of men on the ships.

When the waitress approached her and asked for a small quantity of salad dressing, she placed her drink on the table and her cigarette in the corner of her mouth. Smoke curled up her cheek and into her eye, causing her to squint as she poured the dressing into a spare teacup. Her head barely made it to the waitress' shoulder when she stood to hand over the dressing.

The waitress returned to Ben's table carrying the teacup very carefully.

"Nel said she could only spare this much. She's had a lot of requests tonight. Don't waste it."

A cloudy liquid with small flecks of herbs filled the teacup. Small glistening circles of oil covered the surface. Ben dished himself a bowl of salad and spooned a small amount of the dressing over top. He tasted the salad then swooned at the light, fresh, flavorful experience blooming in his mouth.

"Rudy, don't take any. She said not to waste it," he said.

"It's okay, I don't eat salad. Green stuff makes me sick," Rudy replied.

"You've got to try this, Miss Malloy. I don't know how to describe it. The way Garth went on about this lady's salad dressing, I found it hard to believe it could be that good. But this is something!" Ben said to Miss Malloy, whose eyes remained attached to his face as she sipped her martini.

"Do you rave about everything you shove in your mouth?" Rudy asked.

Ben ignored him as he prepared a bowl of salad for Miss Malloy. She tasted. When the flavor struck, she raised her eyebrows and nodded, then finished the bowl of salad as if nothing else existed in her world.

Duane's curiosity forced him to take a bowl of salad, and he reacted even more favorably than either Miss Malloy or Ben. "Christ, what is this? It's light, it's sweet, it's spicy, it's . . . " Duane ran out of words and decided to eat more of the salad.

Soon the large bowl of salad had been eaten, and Ben ran a chunk of dinner roll around the inside of the teacup. The waitress delivered foil-wrapped potatoes to the table. Ben took the steaks to the grill. He tossed Rudy's slab of beef, intended to be medium-rare, on the grill first to make sure he cooked it all the way through, nice and dry. Then he labored over Duane's and Miss Malloy's steaks, cooking them to perfection. A minute before they were done he placed the ahi steaks on the grill to sear their outer surfaces.

They enjoyed the beefsteaks—even Rudy—but all abstained from trying the rare tuna. Ben accepted their unwillingness to try something new with mixed feelings. He wanted them to enjoy what he enjoyed, yet was eager to consume the additional ahi dipped in a mixture of soya sauce and powdered mustard.

One large group of members at a nearby table boisterously celebrated a birthday. They had purchased a five-gallon container of rich, high-fat ice cream and offered the excess to everyone in attendance. Ben enjoyed two large bowls after Duane had left. When he finished, he, Miss Malloy, and Rudy sat in silence until Rudy couldn't tolerate the silence any longer. "Boring," he said, "I'm going back to the Korean bar, unless, Purrette, you want to go back to my berth for a private grope."

Miss Malloy looked at Rudy with a blank face and spoke in a flat expressionless voice. "More than anything else in the world."

"Well, I'm not stupid, so I'll take that as a no. If you need me, you know where I'll be."

As Rudy disappeared beyond the light cast by the outdoor lamps of the yacht club, Miss Malloy asked Ben, "How come you never go to the Korean bars with Rudy?"

"I made the mistake of going with him once, that's how come. I suppose if I wanted to live a real-life porn movie I'd go with him again."

At the mention of porn, Miss Malloy took her eyes off Ben and looked at the grass where she shuffled her bare feet across the blades. Ben cleared his throat and also looked away for a moment, then said, "Looks like your relationship with him isn't going so good."

She looked up at him with a hard stare. "I have no relationship with him and I never did. I admit I did have sex with him. I also admit that I like sex. Just because I don't have someone I care about to share in the experience doesn't mean I'm going to deprive myself of that pleasure. The porn during the drive to Las Vegas made me want to have sex. It could have been you, it could have been Rudy, or it could have been both."

"See, I don't get that. I don't know how it could be both. And what about the porn? You looked like you were really into it."

"I like sex," she said.

"Is it part of your job description?"

Miss Malloy sat silently, continuing to stare until she made Ben shift positions in his chair. "Carl would not want Miss Malloy to be a slut. As Miss Malloy, I am a virgin, sexual but not available. If anyone approaches me, I fend him off any way I have to. As Purrette, I have sex with whoever I choose, but rest assured, I do the choosing."

Ben nodded contemplatively. "I don't get the Miss Malloy/Purrette thing either. Why is that necessary?"

Miss Malloy leaned back in her seat and answered, "Carl needed a Miss Malloy. He saw that I could be that type of person quite effectively, even though I don't want to be a Miss Malloy. To remain who I really am, Purrette and Miss Malloy both have to exist."

"Why do you work for him if he's turned you into a different person?"

"I haven't turned into a different person. I have to be Miss Malloy for business reasons. And why I work for Carl is none of your business. I told you I wouldn't discuss him."

"Do you have sex with Carl, too?"

She smiled and said, "You've been dying to find that out, haven't you?"

"Curious. So?"

She shrugged in answer.

Ben looked off at the docks.

"I've thought about your green eyes a lot since Catalina. Did you think about me?" she asked, staring at his profile.

He didn't change the direction in which he peered, but continued to watch the imagined horizon for a long while before dropping his head to stare at his clenched hands, thumbs dancing over each other. He turned to look at her. His lips pressed tight together. He met her eyes, then looked down at her shoulder, down her arm beside her breast, down her leg to rest his gaze on her knee. "I did," he said, "at night, after I did the watch I would sit in the hatch. There, in the dark, I strained to see anything other than the stars and the bow of the ship. I thought of you, and I tried to see your face."

"I'm glad."

"You don't know what I thought."

"From what I know of you so far, I know you thought too much. Keep it simple. A guy, a girl, maybe they'll get to like each other."

"Wait a minute. In Vegas you wanted to go straight to having sex with me."

"Still do. But I thought about something you said. I want to have sex with you when it will mean something to *you*. You're a good thing, Ben. I want it to mean something to you. I know it will mean something to me."

When she stood to leave, without thinking, she rested her hand on his shoulder while she slipped on her sandals. He felt the warmth of her hand long after she had returned to the *Aurawind*.

Upstairs, Ben sat and talked with Garth as he closed down the bar. Tonight he didn't hear much of Garth's chatter, and each time he sipped his Mai Tai, he couldn't believe how little of the drink he had consumed. It seemed like no time had passed when Garth called over from the light switch telling him to move his ass and get out of the building. As he walked along the docks, he heard the crash of a cat or a rat toppling over someone's garbage and the distant sound of music thumping from one of the clubs along the beach. The warm breeze felt thick and soft as it lifted his hair.

He stepped onboard the *Aurawind*. He walked aft to check the pilothouse and look down into the main salon. The darkness meant Duane had turned his lights out, as had Miss Malloy. Rudy, who would be Ben's bunkmate when they were at sea, had remained ashore most nights in Honolulu. Ben turned and walked forward. He opened the hatch the rest of the way and stepped down the ladder. Once on the floor, he started a little when he heard rustling in the bunk that would be Rudy's.

"Rudy?"

"No," came Miss Malloy's voice.

"Oh. What are you doing here?"

"I thought I'd sleep close to you. No sex. I'd like to feel your warmth."

Ben stepped closer to her and stood beside the bunk. In the dark he couldn't see her, not even the outline of her head and shoulders, the lightlessness was so complete, but he could feel her. He knew exactly how close he stood to her, and he knew how warm her skin would feel if he reached out to touch her. He shook his head in answer. Though she couldn't see him, she knew he had pulled away. He took off his shoes and placed them where he always placed them. He removed his clothes and hopped into his bunk wearing only his boxer shorts, then lay with arms behind his head, eyes open, unable to speak. The sheets from the other bunk rustled, and he froze when he heard the weight of her foot land on the floor. From very close beside him he heard her speak. "Is the head down this hallway?"

"Yes."

"I'll wake you up if I pass you to go use it."

"Yes." He'd managed to get the first yes out the first time he tried his voice, so he decided to stick with it.

"I'm just going to lie beside you for a while. Is that okay?"

"Yes."

He scooted over as she climbed up beside him. She rested her head on his shoulder, her hand on his chest. He felt her breath crawl across his skin and squeezed his eyes shut each time she exhaled.

"Relax. Just hold me for a minute. I've wanted to feel what it's like to be up against you ever since you left. I'll go back to the other bunk soon."

"You don't have to."

She stayed beside him long enough for him to begin to get dozy, something he didn't think he could do with her in the bed. Before he was able to fall asleep she slipped back to the other bunk. The empty spot she left heightened his memory of the warm spot she had become while she lay along his side.

Some time later, still in darkness, he heard her climb the ladder.

***

Maintenance on ships that go to sea is never ending. Ben had learned this very early in his budding career as a sailor. He labored at a new task while Duane and Miss Malloy went to pick up Carl. A job he could see would take a long time if he oiled all the teakwood the ship displayed. He rubbed the rail that surrounded the upper salon with a rag soaked in teakwood oil, his fingers slick, shining and slippery from the saturated cloth. The wood seemed thirsty, and drank in whatever amount he applied. He hoped he wouldn't be asked to do the walls of the lower salon.

A yell came from the dock. When he walked mid-ship, he saw Carl standing near the gangway, crisp as ever in cream-colored slacks and matching short-sleeved silk shirt. His hair glinted with sunshine as he walked the gangplank to come onboard.

"Hi, Carl. Duane and Miss Malloy went to get you," Ben informed him.

"I arrived early and took a cab to the hotel." Carl craned his neck around slowly to take in the ship and said, "They know enough not to wait too long. I've missed them before. They'll try the hotel and then figure out I came here. What are you doing?"

"Oiling the wood."

"Shitty job. Make sure you don't use too much. The wood will swell and crack if it gets too much."

Ben looked over at the railing he had been working on and said he'd be careful.

"How did the sail over treat you? You like the open sea?"

"I enjoyed it. I don't have anything to compare it to, but I guess we had a good sail. We had a slight navigation problem but we got here."

"Yes you did," he said without paying much attention. "I don't suppose Duane would mind if we had a little scotch while we waited, do you?"

"No. I'll get you some."

They walked back to the salon and Ben went below to get Carl his drink. He brought the bottle, a glass, a bucket of ice, and a beer for himself. Carl winked as the glass of scotch landed on the table in front of him. He lifted the glass to eye level and glanced at the liquid. He looked over the rim at Ben and smiled before tipping the glass and pouring most of its contents down his throat.

"Good stuff," he said. "So what kind of navigation problem did you have?"

"I don't know the details. Duane noticed we were off course a couple of times and corrected for it. He figured it cost us a day getting here."

"Hmm, that's not good," he said. He drained his scotch and slid the glass across the table to Ben. "I think I can handle one more."

Ben poured more scotch. "Carl? You asked me to let you know if I wanted to stay in the deal when we got here to Honolulu. And I want to let you know that I will be staying on. I think things will work out okay."

"That's great. I hoped you'd stay with us. And I also think things are going to work out. In fact, they're starting to work out already. We have our first clients booked. They're going to sail with us in three days. That's why I'm here."

When Duane and Miss Malloy returned, Carl accepted all apologies for having been missed, without acknowledging that his own early arrival and impatience had caused the mix-up. He broke the news of the first client's arrival and then he, Duane, and Miss Malloy got serious about planning what they had to prepare over the next two days.

Ben waited on them while trying to listen in on the plans. On one return to the upper salon with a new bottle of scotch, he noticed Duane giving him a stern look as he approached. When he met Duane's eye and acknowledged the look, Duane looked away.

When they completed their first round of planning, they went to the yacht club's dining room for dinner. Ben cleaned up the small mess in the upper salon and joined them at their table. As he sat down, the waitress placed a Mai Tai on the napkin in front of him. All three of his companions stopped their conversation to look at him silently for a few seconds then turned back to their discussion.

"So the biggest problem is going to be the cook. The person I want to join us later can't make it for this one, so we have to find somebody here. Unless, Ben, you can do it. I remember Duane enjoyed the food you cooked before. Can you cook decent enough to impress clients?" Carl asked.

Ben looked at Duane, whose expression was just short of seething, and swallowed.

"No. I cook edible stuff, I don't cook meals."

"That's what I thought. Well, everybody ask around. See if you can find somebody local. If not, you're it," he said, looking at Ben.

When the meal ended, Carl asked who was going with him to meet Rudy. Duane agreed to go, Ben shook his head, and Miss Malloy stared at the table.

"Miss Malloy, will you be joining us? If this place is as good as Rudy says it is, then it sounds like we're in for a pretty good time," Carl said.

"If Rudy says it's good, then his has to be the dead body I go over to get inside."

"I see he's been working his charm again."

When they stood to leave, Duane guided Ben off to the side and stopped to have a private chat.

"What the hell do you think you're doing?" he said to Ben in an angry whisper.

"What are you . . . "

"Shut up and listen. There is no reason for Carl to know about the navigation problem we had. Do you read me? What goes on at sea stays at sea, unless I decide it doesn't. The *captain* reports to the owner, not the crew. If we're going to get along, you have to keep your mouth shut about what happens onboard the ship. I ask you again, do you read me? And I'll answer for you as well: You damn well do."

Duane stormed away, leaving Ben a pulsing rage.

At the bar, Ben took his usual seat. As he landed, so did his usual Mai Tai. Miss Malloy occupied the adjacent seat.

"Who's the new guy?" Garth asked.

"The admiral of the fleet," Ben replied.

"He sure can knock 'em back."

"There is a certain amount of 'keep 'em coming' to him, isn't there?"

"Why's he here? You guys in trouble?"

"No, we've got clients coming for a sail in a couple of days. He and Miss Malloy are the planning committee and greeting party."

"What did Duane say to you that made your kettle whistle?"

Ben smiled. "Oh, he's mad at me again. And probably rightfully so."

"What did you do?" Miss Malloy asked with a curious grin.

"Nothing, and I'm scared to mention it again," he said waving it off. "Say, Garth, we're looking for a cook to sail with us while the clients are onboard. You know anyone?"

"Yeah, ask Nel."

"Nel?"

"The salad dressing lady. She's a cook."

# Chapter 9

The *Aurawind* stood polished and well stocked for her maiden voyage as a vacation ship. Whenever Duane took time to look up from his charts, he did so in order to get Ben to check some other element of the ship, keeping him busy before the clients' arrival. The busywork became tedious. Ben felt considerable relief when the limo pulled up at the end of the dock and out stepped Mark and Janice Labrio, escorted by Carl and Miss Malloy.

They came aboard. As Mrs. Labrio looked up at Ben, she stopped and said, "Oh, I'd forgotten about you. I'm glad to see you didn't fall overboard on the trip over."

Miss Malloy stared icily at Mrs. Labrio, who smiled wryly at Ben, tilting her head slightly.

"It's nice to see you again, Mrs. Labrio. I thought you weren't joining us until we arrived in Tahiti," Ben said.

"Beats the shit out of me where Mark planned on meeting up with you, but here we are. Tell me. Where exactly are we going?"

"Duane has planned the ports of call, so I'm sure you're going to visit some interesting places." He turned to Miss Malloy. "Can you take Mrs. Labrio to the salon while I go and get the bags? I've set out some snacks that Nel prepared."

While Ben performed his new chores, Duane outlined the cruise to the Labrios, Carl, and Miss Malloy. When he finished, the Labrios went below to the main cabin after a top-me-off of champagne. While they were below, Carl discussed last-minute items with Duane in the pilothouse, Nel chatted with Rudy on the forward deck, and Ben spoke with Miss Malloy at the stern.

"I want to go on a sail. You're so lucky," Miss Malloy said.

"We'll see. I admit I'm looking forward to getting started."

"I'll bet you are. That woman's going to be all over you. I say she tries to stick her hand down your pants at least once before you get back."

"That's not going to happen."

"I'm going to miss crawling in beside you."

"What are you and Carl going to do while we're gone?" he asked.

"We're going back to the mainland, returning before you come back."

"Well, I'll tell you now, I'm going to be thinking about you. I don't know about this cuddling we do every night. I don't know if it's a good idea. I mean we work together. Maybe we shouldn't be mixing the business with the pleasure."

Miss Malloy looked at him. Her mouth dropped open slightly. "You don't like it?"

"Yes," he said in a breathy voice, "I do. But I don't know if it's right. There could be all kinds of complications."

"Like what?"

He looked up at her quickly, responding to her snappy tone.

"Like lots of things. Think about it. Think about how it would work. You're on the inside and I just work here. You know more about this operation, and you've had some sort of relationship with everyone involved, so figure out how complicated this could get."

He could see her slipping into her Purrette-stare, but before she got too deep the Labrios emerged from below. The time to shove off had arrived. Carl and Miss Malloy left the *Aurawind*. Ben, Rudy, and Nel cast off. In all the hustle of the departure, Ben didn't look back to shore until they were clearing the entrance of the yacht club and heading for the open sea. When he did look back he saw Carl and Miss Malloy leaning against the limo. Her hand shaded her eyes. He watched her for a moment, a moment cut short by Duane's order to prepare to raise the jib.

\*\*\*

Two days later, the gentle roll of the ship soothed their tattered nerves as they lay in calm water off the forbidden island of Ni'ihau. For the first time since leaving Honolulu, Mrs. Labrio didn't have to hunch over the side rail and retch. When they had come to the leeward side of Kauai, her color began to change for the better. The bellowing and screaming she directed at her husband had kept them all on edge. They tried to avoid involvement in her misery, but had to attempt to placate her in order to settle her down so they could have a little quiet. On top of lending assistance to Mrs. Labrio, they also had to sail the ship. Duane zealously made sure they stayed on course. Ben and Rudy hopped from task to task to please Duane, who wanted everything dealt with promptly and to his satisfaction.

Now, with a few hours' rest in the settled waters off the shore of the small island, Mrs. Labrio thought she could hold down a drink.

"Do you have ginger ale? That always settles my stomach," she asked Ben.

"Yes, we do. Would you like it with ice or would you like it flat?"

"Ice and bourbon, I think. Then I'll try a little food."

Mark Labrio stood at the stern, looking over the skiff and the mechanism that lowered it from its current point of suspension to the surface of the water. Before Ben went below to get Mrs. Labrio her ginger ale, Mark called to him.

"Ben, come on. Let's get ashore. Let's go check out those caves . . . and bring the fishing gear."

Ben stopped halfway down the companionway and looked to stern, hesitated, then took a step back up, but stopped and shook his head before going down to get the ginger ale and bourbon. After delivering the drink, he went to the stern of the ship to find Mark and Rudy trying to lower the skiff. They yielded control to Ben, who sent them to get what they wanted to take on their excursion while he moved the skiff to the ladder. After the launch, he motored around to the side of the ship and tied up. He climbed the ladder up to the deck, then went below to inform Duane of Mark's plan to go ashore.

"Who's going to take care of Mrs. Labrio?" Duane asked.

"You and Nel."

"No, no, no. She likes you the best. You stay and help her."

"You want Mark and Rudy on their own out there with the skiff?"

"What, you think you're any better?"

Ben lowered his head and stared at Duane. "I have handled it on my own and we still have it."

"Yeah, you're right. We'll take care of Janice."

Ben turned to go, but stopped in the doorway. "Oh yeah, nice job of getting us to where we intended to go."

"What the fuck's that suppose to mean?" Duane snapped.

"Nothing. You navigated well. We're here, aren't we?" He turned and left.

Mark had fishing gear and snorkel equipment stacked near the ladder. He stood watching Rudy bringing towels.

"That should be all we need, Rudy. Are you ready, Ben?"

"Ah, sure. I was thinking, though, maybe Mrs. Labrio would like to come ashore and feel solid ground for a while. Should I check?"

"You may be on to something there. But I suggest we give the alcohol a chance to work and see how she feels in an hour or two." Mark smiled and jerked his head toward the shore.

"Rudy, you coming?" Ben asked.

"I would, but I better stay in case Duane or Mrs. Labrio need anything."

"Nel is here."

"I'll stay anyway."

Mark and Ben both looked at Janice to say good-bye, but when they saw her with eyes closed and head tilted back enjoying the sun, they decided to just leave.

They tore off in the direction of the island, their engine screaming to life. They slowed as they approached the caves. They passed in front of the stretch of six openings a number of times to glimpse their interiors. The small engine idled as they passed by the mouth of one cave carved into the face of a high cliff, the top overhung with green vines spattered with small white and violet blooms. The arch of the cave reached high up into the gray walls. The ceiling inside tapered down and back to a dark black hole.

They brushed by the entrance but didn't cross the line that would place them inside the cave. Their third attempt to steel their nerves to the point of exploring inside still didn't achieve the desired results. They carried on past this cave to the next one, where they would surely be ready to plunge in. The gin-clear water allowed them to see the gray rock of the walls descending very deep below the surface. When they reached the last cave, Ben gunned the engine and arced out away from the cliffs and circled back to the first cave to make another pass.

"Which one did you think looked most interesting?" Ben asked.

"They all look the same. What do you think it's like inside them?"

"Don't know. Maybe there's a strong current."

"Let's go in."

"Which one?"

"Don't know. Any one."

Ben started to turn into the cave, but Mark shouted to go to the next cave, causing Ben to veer back along the face of the cliff. When they got to the mouth of the next cave, Ben didn't slow down for discussion, he just turned and went inside. At first nothing seemed different. The light stayed the same, but they had a better view of the reflections of light created by the waves on the roof of the cave. As they watched the light dance, they drifted deeper into the cave. When they noticed the increase in sound from the engine and felt a greater swell in the water, they looked back at the cave's entrance.

"We're getting in too deep," Mark said.

"Yeah. This is the forbidden island. We better get out of here and check with Nel to see if this is okay."

Ben turned and fled. Once outside, he turned hard to port until they faced the cliffs again, and stopped the engine. They stared back at where they had come from, bobbing silently in their own wake.

"Let's go fishing," Mark said. Ben started up again and headed away from the cliffs. With no idea what they were fishing for, they cruised out to sea but made sure the *Aurawind* remained within swimming distance. They stopped and began to prepare a pole. Mark tied a hook and sinker onto a line and they were almost ready.

"What kind of bait are you going to use?"

Mark looked up when he heard the question. His smile provided the embarrassing answer. "Any ideas?"

"Hmm. We brought nothing? We have any bright-colored cloth? We could tear off a chunk and put it on a hook."

Mark sliced the side of his swim trunks with the gutting knife and cut off a strip of the material. He ran the hook through the middle and started to pay out the line. When he had let out his estimate of enough, he looked at Ben.

They sat and waited.

After a while, Ben said, "Is ocean fishing like lake fishing? Are you supposed to drop a line and wait to see if something hits?"

"Depends. Near shore I think you can do it that way. In deep water you probably want to troll."

"Should we move around?"

"We could try."

Ben started the engine. Keeping it quiet with an idling throttle, he slowly trolled away from the *Aurawind* for a few minutes, and then turned to troll back. They grew restless. After a few laps, Mark suggested they land on the beach down shore from the caves and explore a little by land. He reeled in his line, and they conceded they wouldn't be having fresh fish for dinner.

"We'll have to ask Nel how we should go about catching some fish," Ben said.

On shore, they found a trail and followed it along the beach toward the cliffs, hoping to climb them to see what was up on the plateau. When they'd walked the trail for what seemed like a long time without getting closer to the cliffs, they stopped to re-evaluate their intentions. They were, after all, on the Forbidden Island. The heat and humidity became uncomfortable, and when rivulets of sweat trickled down their temples and backs, they decided they'd seen enough and turned back toward the beach where they sat down to rest before returning to the ship.

They looked out at the *Aurawind* and spotted Nel standing by the rail waving at them. They returned her wave.

"Although we didn't get much accomplished, I found all this activity enjoyable, and a little tiring," Mark said.

"You bet. I thought it was great. We gotta get the scoop from Nel and do all this stuff again."

"I'll say. I hope we can go farther into those caves."

"The sound, the light and the distant feeling in there kind of gives you the creeps. Imagine what it would be like to keep going until you get to the dark."

"Yes. Something to look forward to." Mark sat and smiled for a moment. "I've enjoyed this trip so far, despite the travails Janice has exposed us to. I didn't think she would react that badly at sea. She's had problems before, but not like that."

"I feel bad for her," Ben said, trying to sound as genuine as he felt about her discomfort.

"Ben, how do you feel about this outfit you're working for? Do things seem okay to you?"

Suddenly Ben raised his guard. He told himself to be careful. Since he had signed up for this adventure, his words had come back on him too many times, and he didn't want to piss anyone off again. "They've been good, I guess. They've lived up to everything they told me they would do. I'll tell you one thing, they do everything first class."

"Good. I'm thinking of buying in."

"Buying into what?"

"The whole concept. The private cruise business. I know it's only been three days, but I'm impressed by what you get on one of these cruises. You charge top dollar, but deliver first-class private sailing trips. I like it. Don't know if the sailing end of the business will turn a profit, but the resale of the ship certainly will."

"But we already have owners of the *Aurawind*. Is Carl selling you the ship already?"

"No, just a share."

"A share?"

"Part ownership. I like the idea. I like the sailing. Maybe we'll do this again once you get to Tahiti."

Back onboard ship, Mark raved about all they had accomplished during their day of activity. Exploring caves, hiking, hanging out on a beautiful beach, and even getting in a little fishing. The active life at sea. Nel smiled, waiting for an opportunity to pull Ben off to the side.

"Ben, this is the Forbidden Island. You can't land there," she said.

"What do you mean?"

"Only Hawaiians are allowed on this island. It's ancient and very private."

"Will we get in trouble?"

"Maybe, if someone saw you. There are only about two hundred people living on the island."

"Wow. That's cool. We landed on the Forbidden Island. I gotta tell Mark we shouldn't have done it." He turned to go, but Nel grabbed his arm.

"Yes, let him know it's not cool. It's their island. And, if you sail this way again, make sure you stay the hell off of it." She turned abruptly and left.

They decided to sail northeast to Kauai's Na Pali coast. They were free to sail when they wanted, and where they wanted. Duane put the ship on a northeast course and they viewed the bigger island through the mist that distance provides. It rose from the water looking like a half-submerged torpedo.

Ben asked Nel about trying to fish. After she explained a little about fishing in the strait, he and Mark asked her to drop a couple of lines to test their luck on the way. Once they were moving, she showed them a mind-bending knot used to attach a series of hooks on a leader, and then baited the hooks with a variety of items both natural and rubber. She paid out the line a long way, then showed Ben how to draw in some slack in the line, to attach it to a portion of the line adjacent to the pole with a heavy elastic band. She explained that when a fish hit the hook and took off on its run, the elastic would snap and let them know they had a fish. She made Ben do all the work on the second line, because he kept interrupting her with attempts to take over the duties while they set up the first.

With the bait in the water, Ben and Mark couldn't take their eyes off the elastic bands attached to the poles set in holders on either side of the ship. Duane steered from the cockpit while Rudy lounged on the stern deck. Nel joined Janice in the upper salon. Although the sea dropped and rose with regularity, it remained tame and didn't affect Janice. They watched the two fishermen who sat riveted to the elastic bands, waiting. Periodically, Duane called for Ben to trim a sail and Ben tore himself away from his fishing. Ben made Rudy join him in his adjustments, trying to get Rudy to be more helpful as a sailor.

Na Pali grew closer. Ben had to make himself available to Duane and help him to find a mooring. Standing up front near the jib, he heard the twang of an elastic snapping and turned to see Mark rise in bewilderment and approach the pole, all the while looking over his shoulder in a plea for help.

Nel yelled out, "Fish!" as she left the salon to go and provide instruction to Mark.

Duane turned the *Aurawind* more northerly, away from land. He called out to Ben to lower the jib while he adjusted the mainsail for their new heading. When they had both accomplished their tasks, Ben stood looking at Duane who finally nodded, releasing Ben to go back and watch the fishing action.

All eyes watched down the line. As Ben arrived, Nel, Rudy, Mark, and Janice all hooted when the fish broke the surface, wiggling to free itself from the hook.

Ben arrived too late to see the fish and asked excitedly, "What? Did you see it? What is it?"

Nel, still looking down the line, answered, "Mahimahi."

Ben scampered in front of everyone to get a better view. Nel asked him to get the gaff ready. As he turned to retrieve the hook, a second chorus of fish-sighting amazement sung out, and he turned to see only a taut line entering the water. He retrieved the gaff hook and returned to the side of the ship where the line from Mark's rod now took a steep angle down into the water.

"Pull steadily, release, then reel in the slack. That's good. Again," Nel said.

"This thing weighs a ton." Mark's voice sounded strained.

Finally Ben could see a glint of silver below the surface. It rose, and its back shimmered partway out of the water. It splashed with a violent twist then dropped back down under the surface. Mark reeled in more line. The next time he pulled, he brought it to the surface and held it there. Nel took the gaff out of Ben's hand, leaned over the side, and in one strong swipe, hooked the fish just behind the gill and lifted it out of the water, over the rail, and onto the ship, where it thumped with its head and tail, splashing bloody sea water in fanning red lines over the deck.

Everyone backed away from the flopping fish except Nel, who looked about for something heavy. She found nothing and yelled, "Duane, you got a club up there?"

The fish scooted along the deck toward the retreating Ben, Mark, and Rudy until it reached Nel's feet. She kicked it back toward where it had come. Duane called out for Ben. When Ben turned, a baseball bat flew toward his face. Not expecting it, he jerked to one side and instinctively sent his hands out to protect himself, and in so doing caught the bat. He turned toward Nel, offering the bat, but she pointed to the blood-splattering fish. Ben's eyes widened and so did his stance as he circled in on the flopping silver creature. He raised the bat and brought it down on the fish's head, but the blow only made the fish jump more. After a quick backward step, Ben moved forward again. This time he brought the club down with force. The blow stilled the fish. He hit it once more with a strong smacking stroke that sent watery blood flying in all directions.

He stood and turned with the murder weapon in his hand to face the silent witnesses. "Yahhhh!" he screamed, as he raised his hands and the bat over his head. Mark and Nel rushed forward, and the three fishermen slapped each other on the back.

Nel gutted the fish and disappeared below with the carcass. When she returned, she brought a plate of raw fish to eat the way the Hawaiians enjoyed eating fish. She, Mark, and Ben sampled the fish immediately. Janice turned green at the thought of eating raw fish. Duane and Rudy shook their heads and declined the offer to taste the fresh food.

At dinner the seared fish steaks, served in a lemon-garlic sauce, had a somewhat similar reception. Rudy asked if Nel had cooked any real meat. Nel went to the bow and smoked. Ben joined her after he had cleaned the dishes.

"Will you show me how you cooked the fish?"

"Sure. You want some for breakfast?"

"You bet."

"You cook."

# Chapter 10

In a posh restaurant in an industrial marine area of the harbor, Carl, Miss Malloy, and the Labrios sat enjoying dinner the night before the Labrios' departure. A small artificial concrete river lined with rounded stones and teeming with bright orange koi meandered through the restaurant. The lighted fishing boats moored outside swayed gently each time a slow-moving vessel returned to the docks.

Janice Labrio, being back on firm ground, had recovered her appetite and eaten mightily for a woman of small stature. She dedicated herself to the replenishment of calories so single-mindedly that she had not consumed her normal quantity of alcohol, and therefore contributed coherently to the after-dinner conversation.

"When we had calm water, I was fine, but from a cramped-up hunching position overlooking the sea, it was difficult to stop and smell the sailing. Mark is going to be hard pressed to get me to do that again," Janice commented.

"We'll see, dear. I do think I would like to do this again. Once we figured out how to fish, we were catching everything in sight. Carl,

I can't tell you how much I enjoyed the week. And Ben is an excellent first mate."

"And God, is he handsome," Janice added.

Miss Malloy's smile drooped a fraction as she swung her eyes to look at Janice.

Mark continued, "Duane is a great skipper. I had great confidence with him at the helm. And Nel is a phenomenal cook. But what's up with Rudy? He seemed so pleasant in Catalina."

"Hmm. It surprises me that you found him a little off," Carl said.

"Not *off*, Carl ... creepy. But that's not a consideration. I want to buy in. How many units do you have available?"

"That's good news."

"I think you have a pretty good plan with this setup, and it makes a nice little feather in the investment cap."

Carl tilted his head and looked at Miss Malloy. She met his gaze and made the slightest movement with her eyes, opening them a little wider.

"You're sure now? How many units are you interested in?" Carl asked.

"Very sure. Two."

"Well, I hate to disappoint you, but there's only one left on the *Aurawind*. However, I'm about to make a deal on another ship, and I can get you in on the ground floor on that one. Nice thing about that is you'd be spreading your investment around, staggering the payoff."

Mark leaned back in his seat, crossing his arms over his chest. He took a glance at Janice and saw that her eyes had begun to show their familiar gloss. He puckered his lips, leaned forward, placing his elbows on the table, looked Carl straight in the eye, and held his stare for a long period of silence. Finally, Mark said, "I'm still in. How much per unit?"

"The same. Fifty."

"Okay. I'll have a check to you as soon as I get back. Send me the prospectus on the other ship."

***

Ben joined Nel and some members of the yacht club for open-grill and yacht races. The evening offered gentle wind, clear stargazing, the occasional clang of the finish bell, and the frequent arrival of Mai Tais.

"You should come with us, Nel. We need your help," Ben said.

"I've got a commitment. I'll be at sea for three months."

"Come after that. We can find a temporary chef until you meet us."

"I thought you had a cook but he couldn't meet up with you until later."

"Who knows? The cook's been a mystery to me through this whole thing. Have you ever been to Tahiti?"

"Yeah."

"What's it like?"

"This." Nel stood up and spread her arms out, palms up, and turned a panoramic turn. "Only more rustic, a little dirtier, decidedly French, and a lot further away." She sat down again.

"You sure can sell a guy."

"Rudy sailing all that way with you?"

"As far as I know."

Nel kept her eyes focused out over the harbor while her group ate their salads.

Ben took a large bowl, knowing he would be away from Nel's cooking for a long time. "You have to give me the recipe for this salad dressing," he said, while chewing a large mouthful of greens.

"No."

Ben stopped eating to look and see if she had smiled as she responded, but he only saw the back of her head as she continued to stare out at the darkness over the water.

\*\*\*

While they remained in port, Rudy continued to stay onshore during the nights. So Ben relaxed, enjoying the luxury of being the lone occupant of his berth again. Carl had returned to the mainland while the crew awaited his instruction to leave Honolulu and head for Papeete.

When they had returned from the Labrio trip, Miss Malloy had tried to enter the berth and resume the late-night contact with Ben. But he had told her it had to stop. A relationship between them couldn't happen. He told her it didn't make sense to be involved when they wouldn't see each other for long periods. These reasons he used so he didn't have to explain the level of discomfort he had regarding her idea of relationships with men.

For the next two days, if he found himself working somewhere near her, he would perform his work silently and as quickly as possible, then move to another part of the ship. The night before she left, he lay in his berth unable to sleep and undecided whether he wanted her to return one last time. She didn't. Instead he basked in the most vivid memory of her scent as she lay with her head so near to his nose, the chilling scorch of her breath on his bare chest, and the full-length warmth of her body underneath the light pajamas he insisted she wear.

The next day he carried her luggage across the docks to the entrance of the yacht club, where he waited with her after she called a taxi.

"Do you know when we'll be leaving?" he asked, so there would be no silence.

"No, but I don't think there's anything lined up here, so I think it will be soon."

"Oh really. I guess that's good. You know, when Mark and I went to the beach on Ni'ihau, he said he was going to buy into the *Aurawind*. Do you know what that's all about?"

Miss Malloy hesitated briefly before answering. "No."

"He said he was thinking about buying a share of the ship. Does that change my deal with Carl in any way?"

"I don't know what your deal with Carl is so I can't give you an answer. Carl did say he would probably buy another ship and do the private cruise business again. Maybe that's what Mark was referring to."

"Yeah, maybe. Would you mind asking Carl to let me know what's going on?"

"I'll let him know you're curious."

The whole time they talked, she watched the opening between the hotel and office building across the parking lot, searching for the cab. She had the stare of Purrette while she spoke of Miss Malloy's business.

"I thought you might have come to see me last night, to say good-bye."

She closed her eyes as she turned toward him then sat down on the end of her suitcase, turning her eyes toward the ground.

"You made it pretty clear that you didn't want me doing that anymore."

"I know. I didn't mean to come down and lie with me, I meant to come down and just talk." Now Ben stared off looking for the cab. The breeze seemed to die, and the heat radiating up from the sidewalk closed in on him.

"Are you going to be in Tahiti at some point?" he asked, to avoid a silence again.

"I imagine so."

"Good. It will be good to see you again."

She looked up at him, tilted her head, and squinted one eye, an inquisitive expression on her face.

"You know, Ben, I told you you were something good, and I still believe that. I still want to feel what it's like to lie beside you. I still want to make love to you. I still want you to want it, too. But, when it comes to dealing with what you want, you never explain yourself, so I don't know where you're coming from. You're kind of a prick on that front.

"All that shit you were trying to feed me the other night, about why we would have a difficult relationship, makes me puke. You spouted a bunch of reasons that I don't really think you actually believe. If you can't make up your mind, then I guess I have to reconsider what kind of guy you really are. If we were to start this *difficult* relationship, I don't want to start it with you leaving yourself a back door that's wide open." She turned away to look for the cab again. Not seeing it, she turned back to him and said, "I can wait alone. Why don't you go back to the ship?"

Ben wiped a wisp of sweat off his upper lip. He stood and looked down at her profile. She stared vacantly as words eluded him. Finally he gave a slight nod, which she didn't see, and walked behind her and away toward the clubhouse.

Upstairs at the bar, Ben sat at his normal place. When Garth appeared he carried a box of napkins and two bottles of fruit juice.

"Ah, it's a good thing I went to get these, now that my champion Mai Tai drinker has arrived." Garth stopped short when he took a good look at Ben. "You're looking a little down, man. Mai Tai's don't come as doubles, but I could bring you two."

"That would help."

***

Two days after Miss Malloy departed, Carl contacted Duane and told him to leave Honolulu. Ben spent the next two days with Nel, outfitting the ship for the long sail. He still hadn't convinced her to join them when she got back from her own long stint at sea.

On the morning of their departure, Ben had breakfast one last time inside the club. He'd said good-bye to Garth rather late the previous night and now waited for Nel to meet him to help them shove off.

He finished his meal early, signed the chit, and decided to walk to Nel's mooring and meet her. When he arrived, he found her with coffee and a smoke in the stern of the small yacht she lived on. She offered him the chair that she had been resting her feet on and told him to help himself to the coffee, if there was any left. He declined.

"There were times during the ten days at sea it took to get to Hawaii that bored me to tears. I don't know how you're gonna make it through three months of it," he commented.

Without taking her eyes off of the horizon, she said, "I work almost constantly when I'm on a freighter. Time goes fast. You, though, are going to have a lot of nothing time. That's what's really slow."

"You've sailed long passages on yachts. Any tips on keeping occupied?"

"First, if you don't want to go crazy, I would tell you to spend as much time as possible avoiding Rudy. Maybe it's me, but . . . Wait, maybe I better not knock the guy. You have to live with him for a long time, so let me cop out and tell you to take plenty of books."

"Thanks. Ready to go?"

"Yes, but I still have to go over to the clubhouse. I'll see you at your slip."

With everything ready to go onboard the *Aurawind*, they had only to wait for Duane to return and for Nel to come help them shove off. Rudy had returned to the ship the afternoon before and moved all of his belongings into the second stateroom, which Nel had occupied during the Labrio excursion. Ben had his berth to himself for a good long time. Duane soon returned and went below to retrieve his charts.

Nel came aboard, went straight to Ben, and addressed him rather sternly. "When were you going to tell me?"

Ben smiled the innocent smile of the unknowing and shifted his eyes from right to left, then back to Nel. Shrugging and lifting his hands, he asked, "Tell you what?"

"About your change in destination."

Ben shook his head in quick little shakes and said, "Don't know what you're talking about."

"Come here," she said and led him to the bow away from Rudy. "The commodore just told me that you're setting sail for the Galapagos. He said that's what Duane told him. This surprised him because I'd told him I might join you when you get to Tahiti. You don't know anything about the Galapagos?"

"No one's ever mentioned it to me. That's the island with all the lizards, right?"

"Right."

"Hmm. Well, then I guess I don't know where we're going. When we get there, and if we still need a cook around the time you finish your contract, I'll call you somehow and let you know where we're at."

"It's weird, Ben. Here comes Duane, you going to ask him?"

"Not now. He's been wound so tight the last couple of days, it would only piss him off. I'm going to have to go wherever they go anyway. I'll ask him when we're at sea."

"Okay, let's get you guys shoved off."

After she tossed Ben the last line, she waved and called out to have a good sail. Duane chose to embark under engine power, so Ben didn't have to run off to deal with any sail setting. He waved to Nel and watched her shrink as they pulled away. The long waving session grew embarrassing, so he yelled out, "You never gave me the salad dressing recipe."

To which Nel yelled back, "Tough!"

Once outside the harbor, Duane killed the engine. They set the sails and headed due south. Ben walked to the stern to look back at the island, once things were settled. He smiled, remembering how comfortable he had felt in Honolulu, and hoped that the next port, wherever it may be, would prove as pleasant a place to live as this one. He waved to the city and heard Rudy's voice come from behind him.

"Ah, isn't that sweet. Ben is saying good-bye to all his friends."

"For once, you're right. I feel a little corny," Ben said and turned to go find some busywork.

***

The next day, still on a southerly course, Ben stood in the cockpit and listened to Duane explain the trim of the sails. When Duane finished, he started to explain their heading, and that they would stay on this course for the next six days. Once they crossed the equator, they would make a slight easterly change. Without thinking about his question, Ben asked Duane if their heading would take them to Ecuador.

After a very slight hesitation, Duane spoke at a very fast pace. "Ecuador? What the fuck are you talking about, man?"

"Ecuador. I heard we were sailing to the Galapagos. Isn't that off Ecuador?"

"Yes, it is. But why in hell would we be going there?"

"I don't know, that's why I'm asking. Nel said she heard you tell the commodore we might have clients to pick up and sail to the Galapagos."

"That's bullshit, man. She don't know what she's talking about. We're heading for Tahiti like we always said we were. What the hell does she care where we go, anyway?" Duane shook his head while speaking.

Ben smiled and cleared his throat. "I told her we might want her to come to Tahiti if we needed a cook. She was just . . . "

"You what?" Duane said incredulously, "You told her she could join us in Tahiti? What did I tell you about shooting your mouth off about this ship? What gave you the idea you could make a decision like that without Carl's input? Let's get it straight this time and let's keep it straight: You have no say about what is going on onboard this ship. We don't need no dumb-ass ideas coming out of your dumb-ass mouth. Do you understand me?"

Ben stood and took the verbal abuse Duane dealt. His arms tensed as he listened, and he could tell that if he didn't speak out, he would lash out. "If you recall, it was my dumb-ass idea to sign on Nel as the cook in Honolulu, and you may also recall that she saved our asses when she said she would help. You weren't calling me a dumb-ass then. You and Carl and the rest of this dipshit crew couldn't acquire the right personnel in Honolulu, so I figured I better have a backup plan for when you all hung your heads and started whining that you wanted me to do the cooking in Tahiti. Now, you want me to keep my mouth shut. I guess that's what you'll get. Tell me when you need something done and I'll do it, because you know the best goddamn way to do everything, don't you? You know the best way to trim the sails, you know the best way to hire crew, you know the best way to calculate the course we need to sail, and you know the best way to correct the course you calculated. Of course it takes you a few days to realize you miscalculated, but what the hell, we'll make up for it with a few extra days of sailing."

If skulls could smolder, a thick cloud of smoke would have filled the air above Duane's head. Words could not escape his mouth as he watched Ben walk toward the bow. He turned rapidly to pursue Ben, but stopped when he saw Rudy leaning against the half-wall of the salon with a smile on his face. When their eyes met, Rudy raised his brows.

"What, you think this is funny?" Duane barked at him.

"Looks like we got to get rid of him." Rudy said.

Duane lifted his head and stood like he'd been coldcocked. "When I say so," he said, and turned back into the cockpit.

When Ben arrived forward, he placed his hand on the jib sheet and pulled lightly, then checked the wrap on the cleat. His hand trembled with each move, but he continued to check and adjust everything in sight, trying to get his heart rate back to normal.

# Chapter 11

A thin crumbling two-lane sheet of asphalt covered with cracked crab slithered through the dense undergrowth of brush and ferns. Foliage crept close to the shoulder, almost to the gray edge, ready to reclaim the road. Ben pushed the rented scooter along the shoulder, spotting large land crabs retreating down their holes or raising their claws to defend themselves. He began to wonder if he had misunderstood the desk clerk's directions to the old man's compound.

"Up the road about four kilometers, on the right there is an opening in the bush barely wide enough to get a van through. You can't miss it," he'd said.

Thinking he might miss the opening, Ben stopped the scooter and walked along in the high humidity. It didn't take long before he second-guessed his timing and began thinking he had already passed his destination. At a slight bend in the road he spotted a break in the grass that opened up into the bushes. Two grooves cut by tire treads led into the wall of maple and bamboo trees. The smell of fresh-baked bread filled the air. As he filled his lungs with the homey scent, he remembered he had seen a number of locals riding bicycles with long baguettes pinched between their fingers.

He closed his eyes to take in the smell again, then proceeded down the tire tracks into the deep-green wall. He passed the scrub and fern, moved into the taller line of trees and walked a short distance in their shade. When he reached the other edge of the trees, he stopped and leaned forward past the tree line to look into a clearing. He saw a small wooden tabletop sitting on metal legs. A seat from an old tractor had been welded to the legs of the table, and a stump of wood supported the seat. In front of the seat stood an odd-looking metal object resembling the footrest on a shoeshine chair. To one side of the table sat a European van whose model was unfamiliar to Ben. Its sides and top were entirely made of glass.

The chewed-up earth had a sprinkling of wood shavings and coconut husks. Next to the table with the strange apparatus in front, a pen had been constructed from old cattle gates. Some corners were held with welds while others were wrapped with orange twine. Inside, a small heap of gray coconuts waited for their trip to the grinder. Old track marks, wider than the ones on which Ben had entered, led away from the coconut prison to another opening into the jungle at the far end of the compound.

As Ben scanned further, he spotted a hut on stilts that seemed to be built into the towering green wall of bamboo. Deep in the dark interior he could see the unfinished plywood of the hut's back wall and the poles that supported the roof. A fire pit smoldered a few feet in front of the three steps that led up to the platform floor of the hut's full-length opening. Beside the fire pit stood a few wooden stumps and two kitchen chairs with torn vinyl seats, their dirty-white cotton stuffing exposed. Beside the kitchen chairs a large white wooden deckchair seemed to hold a place of honor.

Something else, also white, moved in the chair, causing Ben to pull his head back from looking into the compound.

"Bonjour, mon ami," called a strong tenor voice. Ben pulled back behind the cover of the trees and stood frozen for a few seconds, considering whether or not to turn and go. The rustic look of the compound hadn't impressed him. He wondered whether he really wanted to go into the opening. Then the tenor voice spoke again. "Monsieur, voulez-vous entrer? Puis je vous aider?"

Ben didn't understand a word, but he heard a friendly tone in the voice so he pushed his scooter into the compound. His feet sank into the soft dirt. The tires of the scooter cut deep ruts, making it heavy to push. He decided it need not accompany him any further, and placed it on its kickstand. He approached the older gentleman, who now stood in front of his chair. Through the thin twisting threads of smoke rising from the fire pit, the old man stood smiling, waiting for Ben to speak.

"Jem appel Ben Beck. Moi avec le bateau avec le harbor," he said in a jagged tempo. The older man's eyebrows closed together as he looked away to comprehend what he had heard. When he looked back, Ben continued, "Moi avec le opportunity avec vous."

The man shook his head in quick little movements and lifted his hands, still not understanding.

"Comment est-ce que je peux vous aider?" he asked.

The speed with which the words were spoken made it impossible for Ben to understand them. Again he stood and smiled, not knowing which direction he should attempt to take the conversation. His limited grasp on the language provided few choices.

"Vous avec bon maison," Ben said.

The man looked off toward the jungle for a second, and then said, "Merci."

"Parlay vous manger onglish?" Ben asked, causing the man to tilt his head and twist the muscles in his face as he tried desperately to pick up on what Ben might be talking about.

A woman's voice came from the shadows inside the hut. "My father can speak English, but he can't understand poorly spoken French."

Both men looked toward the hut, then back at each other. The older man's expression became more relaxed. "Tres bon, you speak English," he said, "That is good. If we had to continue in the language you were speaking, I'm afraid we would never be able to have a conversation."

"Oh, this is great. I'm new to French, just started trying to speak it."

"Yes. In a few years we may be able to converse in that pleasant language, but until then we will be forced to use this one. My name is Rene Argent. Somehow I discerned that your name is Mr. Beck, and it seems you have an opportunity for me to eat all the Englishmen you have onboard your ship."

"Is that what I said? No, there are no Englishmen to eat. I want to talk to you about tourists."

"Much better, Monsieur Beck. I do enjoy eating tourists."

The woman spoke again. "Papa, ne gosse pas."

Mr. Argent turned to the hut and raised his voice to say, "I'm not being rude. This young Monsieur is offering people to eat, and I'm letting him know my tastes. We are two gentleman having a conversation regarding an unusual topic, and we don't need you coming between us." He turned back to Ben with a smile and continued in a calm, formal voice, "Now, Monsieur, how many tourists do you offer for this feast?"

"Papa, arrête la plaisanterie avec cet homme." The woman stepped out of the shadows to look sternly at her father. She wore a faded, but once deep blue, pareo with a pattern of white flowers. Her slight but curved body leaned against the bamboo post in the center of the hut's opening. Her smooth hair, dark blond with sun-bleached streaks, hung down to her waist as she tilted her head back to keep it from falling over her face. Mr. Argent didn't turn this time, but waved his hand dismissively behind his head. To Ben he said, "She is very persistent and also very perceptive. I apologize, Monsieur Beck, for having a little fun with you. Please, tell me what you wish to talk to me about."

"I'd like to send you some tourists. In return, I'd like you to send some to me."

"Maeva, bring the young monsieur a bottle of beer. He is hot and looks like he could use a cold drink."

Ben outlined his intention to recommend island tours by Mr. Argent to the tourists that he brought onboard the *Aurawind*. In the four months the ship had been moored in Papeete, Carl had only sent them three clients to take out on private cruises. The remainder of their time had been spent sitting and waiting. They had sailed to a few of the closer islands on their own to gather information and plan trips for their eventual clients, but they had to remain close to the capitol city in case Carl tried to contact them. Some of the time they spent on land, but in general they received a large ration of boredom sitting onboard while moored at this island paradise.

Most mornings, Ben walked down the dock to the marina to sit in the small café and drink the strong French coffee with a croissant or a piece of baguette. The lack of cow's milk made it hard to get used to the strong coffee. He tried flavoring it with coconut milk, but he couldn't get accustomed to the cloying flavor contrasted against the edgy taste of the dark-roasted coffee, so he learned to live with it straight up. The first morning he had breakfast in this manner, he took a table at the edge of the open café so he could look down onto the beach. Shortly after Ben sat down, the waiter banged an ashtray onto the countertop to get his attention. When he had Ben's eye, he indicated by stretching his neck toward a point behind Ben, that he should look down the beach. Ben turned to see three men, with skin as worn and tired-looking as their clothing, walking toward him. They had come from the scrubby bushes that lined the concrete wall of the beach. They walked heads-down in single file, the two followers intent on using the first man's footprints.

The leader looked up to see inside the café. His eyebrows curved severely downward and overhung his eye sockets. The gray sun-faded baseball cap he wore showed dark lines in front where a New York Yankees logo had once been attached. His grime-infused T-shirt had a hole on one side stretching from the armpit to the bottom seam where it held on by a thread. On the front it said "Rice University 1978." His jaunty walk made the foot-steps game more interesting for his followers, and he dragged a thin stick of driftwood to create a wobbly line for them to trace with their own sticks. As he spotted Ben sitting alone at the outside table of the café, he stopped and lifted the stick, swinging it across in front of his body to slap it with military precision into his other hand. He held the stick parallel to the ground in front of his thighs. His two companions, a few feet behind, looked up when the line they were tracing ended. They noticed their leader's attention was on Ben. Now, they stood upright to appear as their leader's bold companions rather than his silly followers.

When the trio reached the gray wall that supported the floor of the café above the beach, they stopped and stared slightly upward at Ben, their heads about table level.

"Bonjour, monsieur," the leader said.

"Hello," Ben replied.

"Merci. Thank you for letting me know to speak English. One must always assume French first." The leader spoke with a heavy French accent.

"I see you're a fan of the Yankees." Ben pointed to the leader's hat, causing him to turn around quickly and look down the beach in the direction Ben pointed. When he didn't see anything, he turned back and said, "Monsieur, I love all Americans, and you, sir, have very little in the way of an accent." The leader smiled and bowed his head slightly, pausing briefly at the bottom. "My name is Yves Tremblay.

My two associates here are Luc Houle and Le-hiro-de-biere." He placed his hand beside his mouth and leaned closer to Ben to speak in confidence. "Not his real name, Monsieur, but his reputation." Leaning back, he dropped his hand, nodded, and waited for Ben to respond. After a second or two with no response, he continued, "We work along this part of the beach providing services to people who are unfamiliar with Papeete, and gladly offer our assistance to you. How may we serve you, Monsieur . . . "

"Beck."

"Oui, Monsieur Beck?"

"I'm not sure. Have you had your morning coffee? May I buy you a cup?"

"We would all enjoy your company, a cup of coffee, and perhaps a piece of bread if you are willing, but the waiter does not allow us to enter the café. He mistakenly believes that we assaulted him some time ago, but of course it was an accident that caused my stick to strike him. I jumped, having been frightened by a large crab, and in my haste when I pulled my stick back to strike the crab, I did not observe the direction of my backswing, and the stick smacked him soundly across the lower part of the back of his legs. I did not appreciate why my two friends were laughing so hard until I turned to see the waiter performing a wild kick-step, his back arched very far backward as he distanced himself from my stick. From that day until this morning, he has not allowed us inside, and he has never accepted my apology."

Le-hiro-de-biere said, "But you have never apologized."

"Of course not," Yves said, agitated, "after the insults he threw at us, once he had reached the safety behind his counter."

The waiter didn't look directly at them, but he watched them converse with Ben from the corner of his eye.

Ben shook his head and asked, "What kind of services do you offer to someone new to the city?"

"If you have questions about anything on the island, I can answer. If you need to know who the most important people are, I can answer that, too. We are here to help and have many things to offer. Now, as far as the coffee is concerned, what has worked in the past is that the patron of the café orders coffees and a baguette to go, then passes them outside to us so we can have a decent conversation. N'est pa?"

Ben smiled as he turned to the waiter. He held up three fingers and pointed to his coffee, then pointed at his bread and indicated he wanted a whole loaf. He had to communicate with the waiter in sign language. When he first indicated that he only spoke English, the waiter had stared blankly and made no attempt to accommodate him in his own language.

"I think he knows what I ordered," Ben said.

"Monsieur, the waiter speaks very good English."

Ben turned back to place his order in English, but the waiter had already begun to pour the coffee into paper cups.

This became his established breakfast routine: coffee and croissant along with the rapping of the ashtray on the counter, followed by the visit of Yves and his two companions. Within days he noticed the waiter would occasionally point him out to tourists occupying the prime tables at the front of the café near the water where they had the best views of the ships in the marina. The tourists would nod to him if they caught his eye.

One morning, after such a nod had occurred, the gentleman walked over to his table. After brief introductions the tourist asked about the ship, and then hesitated before asking if it would be possible to come onboard to take a look. Ben smiled and said he would check with his captain. He disappointed the tourist the next morning when he told him the captain had declined the visit. Eventually, tourists began to ask him if they could charter the *Aurawind* for the day. He responded that, indeed, the *Aurawind* was a charter yacht, but he disappointed the tourists when he explained the nature of the ship's private cruises of a week's duration, mainly booked by their principal partner located in the United States.

The frequency of the requests amazed Ben. Given the lack of clients being generated by Carl, he broached the subject of providing day cruises to tourists with Duane. It took almost a month to get him to agree, and the agreement came only after Ben committed that, first, he would do all the work required to find the customers, and second, that Duane would keep half the fee, after expenses, while Ben and Rudy split the remainder. To acquire the customers, Ben had embarked on a systematic canvassing of the island's resorts, many of which had been identified to him by Yves. He left information regarding the *Aurawind* with the concierge at each location, hoping they would recommend the ship to their guests. His plan had worked, and they had been out on a number of day cruises. Even so, they had time to take out a few more, so he began to expand the number of resorts that might provide them with customers. The concierge at Bali Heiva had recommended that he contact Mr. Argent, and since he was in the area, he had sought Mr. Argent that day.

"This sounds like a good opportunity for one hand to wash the other, Monsieur Beck. So why don't we talk about the soap?" Mr. Argent said, tilting his head forward and smiling at Ben.

"Soap?"

"Oui. The greasing of the palm. How much will you pay me for each customer I send to you?"

"I'll be sending you customers in return."

"Oui, Monsieur, but you will receive fifty times as much soap from the customers I send to you. I see eight tourists five days a week and will gladly tell them about your ship. My guess is that you see fewer, and therefore will not have the opportunity to recommend my services to so many. As well, the fee you charge just one tourist I send to you will be so much more than what I charge the few I get from you combined. Plus, I'm sure that the men at the resorts expect something in return for the customers they send to you."

"Why don't we try it out first and then make a deal?"

"It's not that I don't trust you, Monsieur Beck, but this type of arrangement should always be made clear up front. Can we say twenty-five percent finder's fee?" Rene leaned back in his chair and sat with a content expression that implied he would wait all day for Ben's answer.

Ben watched him for a few seconds. Then, without saying a word, he poured the dregs of his beer onto the ground beside his chair, stood up, and walked toward his scooter.

"Mr. Beck," Rene called after him, "I think we have something here. Please come back and sit. I think twenty percent would be fine for a beginning."

Ben stopped and turned to look at Rene. He said nothing, waited for a few seconds, and turned back toward the scooter.

"Okay, Mr. Beck. Fifteen percent."

Ben turned to Rene again, gave him a quick nod, and walked back.

Maeva had come to gather the empty bottle and said to Ben as he took his seat, "Another beer, Ben Beck?"

Ben looked up at her face. Strong smooth jaw, fine wide lips, high cheekbones, and oval eyes with dark black pupils. Captivated, he didn't answer her question until she raised her thin, sun-bleached eyebrows to remind him.

"Ah, no. I better not. I have to drive that thing," he said, waving somewhat in the direction of the scooter, but still focused on her face. She smiled and stood to let him gaze.

"It will be dark soon. I hope you rented one with a headlamp that still works," she said, then turned and disappeared inside the hut.

He watched her hips roll slowly while the triangle from her shoulders to the center of her waist remained very still during each of her steps. When she could no longer be seen, he turned to Rene. "I should be going," he said.

"Fine, let us begin under these conditions. Please return tomorrow and take the tour, so you are familiar with your recommendations. Maeva and I will both be guiding, and I will give you a reduced price because we are in business together."

Ben stood and extended his hand, but Rene reached out and grabbed his shoulders. After holding eye contact for a few seconds, he kissed Ben rapidly on both cheeks. Ben pulled his head back because he couldn't pull his shoulders out of Rene's grip.

"Okay," he said, shifting his eyes from side to side.

Rene let go. Ben turned and walked to the scooter without saying another word.

Dusk began to settle over the bamboo forest, and what little could be seen inside the jungle lived in complete darkness now. He rode down the road, the sputtering whine of the scooter filling the space between the thick dark rows of trees. The noise so loud he didn't hear the warning sounds of barking, and could only react to the pack of bony dogs when they came at him from the front and side of the road, just a few feet away. His first move to the right side of the pack took him off the hard surface of the road and halfway down the gradually sloping shoulder. The thin limbs of the brush whipped at his bare legs, and at first he thought he had been bitten. The dogs, now on his left, turned toward him. The ones farthest away collided with those that had not yet adjusted to his position off the road, and three of them went down in a heap of legs, ribs, flying slobber, and a chorus of yelps.

Ben lifted his left leg up by the handlebars as he passed the remainder of the pack and swerved back onto the road. He could hear their barking close behind him, so he twisted hard on the throttle and bent forward with his chin resting on the headlight that didn't work. The barking grew faint in the additional noise of the engine, so he rode in this fashion for a long time before he looked back and saw no trace of the dogs.

After returning the scooter, he walked past Le Marche. The Papeete Market's lights illuminated the surrounding streets where the food stands prepared and served foods of many varieties. Food the locals could afford to eat. The air was hazy with smoke that glowed from the background lights. The smell of grilled fish made his stomach growl, so he stopped to eat before going to the ship. He bought a plate of grilled tuna that came with a banana-leaf packet of mashed breadfruit. He'd had the breadfruit on his plate before, but tonight he decided he would actually try to eat it. The vendor opened the packet and drizzled coconut milk over the mash. Ben paid for the fish and beer, then walked to an open spot along the curb and sat to eat. The fish had a wonderful grilled flavor on its surface, and the flesh was still quite pink in the middle. He ate almost half of it before he built up the nerve to try the breadfruit. Before he scooped some onto his fork, he cut a piece of fish so he could get it into his mouth quickly in case he needed to kill a bad taste, then he touched his beer to confirm its location. He took the forkful of breadfruit, swished it in some of the coconut milk, and popped it into his mouth. At first he chewed with his teeth, expecting some resistance, but realized the soft mash could easily be chewed with just his tongue. He rolled it in his mouth and detected a taste of bland nothing with a hint of coconut. He swallowed, shrugged, and ate the rest of the fish without trying the breadfruit again. He left, still feeling hungry.

When he returned to the ship, he turned forward from the gangway to go to his berth. He knew Rudy and Duane could be found in the stern but he had no desire to see them. A lamp at the top of the pilothouse created a circle of light that prevented his vision from reaching the very back of the ship. He could feel eyes coming from the dark, straining to watch him, but he knew they couldn't penetrate the circle of light, either.

# Chapter 12

The ashtray banged twice on the counter, and Ben knew Yves would soon arrive. As he and his companions approached, Ben ordered coffee and bread for his three friends in English. The waiter looked at him with a blank expression and shook his head while holding his hands out, palms upward. Ben's attempts to trick the waiter into revealing that he understood English had not been successful, so he spoke the French words he'd learned in order to get his breakfast.

When the three ragged men arrived outside the restaurant, Ben told them about the dog attack.

"Ah, les chiens fous," Luc said and pursed his lips.

Yves turned quickly to gaze at him. Luc lowered his eyes and stared at the sand.

"You were attacked by one of the many packs of wild dogs, Mon Ami," Yves said.

"Really … Do they bite?" Ben asked.

Agitated, Yves broke into a rapid French, "Ne m'avez-vous pas entendu les dire étiez-vous les chiens sauvages?" When he saw Ben's expression he slowed down and said, "Pardon my French. I just told you they are wild dogs, of course they bite."

"I thought maybe they just made a bunch of noise and tried to scare people."

"They bite."

Luc and Le-hiro-de-biere sat on the beach while Yves leaned with his elbow and coffee bowl on top of the concrete wall. They stared out at the marina and sipped their brew until Ben asked them about Rene Argent.

"He is a good Frenchman," Yves said without looking at Ben. "He, like us, is one of the ones that stayed. He fell in love with a vahine and married her. She left him and the afa to go live in a village on Tahiti-Iti. She worked the coppa; she ground the coconut meat for him. When she left, so left much of his income. They say she could grind as fast as three women. The afa isn't quite as good."

"Afa?"

"Demi, mixed blood."

"Maeva?"

"If that is the daughter's name, then yes."

"I'm taking his tour this afternoon," Ben said.

"Then you will see the island from the tourist's viewpoint. It's much nicer that way."

That afternoon Ben did see the island as a tourist. Rene had changed his mind about giving Ben a discount for the tour, but when he went to pay Maeva she scowled in the direction of her father and refused to take his money. "I couldn't tell if my father was joking with you or not, Ben Beck, so let's assume he's not the money grabber he chooses to portray."

The three of them climbed into the van made of glass and drove out to pick up the tourists at the resorts. They saw the high points of Papeete, including two that Ben had already discovered, the Marina and the Market. It piqued his interest to hear the description of the Market provided to the tourists. He hadn't realized that most of the vendors came from the rural villages; he'd thought they shipped their products to permanent Market vendors. It made sense for the farmers to man the booths themselves. Since they grew the produce sold in the Market, they earned more profit by eliminating the middleman.

When the tour left the city, they drove through farmland to visit waterfalls and rivers and to get a view looking down at the city and its harbor. They visited a pineapple plantation, where everyone stretched their legs and sampled the fruit. Ben welcomed the leg stretching. Rene had filled all the seats in the coach. With Maeva in the small fold-down jump seat facing backward to narrate the tour, Ben had to sit on the top step of the entrance. This put his feet one step lower than his hips. His heels were directly under his haunches so his knees bent at an acute angle. He took the tour staring out the door.

Ben stood back and watched the two small pods of tourists circle Rene and Maeva, asking questions. Most of them knew their own answers, but felt compelled to show off their knowledge of the island. The hosts stood out at the center of each of their groups. Rene wore a crisp white linen suit and a bright white straw hat; Maeva wore a purple and yellow pareo wrapped very tight to show her curved hips and slight waist. In her hair she wore a white flower, the Tahitian Tiara, stuck behind her ear. The tourists wore a mix of blue denim cut-offs, tennis shorts, T-shirts and sneakers. One or two of the women showed bits of color by wearing pareos tied around their waists as sashes or draped through the straps of their massive handbags.

Maeva spotted Ben watching her as she explained the history of the large snails that could be found all over the island. The French airline pilots had brought them to Tahiti so they could eat escargot during their stopovers on the island. The novelty wore off, and the locals they had entrusted to cultivate the creatures dumped them out into the jungle. They flourished in all the lush vegetation, and soon the island had another imported species that loved to live in Tahiti.

Although she continued to tell the snail story, her eyes remained on Ben, and they warmed him with their smile.

As always, Rene ended the tour back at the Market. He offered to drive the tourists back to their resorts if they wanted, but most of them chose to stay and shop. Before he officially ended the tour, he introduced Ben and spoke of the day cruises that Ben offered on his yacht. Ben smiled and handed out small photocopied brochures with rates and information.

After the departure of today's tourists, they stood on the curb beside the empty van. Soon the sun would begin to set and be gone very quickly. Ben invited them to come aboard the *Aurawind* so they could see the ship they would be recommending. Rene declined, saying a ship of that size must surely be luxurious and that he had no reservations about elaborating its finer points sight unseen.

"Probably a good decision. You'd have to meet Rudy if you came onboard," Ben said. "Well, I guess I can just head back from here.

I'll keep in touch . . . and let you know if something develops from any of your tours."

"Oui, I'm certain that none of that lot will be able to resist the dream of sailing on your ship. Please come by with my commission the minute you have the funds," Rene said boisterously.

Ben turned to Maeva and held her eyes with his for some long seconds. "I enjoyed your stories of the island. I learned a lot."

Maeva smiled and looked down at the sidewalk. Ben lowered his head a little to see her expression. When she rolled her eyes back up to look at him, he smiled. She smiled briefly, and then looked down at the ground again.

He turned back to Rene. "So long, Monsieur Argent. Good-bye, Maeva."

Maeva looked up and smiled a wide smile that showed none of her brilliant white teeth. "This is not good-bye, Ben Beck."

Ben stopped and returned her smile. "I hope not."

"You left your rented scooter out at our house. Won't you come home with us and get it?" she asked, smiling bigger.

Night had fallen when they reached the compound. Rene bounced the van across the rutted dirt and swung it around so that the headlights illuminated the front of their hut. Ben walked to the scooter and tested the headlamp and discovered he had rented another scooter with no light.

"You will be riding in po, Ben Beck, which in your language means the unknown dark," Maeva said. "Would you like to stay here instead?"

"Thank you, but I've ridden the roads in the dark before."

"We have an extra hammock. You are welcome to stay. At least have a beer before you go."

Rene disappeared into the hut as Maeva began to stack kindling to start the fire. Ben walked to a pile of wood and loaded up. When he returned, she admonished him for carrying wood, but he went and loaded up again. As he turned back with a second load in his arms, a loud whoosh and a large blue and yellow flame tore into the darkness, lighting the walls of the jungle that surrounded them. Maeva stood holding a small red gasoline can. A good healthy fire burned strong a few seconds later. She went into the hut and returned with a bottle of beer.

Ben stood as she approached. When she stood in front of him they looked at each other with serious longing and intent. Maeva stepped closer and placed her free hand on his shoulder, then traced down his arm slowly. She stepped closer and laid her head against his chest, her body pressed gently against him, sending a warm vibration along each of his tingling nerves. He could smell the ylang-ylang and frangipani flowers she wore, so fresh he could taste them. He lifted his hands and let them rest on the soft bare skin of her shoulders and felt her breathing as she pressed in more firmly. She lifted her face to him. His lips descended uncontrollably onto her mouth, and he kissed her and felt her lips and tasted her and warmed to her willing response.

"I think you should stay, Ben Beck. The po in my room is more pleasant than the po you will find on the road."

He put his arms around her and held her tight against his body while he kissed her again. She held the kiss for a long while, then broke to whisper, "Come." They turned and walked up the three steps of the hut and turned to go to her room, a room defined by a thin bamboo-slat wall that separated it from the great room of the house. Her bed sat in darkness at the rear of the room. She took him there and pulled on his arms to make him sit, and as he lowered himself she unwound her pareo and stood before him naked.

Like the rest of the house, her bedroom had no front wall. The light of the fire flickered against her skin and against the rear walls of the room. He looked at her smooth black silhouette against the firelight, then placed his hands on her hips and pulled her to him so he could kiss her soft stomach. His head filled with the scent of flowers and ripe fruit as the tip of his nose brushed her skin. She overlapped her hands and held the back of his head as he kissed her nipples. She arched her back when she felt the slight pressure of his teeth on the taut raised centers. He held her tighter and moved her gently down onto the bed. As she lay there, he traced the curves of her body over and over again with the firm tips of his fingers. He traced the line from her neck down to her collarbone and out to her shoulder. He traced the line down her shoulder to the curve under her breast, then down her belly to below her navel. He traced the line of her hip down her outer thigh to her knee, then over her knee and up her inner thigh to pass over her pubic mound. He reversed the lines on the other side of her body to return to her neck and start over.

Flecks of fire glinted off her black pupils as she searched his eyes and told him how much she wanted what he was to give her now. He removed his clothes and entered her. They moved slowly, concentrating on the sensations of each other. He looked straight into her eyes. She held his stare. His hand slowly moved up across her soft belly, up over her breast where it lingered as he felt the silky firmness. The hand began to move upward again until it came to rest with the back of his fingers barely touching her warm cheek. Without taking her eyes away from his, she turned her head and kissed the back of his hand. They maintained a slow deliberate motion between their torsos, both conscious of the exchange between them. They gave themselves to each other in the heat of a tropical night, in the moisture of fragrant air, in the light of the golden unknown dark.

***

The wild dogs slept as he passed their location on his trip back the next morning. When he arrived at the ship, Duane and Rudy were still asleep below. Ben performed a quick, quiet inspection topside, and then went down to sleep in his own berth. Hours later he heard the thumping of Duane's and Rudy's heavy footsteps on the deck above and got up to join them. He found them sitting in the aft salon. Neither acknowledged him as he went below to the galley to scrounge up a cup of coffee and something to eat. The pot sat empty in the sink. He turned the coffee maker off and threw the used filter and grounds into the overfilled garbage container. Before he made a fresh pot, he checked the cupboards for food and came up empty-handed. Waste of time to make coffee now, he might as well go ashore.

Duane and Rudy watched him as he climbed back up the stairs. They waited for him to speak. But when it appeared he would ignore them by turning and going forward to his berth, Duane said, "When are you going to get us more trips? We haven't been out for a while."

Ben stopped and stared at them without expression. Finally he responded, "When they come, they come." He turned to leave.

"You're the one who's supposed to be lining up the trips, but you haven't been getting too many lately. Why is that?"

"You're welcome to line them up yourself," Ben responded.

"You said you would do all the work."

"And I do."

"Right, sightseeing and taking tours all day. Is that what you call doing the work? I noticed you didn't come back onboard last night. You got something going on onshore?"

"I think he's got himself a Tahitian girlfriend," Rudy said with a leer.

"No. I'm looking for tourists," Ben stated.

"You call those three bums you have coffee with every morning tourists?" Rudy said in the same tone.

"You better get some more tourists quick. You said you'd do all the work," Duane said, as if giving an order.

"Right. Did you tell Carl to do more work and get you more trips?" Ben asked, and then turned away, not expecting an answer.

"Fuck you," Duane said to Ben's back.

Ben went to the café for his usual coffee and bread. When he walked in, the waiter waved him over to the counter and handed him a note. Ben saw the date and time written in French and the name of an American tourist. At the bottom of the note appeared the name of a resort. He had a customer for the next day.

The lateness of the hour meant he had a lot to do, and he had to do it in a hurry. He tipped the waiter, thanking him for taking the message, and then ran back to the ship without taking his meal. He told Duane and Rudy about the trip and suggested they clean up the galley and salons while he went to the resort to collect the payment. He rented a scooter and set out to arrange the trip. The concierge at the resort had the full amount in cash waiting. Ben paid him his commission and, with the business end of the transaction out of the way, he went to Rene's compound. He had an excuse to see Maeva again, to ask if she would help him buy supplies for the next day.

When he arrived, he found Maeva sitting in the strange seat welded to the table by the coconut corral. She stopped grinding the coconut she held when he pulled his scooter into the compound. She stood and took some tentative steps toward him, and when he dismounted the scooter he stood silently watching her, not knowing what he should say. Maeva smiled and looked down at the soft dirt. Her fidgeting movements let him know that what he wanted to do was exactly what he should do, so he walked very deliberately to her, placed his arms around her and held her firmly against him. He said her name. When she lifted her face to look at him, he kissed her. Then he thought of everything they had done for each other during the night, and he kissed her more deeply.

They took the tour van into town to pick up supplies. Normally he bought from the Market, but Maeva took him to a local grocery store that offered a different selection of items. Here they could purchase sliced deli meats and cheeses to make the luncheon onboard more convenient. They stocked up on beer, wine, rum, soft drinks and ice.

She took him to a local fish market. He planned on catching fish during the trip, but having something in the cooler for backup made him feel a little more at ease. Maeva drove him and his supplies to the marina, where he grabbed a tote cart to wheel the supplies out to the boat. When he went back onboard he found Rudy sweeping the deck. He had no intention of interrupting him, so he went below with the supplies to find Duane. The galley hadn't been touched, and Ben knew he would be up late getting it in shape for the clients. Ben went to Duane's cabin where he found Duane charting a course.

"So where do the clients want to sail tomorrow?" Duane asked.

"Moorea. They'll be here at seven-thirty. They want to circle Tahiti first, snorkel off Moorea, then sail back at sunset."

"They won't get much time to snorkel if we go all the way around Tahiti, but it sounds good. Where's my money?"

Ben always made Duane ask for his share of the fee. When he wasn't in a hurry, he would delay giving it to him by leaving to carry in more supplies so that Duane would have to ask for his money again. Yet this time he didn't have time to fool around.

"Here," he said as he handed him his share. "Wear white in the morning. And thanks for helping clean up in the galley."

When Ben and Maeva returned to the compound, the smell of fresh-baked bread filled the air and reminded him to get bread and croissants for the guests' breakfast. He didn't want to leave Maeva. When she asked him to stay again, he had a hard time telling her he had to go. Then it hit him that he wouldn't see her the next day. He felt like something important had been taken away. He asked her to join him on the trip and act as hostess. Since she didn't have a tour of her own to conduct the next day, she accepted happily. She also offered to pick up the supplies from the bakery in the morning before she met him on the dock. He took her in his arms and kissed her, and told her he wanted to see her every day from now on.

It had turned dark, and when he checked the scooter's headlight he found he didn't have one. He chastised himself again for not checking when he rented it. Tonight he had no choice. He had to get back to the ship, so he had to ride in po.

The luminescence of the land crabs crossing in front of him told him he was still on the road. The slow speed meant that the engine wasn't quite as noisy as it had been on previous trips. However, his effort concentrating to stay on the hardtop caused him to miss the dogs' barking until he could see the shiny glare of their eyes. When he did spot them, he twisted the throttle hard and charged right at them, but he couldn't swerve to the shoulder because he didn't know where the shoulder started. It didn't matter. Before he had time to think, along with the eyes, he could also see the teeth. He had to count on his speed to get him through. His front tire grazed the back end of one dog to his left while another dog rammed into his right leg with its snout. The handlebars wobbled in his hands, and he felt himself tipping to his right when he over-corrected. This caused him to take his foot off the peg and shoot it out to steady himself. When he did, he unknowingly kicked another of the dogs. It yelped as it tumbled into the ditch. His leg, after contacting the cur, carried on to find the pavement. He stomped the ground hard to get balanced on the tires again. The rest of the pack seemed less interested in the chase after they heard their comrade wailing in shock and they didn't follow. Ben was still trying to gain control of the scooter and drifted onto the shoulder and down into the ditch, again feeling the sting of thin branches. He slowed and turned back toward the road where he saw the dim beacons of scampering land crabs.

His heart rate began to drop only as he approached the Market. The smell of the grilled fish reminded him that he had gone without food for the entire day. He returned the scooter, then stopped and ate. Sitting on the curb in his usual spot, he took the time to drink a bottle of beer and to realize that he felt good, good because something unexpected had happened to him. The surprise of receiving the affections of a beautiful girl gave him pleasure.

He had not expected to meet someone like Maeva, to have feelings for anyone, to have the feelings reciprocated. When he caught her eye during the tour he felt friendliness. zWhen he caught her eye at the compound that night he knew they had both felt much, much more.

# Chapter 13

In the still dark of the early morning, Ben fussed in the galley, wishing he had more time before he had to meet the clients at the marina. Duane sat in the pilothouse drawing lines on his chart under the light of a small marine lamp. Rudy sat on the deck a few steps away from Duane, leaning against a stanchion while looking out over the dock. He rose up into a squat position when he spotted a ghost moving along the dock, but stayed low behind the hump of the pilothouse so the ghost couldn't see him. Duane noticed his movement and looked over curiously; when he saw Rudy's serious stare directed toward the dock, he turned to see what held his attention.

Neither spoke. Rudy had no idea that Duane had joined him in monitoring the barely-visible grayish patch that floated silently along the dock. It had wisps and streaks that moved in different directions. Its top seemed still; its middle shifted and rolled seductively. It did not get brighter, but it did get larger, as it came closer to their gangway. It stopped, but remained suspended in the air, then the top half of the phantom disappeared while the bottom began to roll again.

A thought penetrated Duane's curiosity. He reached forward and turned on the mast light. At the edge of the cone of light cast out around the ship, they saw a woman. She had been walking away from the ship, but when she saw the light she turned back. She wore a dark-colored wind jacket that she left open over a deep red pareo with a white floral pattern. As she walked back to the ship the men recognized the shift and roll of her hips.

"It's a woman," Duane said.

"It sure as hell is," Rudy replied as he stood and walked forward.

Duane left his seat to go forward as well. When he reached the gangway the woman arrived at the dock end and smiled at them before asking, "Is this Ben Beck's boat?"

Both men heard the question, but stood still, unable to answer in the beam she smiled at them.

"Hello. Is this Ben Beck's boat?" she asked again.

"Yes," Rudy said. "Ben is here."

"Good. I wasn't sure in the dark. I brought his baguette."

Maeva started up the gangway as Duane and Rudy bumped into each other on their way down to help her with the bags of bread. They took the bags and turned back. When they got back on deck, they turned to let her go first, but found that she hadn't followed them. They saw her walking away from the ship toward the marina and felt dejected. They watched her disappear into the darkness outside the cone of light. When they could no longer see her, they looked down at the bags they held then turned to take them to Ben in the galley.

Below, they placed the bags on the counter as Ben arranged the refrigerator. He turned and saw the bags.

"Good. Where is she?"

"She left," Rudy answered.

"She'll be back; she's going out with us today."

"I thought you said the clients were Americans," Duane commented.

"She's not the client, she's going to be the hostess today. I asked her to come."

"All right," Rudy said, "She is one spanking, good-looking piece of Tahitian ass."

"If I hear those kind of words come out of your mouth again, I'll break your teeth," Ben said calmly while staring at Rudy. He looked at Duane and said, "Either of you."

Both men stood frozen by the words and cautioned by the cold tone of Ben's delivery.

"Take it easy, man. You just had to say to lay off. You don't need to go threatening anybody's teeth," Duane said.

"So Ben got himself a girl. That's why you've been so willing to go ashore to hunt down clients, only it looks like you've been hunting down skirts. And it sounds like you got serious about one. Big mistake," Rudy said, shaking his head.

"Shut up, Rudy," Ben said in a low rumble of a voice.

"Big mistake." Rudy began to cluck his tongue. Before he'd made the sound twice, Ben grabbed him by the front of his shirt at the collar and twisted the material so it cut into Rudy's neck. He pulled Rudy across the counter so his heels came off the floor. Rudy tried to balance himself with his arms. Their faces were an inch apart, and Ben held him there so Rudy could only look directly into his eyes.

Duane grabbed Ben's wrists and pulled down on them so that he had to lower Rudy, whose face began to turn dark red. Ben let go, giving Rudy a flick of his wrist, sending him backward against the galley wall. There Rudy remained, rubbing his neck, trying to catch his breath, glaring at Ben.

"What the fuck's got into you? You don't go pullin' off that bullshit with your crew. You do that shit again, and you're outta here, you hear me?" Duane yelled at Ben.

Ben let him finish, shifted his attention to Duane, and said, "You interfere with what I'm doing again, and you'll get the same. Do you hear me?"

"You watch yourself, Ben. He was just trying to be funny. You don't have to get like that. Rudy, you got things to do on deck."

Rudy left them in the galley. Ben reorganized the counter and began to set up a tray of bread and cheese while Duane puttered around doing things he didn't have to do. He opened cupboards to inspect glasses, moved the toaster an inch farther into the corner, and lifted the salt and pepper shakers to see that they were full. After a few minutes, he went to his cabin and sat. When he heard Ben's footsteps going up on deck he quickly got up and walked out after him. As he came up the stairs, he saw Ben moving forward, then glimpsed Rudy's movement behind him. He turned, causing Rudy to stop. Duane had blocked the progress of his attempt to sneak up on Ben. Rudy held a stanchion loosely in his hand, down low by his leg. Duane slowly shook his head and saw the violent tension reluctantly ebb from

Rudy's face. He said nothing, but walked over to Rudy and took the stanchion.

Duane turned and looked forward to see if Ben had noticed, but saw Ben running down the gangway, where the ghost girl carried another large bag.

They returned to the boat, and Ben carried the bag to the aft deck. After he came back to the pilothouse he introduced Maeva to Duane. Ben described the itinerary that Maeva had suggested for the trip to Moorea. Duane liked her plan and asked her to come and look over the charts.

When they were finished, they went below to get the trays of food and make coffee so the clients' breakfast would be ready when they arrived. With that done, Ben and Maeva walked back to the marina to meet their guests. They had waited only a few minutes when a shuttle bus from the resort pulled up at the curb. They greeted the tourists, three of them: Greg, Sandra, and their teenage son Doug. Maeva placed flower lei over each of their heads and led them down the dock to the *Aurawind*.

Duane and Rudy stood waiting at the top of the gangway as they came aboard. Duane introduced himself as captain of the ship and introduced Rudy as first mate. He then led them to the breakfast table and indicated that he would provide a tour of the *Aurawind* once they had dined and were well away from the harbor. Ben poured their first glasses of champagne and orange juice, then left them with Maeva as he helped shove off. The breeze blew down from the mountain and out to sea, so they left their mooring under sail. The brochure had promised a sunrise breakfast looking back at the departing Papeete Harbor. The champagne-enhanced view of the island, the gentle slapping of water against the hull, and the flutter of canvas delivered on the promise.

They sailed south along the coast of the island, then turned north and west to cross the shipping channel toward Moorea. Maeva directed Duane to a point outside the atoll near an opening that would take them to a small, uninhabited island inside the reef. Outside the reef they set anchor. Ben and Maeva disembarked with the visitors in the skiff, taking them through the opening and landing on a small section of beach on one side of a sand spit. Then, each grabbing some of the gear, they marched a short distance through a stand of coconut palms to a long stretch of beach that faced across the water to Moorea and another small island. The stretch of water that lay between the two small islands displayed clusters of floral-shaped blooms of coral smattered about in the shallows.

Ben left Maeva and the tourists to go back and retrieve the baskets that held their lunch.

The three guests stood in awe at the sight of the big green tooth-shaped mountain across the aqua lagoon. They dropped their gear and walked into the water and silently took in the sight, until something in the water caught Doug's eye. He yelled out and ran along, kicking up a splash and pointing at a school of blue- and yellow-striped fish that first darted away from him, then regrouped and disappeared behind a cluster of coral. He looked back at his parents, who had followed as he chased the fish. Before they reached him, he spotted a lizard streaking along the beach back near the line of trees, and came running out of the water to get a look at the creature, but it made a quick getaway into the brush.

He ran back toward Maeva and asked if they could snorkel.

As they put on their snorkel equipment, Maeva explained a little about what they should expect in the coral field and warned them to be careful near the clusters—the scrapes could be painful and cause skin irritations. In minutes they were in the water swimming against the slight current running between the two islands. The water varied in depth from three to twelve feet. In the shallow section they swam through a maze where the coral rose to the surface of the water on both sides of them. Bright red and yellow fish skittered out of their way around the corners of the maze. From time to time, the corridors opened up to deep sandy-bottomed pools with large ball-shaped corals sitting on the bottom like blue-gray pearls in an oyster. When Doug dove to take a closer look, a school of several hundred tiny blue fish swam to meet him and protect their home. Before he knew it, they surrounded him on all sides, and he felt the touch of numerous noses against his skin. Up he went in panic, but when he broke the surface he laughed out loud and his parents, who had watched while floating on the surface, smiled when they heard his laugher. After repositioning his snorkel bit, he dove again and again, and each time the cloud of blue came to meet him. He maintained his position as long as he could while the school encompassed him on all sides. They popped him face to face on the glass of his mask so he couldn't see beyond them. Wiping his hand in front of his face, he attempted to clear them so he could determine how many surrounded him. Though each swipe moved some of the fish away, they soon returned to cover his mask again. In an instant they zipped away from him toward another invader. Before they engulfed the new threat, Doug saw his father diving toward the coral. His lungs pulled hard for air so he surfaced, blew out his pipe and watched his father and the fish. When his father resurfaced, they lifted their heads out of the water and laughed again at being surrounded by the brave little fish.

For the next two hours they explored their private coral reef. They spotted fish of many colors darting about the maze. Sea cucumbers lying on the bottom, anemones with their translucent tentacles swaying in the current, flat bottom-dwellers coasting below, and sponges clinging to the sides of the coral formations. They moved toward the main protective reef, and as they swam across a deep basin to its inner wall, they saw the shiny teeth of an eel. They turned quickly and headed back to the beach.

Hunger fatigued the swimmers. Their legs felt heavy as they walked out of the water and up the slight incline of the beach to the picnic Ben and Maeva had spread out for them. They talked nonstop with mouths full, their conversations full of descriptions of the strange things they had seen. Occasionally they asked Maeva about some creature that stood out as more unusual than the others, but most of the discussion took place among the three family members.

They heard a thump in the trees and the family stopped talking and chewing and looked silently toward the palms.

"What was that?" Doug asked.

"Coconut," Maeva answered. They returned to their meal.

A second coconut fell a few minutes later and they stopped again, but only briefly. When a third one dropped near the end of their lunch, Doug commented, "Can you imagine walking through the trees and one of those things falls on your head?"

Maeva told him that could never happen. Doug asked why not.

"Because the coconuts have three eyes, and they never fall if they see people or animals below them."

"Coconuts don't have eyes."

"Sure they do. I'll show you."

Before they knew what had happened, Maeva jumped up and ran into the trees. They all, including Ben, watched where she had disappeared. Soon she walked out of the brush carrying a large coconut still wrapped in its thick brown husk. She grabbed the machete they had brought along; holding the coconut in her outstretched hand, she hacked away at the husk and very efficiently cleared the entire thick stringy mass from the fruit inside. She used her hand to rub away some of the straggling fibers and then turned the hard shell toward her audience to show them the three dark eyes on the smaller end of the coconut.

"See?"

"Those aren't real eyes," Doug said.

"They must be," she responded smiling, "because they know not to drop on people."

She then held the coconut out in her hand again, and with the back of the knife dealt it a quick snapping blow at its equator. The shell cracked and water leaked out. She broke it open the rest of the way, managing to retain most of the liquid.

"Here, taste the water," she said as she handed the coconut cup to Doug.

He accepted it with wide eyes and drank all the coconut water greedily.

"Can I have another one?" Doug asked.

"Sure, but you go get it." Maeva replied.

Ben and Maeva packed up the picnic, and Ben took the baskets back to the skiff. When he returned, he spotted Doug, who had forgotten about the coconuts, snorkeling out in the water where he skimmed the surface. Greg, his father, stood in thigh-deep water, keeping an eye on his son. Sandra and Maeva sat in the water up to their shoulders and let the mild current wash the warm salty water over their bodies. Ben walked in and joined Greg, who turned and looked at Ben with a smile as he waded out.

"This place is something else," Greg said.

"Yes, it is. This is the first time I've been here. Maeva suggested it."

"This whole day has been something. We will always remember this vacation to your island. It cost us way too much, but Doug's getting to that age where he's not going to want to do much with his parents anymore. If this is going to be our last trip together, it's going to be the most memorable."

"I'm glad to hear that."

"Even this day trip is a little extravagant for us. We're not the kind of people that would even think of a private sail on a yacht like yours. Doug is having a gas."

"That's what we wanted. Now I think I'll join him; like I said, I've never been here either."

Ben got into his equipment and swam to meet Doug, and the two stayed in the water a long time. When they had almost exhausted themselves, they returned and joined the other three for a final beverage before they had to leave their private island.

Greg stood the whole time and watched them swim, and now lowered himself into the water beside his wife. He had almost settled his weight on the bottom when he felt something wiggle and thump against his butt cheeks. In his haste to stand up again, he didn't see anything, but when he took a step backwards to get away from whatever it was, he felt the hair on his legs ripping as his legs parted. Sandra shot up out of the water and now stood ten feet away on the beach, looking back, slack-jawed. Forgetting about discovering what he'd sat on, Greg looked at his legs to find that from his middle shin to his ankles a stringy white substance had become glued to his skin and hair. It didn't sting or burn, so he reached down to pull some of the substance off. As he pulled, he felt the hair ripping from his leg, but when he felt the substance it didn't stick to his skin. He looked questioningly at Ben, who stood near him equally confused by the substance. Ben shrugged and they both turned toward Maeva, who still sat in the water. Greg held out his hands to show her the material and asked, "What is this?"

"I don't know," she said casually.

"Something squirmed under my butt, and then this stuff was hanging all over me."

"Sounds like a scared fish hit you with his protection," she said.

"What kind of fish do you think it was?" Ben asked.

"I don't know, Ben Beck. Based on what it hit him with, I'd say a Silly String fish." She said this with a straight face.

Both men sported questioning looks on their faces.

"You're not serious?" asked Greg.

"No, not at all."

"You don't know what kind of fish it was?" This time it was Ben.

"No clue. If it doesn't hurt, then I wouldn't worry about it. But I would be sure to tell everyone back home that it was poisonous and could have sunk inch-long fangs into your leg instead of shooting string, but you managed to avoid its jaw."

"Is that true?" Greg asked.

"No, not one bit."

They sat back down in the water with Maeva, and Greg slowly picked at the goo strung throughout his leg hairs. It took Sandra a good ten minutes to build up the nerve to join them. Doug hunted throughout the shallow water, trying to find the fish that had attacked his father.

Reluctantly, they left the water and the island, and returned to the ship for the sail back to Papeete. Duane smiled and asked about their snorkeling as they climbed aboard, while Rudy drifted on the fringe of the group.

As soon as Duane had set their course for the sail across the strait, Ben set up the fishing poles and told Doug to watch for the elastics to snap. About halfway across, one of them did, scaring Doug out of a daydream. The whizzing noise of the fast running line froze him in place after he stood. Tongue-tied, he looked about for Ben, who came running up from the galley after hearing the run of the fishing line. Ben spotted Doug and stopped. He pointed to the line and said, "What have you got there?"

This brought Doug out of his state of confusion and he yelled, "Fish!"

Ben pulled the port side pole and moved around the stern, as the fish had gone under the ship to the starboard side. After putting some drag on the line, he called Doug over and handed him the pole, but stayed behind him with his own hands still bearing the majority of the strain. The line came closer to them as the fish dove for deeper water. Ben told Doug to hold steady. When the line stopped running out he told him to lift up on the pole. They did, and when they released, Ben showed Doug how to reel in the slack. They lifted again, and when they released Ben had Doug reel in the line. Repeating the lift and release, they brought the fish close to the surface where it attempted another short-lived run, but it settled down and they landed themselves a nice fifteen-pound tuna.

Ben watched the exhausted teenager flexing his hands, trying to loosen the muscles in his forearms. "Good work. Fresh fish for dinner."

"I don't eat fish," Doug said.

"You'll eat this one. It's delicious. Besides, it's a ritual of the South Pacific. No one else can eat the fish until its captor has tasted it."

Maeva gave Ben a curious look.

Dinner took longer to prepare than they had planned, so Duane dropped anchor outside the harbor as the sun set. The pink to orange to purple clouds entertained the passengers and crew. And then the city took to light.

Doug tasted the grilled tuna, freeing the others to enjoy their meal. He enjoyed the flavor; enlightened to how good fish can taste, he ate like a teenage boy who had been deprived of calories for at least five hours.

Back at the marina, they packed up all of their belongings and walked out onto the dock. Ben informed Duane that he wouldn't be back until sometime the next day and left the *Aurawind*. They used Maeva's van to deliver their customers back to their hotel, and then they drove to the compound where they found Rene illuminated by a strong burning fire.

"Dinez-vous votre, Papa?" Maeva asked her father.

"No, I am hungry. Not even bread or cheese in the house," he said without looking up from the fire.

"I have some tuna. Ben Beck caught it today. Would you like a plate?"

"Oui, merci."

"Ben Beck, would you like a beer?"

"Oui, merci," Ben said.

"Vous aimez encore plus de thon aussi bien?"

"Whoa, I only spoke a little French to be polite."

"Sorry, I just clicked over when you spoke," she apologized. "Would you like some more tuna?"

"No thanks, just a beer."

As the flames licked high into the air Ben noticed that the woodpile nearby had been depleted. He walked to the larger pile by the corral and loaded up. He returned, unloaded, and sat down with Rene. When Maeva returned she placed a plate in Rene's lap. Ben looked at the cubes of red meat and watched, as Rene squeezed lemon juice onto the raw fish then picked up one of the cubes and popped it into his mouth.

He watched as Maeva stepped over to her father, reached down and took a cube of the tuna and put it in her mouth. She closed her eyes and chewed slowly, lovingly. Ben wondered how she could eat any more food, but then realized that she hadn't eaten any of the grilled tuna back on the ship.

He found himself delighting in the way she seemed so lost in her own enjoyment of the fish. He felt happy when she reached down and took another cube, placed it in her mouth and drifted off to her delicious dream place. Her total enjoyment got the best of him. He stood and made his way to Rene's side, where he asked, "May I?"

"Of course," Rene said, lifting the plate of gleaming cubes.

He took one and placed it in his mouth, remembering the poke he had eaten in Honolulu.

After Rene had finished his meal they sat silently by the flames. Their chairs were placed across the fire from each other, and as magically as a burning fire can draw the eye, this night the magic could not keep Ben and Maeva from staring at a different fire. They smiled, and then looked away, but soon their eyes locked together again. They read each other's expressions and teased with minute squints and slight lifts of eyebrow, then smiled and looked away again.

Rene spoke. "I feel like sitting by the fire for a great long time tonight."

Ben noticed a flattening of Maeva's smile and realized he too must be frowning.

Rene spoke again, "You two don't need to keep me company. Go to bed, you look like you've both been ready for a long time."

Maeva looked down and away as heat flushed her face. Ben smiled and said, "We did get up early; I am kind of tired. Good night, Monsieur Argent." He stood up and left the fire.

Maeva continued to sit and fidget in her chair, but her father only let her do so for a minute or so before saying, "Go on."

She began to unwrap her pareo as she climbed the steps. She tossed it on the end of her bed and stood naked before the waiting Ben, who placed his hands on her hips and rested his cheek against her soft, smooth stomach. Her floral scent penetrated his mind. He kissed her skin, bent to kiss her navel, lifted to lick and kiss her dark brown nipples. He pulled her down onto the bed. She lay and watched him undress. He lay down beside her and began to touch her skin, moving his hand slowly over her body while she lay with her eyes closed and drifted off to her delicious dream.

# Chapter 14

Snorkeling on the island off Moorea became a regular stop on all future excursions, whether initiated by Carl or Ben. Maeva became the regular hostess when she could free herself from the island tours her father scheduled.

Although their cruise schedule continued to have large blocks of inactivity, they did manage to make themselves some extra cash. With no real need to spend it, each of them amassed a tidy sum.

Ben parked Rene's van and walked to the café for breakfast before doing his rounds of the various resorts. It soon became a good day when the waiter handed him a note with a booking for an overnight cruise. The overnighters meant twice as much work, but three times as much money. He looked at the dates requested and immediately saw a scheduling problem. Rene would have to drive the island tour the following weekend.

He looked out over the marina to make sure the *Aurawind* hadn't left port without him and realized that he would be onboard very soon to let Duane and Rudy know about the upcoming trip.

He heard the ashtray crack twice on the counter and turned to see his trio of friends plodding down the beach. Their normal listless gate was even slower, and Yves held his head a little lower.

Ben looked to the waiter to order his companions coffee and saw the waiter already preparing their breakfast.

"Bonjour," Ben greeted the men.

"I don't know about that yet," Yves replied as the other two men slumped down onto the beach. Once seated, it didn't take long for Le-hiro-de-biere to roll on his side and pass out in the sand while Luc hung his head, shielding his hooded eyes from the sun. "My friend, where have you been?"

"Argent's," Ben answered.

"Ah, the woman has bound you to her."

"I guess," Ben said. "How come you three look so tired?"

Yves, who had been looking back toward the street, turned to Ben to display a swollen eye, dark in the socket, a line of crusted blood visible in the brow hair.

"Yesterday, your three friends had a very lucky day. We carried some heavy bags for a tourist and his wife. They, of course, wanted to pay us for our much-needed assistance, and we accepted their payment. When we counted the monies much later, too late in fact to go back and correct their error, we discovered they experienced some difficulties with the conversion rate of the Franc and had given more than we normally accept for our services.

"This good fortune required a celebration, and our efforts to moderate our joy became overwhelmed by our eagerness to keep up with each other. If Le-hiro ordered another beer, then Luc ordered another beer, and I ordered another Pernod. So it went, until, minding our own business, we chanced to meet with the constable, who is always making trouble for us.

"Last night, le sac de la merde with a badge and a baton wanted to throw us in jail, so he marched us away. As soon as he left the busy street, he decided to teach us a lesson instead of throwing us in jail. That is why I have the mark over my eye. And, under their shirts, Luc and Le-hiro have welts about their bodies. But the lesson has become a big waste of time. The three of us have no memory of the beating; we woke up this way." Yves finished his recap victoriously.

A gagging hack croaked from Le-hiro's constricting throat, drawing the attention of Ben and Yves. The large man remained on his side on the sand with his back to them. Soon he pulled his knees up to his stomach; the muscles in his back tightened, then began to quake with each straining retch. Great spasms forced his legs further into his abdomen. Each time his shoulders hunched, it seemed his ribs would rip through his skin and out of his tightly drawn shirt.

"You better check and make sure he's not choking on anything," Ben said.

"Oh no, there's nothing for him to choke on. He lost it all earlier this morning," Yves told him matter-of-factly.

The retching stopped and an exhausted Le-hiro-de-biere labored to rise to a sitting position. He ignored the sand stuck to his skin, powdering the side of his face. A skein of hair dangled before his vacant eyes.

"Le-hiro, vous aiment votre café et baguette maintenant?" Yves asked.

Le-hiro closed his eyes and nodded, so Yves grabbed a bowl of coffee and a chunk of bread from Ben's table and placed them in the sitting man's hands. Le-hiro tore a big ragged bite of bread with his teeth. It didn't quite fit in his mouth, but he began to chew.

Yves shrugged and turned back to Ben. "I would like to have a few of those francs to enjoy later in the day."

"Maybe I can help," Ben said, "I'll be ordering some supplies at the grocery later today for pickup and delivery tomorrow. Can you handle it for me?"

"That is our specialty, Monsieur. Where do you want them delivered?"

"The ship."

"Sometime during the morning?"

"That would be fine."

"And the fee?"

"Five hundred francs now, five hundred upon delivery."

"You can count on us," Yves said, extending his hand.

***

Duane sat reading in the upper salon. Ben arrived and informed him of the recent overnight booking, causing him to smile at the thought of something to do and the extra money. Ben told him of his intent to purchase the supplies for the trip and have them delivered, and that Duane would have to pay the deliverymen. He then asked if there were other supplies that Duane wanted him to pick up. Duane informed him of a list he had left in the galley.

Below, Rudy sat at the dining room table eating a bowl of cereal. He turned when he heard footsteps.

"You decided to come back, did you?"

Ben ignored his question and read over the list pinned to the small corkboard beside the refrigerator. He took down the list, then began looking in the cupboards and occasionally adding something more. When he finished, he left the galley and joined Rudy at the table. "We have an overnighter in a couple of days. Supplies will be delivered tomorrow before noon. Make sure and help the guys that deliver them."

Rudy stared at Ben but said nothing, which suited Ben fine—so he stood up and left.

As Ben walked down the gangway to the dock, Duane called out and asked when he would be back.

"Tomorrow afternoon," he answered without looking back.

"Good, bring the money."

Ben drove to the resort to pick up the payment, and then went to the grocery where he ordered and paid for the supplies to be picked up by Yves. In the mid-afternoon he returned to Rene's hut. As he pulled in, he saw an unfamiliar old truck parked in the center of the compound. In front of the truck, a small man turned to look at him as Maeva ran toward him in despair.

"Ben Beck, it's Papa. He's been hurt. Please take me to the hospital." Maeva jumped in the van and Ben backed it up to turn it around. They left the Chinese driver standing, waving at them as they left the compound.

Earlier, Maeva explained on the drive to the hospital, Rene had walked up the road that led into the jungle on the other side of his clearing. He often walked this road. The road stretched a good distance across the mouth of the valley in a softly-curved path and eventually returned to the main road that led back around to the front entrance. The wider jungle road accommodated the truck that brought Rene his loads of wood and coconuts more easily than the front entryway. The height of the trees kept the road in shade, and Rene would often walk this road in order to stay cool while getting his exercise. He walked the shoulder of the outside road on his return.

This day as he walked along, a small vehicle came speeding around the curve behind him. The driver's reactions were a little slow, and he didn't pull away in time to avoid Rene completely. He clipped him on his left hip, spinning him out of sight into the brush beside the road. The driver kept going, and Rene didn't get a chance to see the car that struck him. He lay in shock in a low bush, not feeling the pain of his broken hip right away, but instead feeling the pain of the small punctures in his abdomen where a number of broken branches poked at him. When he grew angry at the insignificant shrub inflicting this stabbing pain, he tried to lift himself, bending his hip in the process. He screamed at the burning grind that shot up his side with a heat he thought would cook his brain, then he passed out. When he awoke, he rolled onto his back, trying to get out of the bush and closer to the road where someone could spot him. The roll caused the pain again, but he toughed it out and completed another roll that landed him on the shoulder of the road in view of the passing cars.

Sometime later, the delivery truck from the Chinese bakery chugged by and stopped when the driver noticed Rene's waving arm down in the shallow ditch. The driver loaded him in the back of the half-empty truck alongside the stacks of baguette and drove him to the hospital. When he finished delivering his bread, he stopped at the compound to inform Maeva of her father's accident.

At the hospital, Ben and Maeva located Rene's room and found him plugged into a variety of machines, but sleeping quietly. She slid a chair over by the bed and sat bent over, holding her father's hand tight against her cheek. She rocked as she cried as she softly chanted a short prayer over and over.

The doctor explained the nature of Rene's injuries and Maeva felt relaxed.

"He'll sleep through the night with the aid of the painkillers. So why not leave him to us and come back in the morning to check on him?" the doctor concluded his comments.

"No, I should be here if he wakes up. He'll wonder where he is and why I'm not with him," she said.

"You sure? You'll be more useful to him tomorrow if you get some rest," Ben said.

"I want to be here."

"Can I bring you anything from home that you might need tonight?" Ben asked. She shook her head, so he left saying he would be back early in the morning.

Just to be sure the compound would be okay, he drove there to check on the fire. Then he returned to stay onboard the *Aurawind*.

He stopped and picked up food for Duane, Rudy, and himself. He parked the van near the marina and walked to the ship. He found the other two in their usual positions in the upper salon, reading. They looked up when he called from the gangway.

"Ben, what's up? Did the vahine throw you out?" Rudy asked.

Ben placed the containers of food on the table and said, "Here, put some of this in your mouth as soon as you can."

Rudy smiled without friendliness and opened one of the containers.

"You said you wouldn't be here until tomorrow," Duane said.

"Maeva's father got into a car accident. He's laid up in the hospital, and she's with him. I thought I'd get some things in order here."

"Good, we were going to do laundry in the morning, but I guess since you're here you can do it," Rudy chimed in.

Ben said, "I think you should stick with your plan. I have some trip-related things I have to get done. It looks like you two are going to have to take the clients out on your own."

"No way, man. You're the one that does all the shit with the tourists. We can't do any of that," Duane said, sitting up and throwing his book on the table. "You work for Carl, man, not the old Frenchman. Besides, this is an overnighter. We can't do the food."

"I work for Carl when it's Carl's trip. When it's one of my trips, I work for myself, just like you do. You want to cancel the trip and give back the money, then say so, otherwise shut up. I'll have most of the food prep done before you leave. You'll have to bring out trays of fruit and bread for breakfast, and meat and bread for lunch. I've seen you grill fish and steaks before, so I think you can handle it. Do you want me to give the money back?"

"You got it?" Duane asked.

"Yeah." Ben pulled out the money. Rather than make him ask for it twice, he decided to get him committed by letting him have the cash right away.

"Okay," Duane said after he counted his share. "Make sure you tell us what to do."

***

The next morning, Ben stopped at the hospital and told Maeva and the complaining Rene that he himself would take out Argent's scheduled tour group the following day. Maeva's ashen complexion brightened slightly with the business worry put aside. He asked if she needed to go home for anything, but she said she wouldn't leave her father's side. He gave her some just-in-case money and left to finish his preparations for the trip.

Back at the *Aurawind*, he tidied up the master suite, galley and main salon. Then when Rudy returned from the laundromat, Ben browbeat him into cleaning his own stateroom while he took the fresh linens and made the bed for the guests.

Later in the morning, he heard Rudy yelling at something. He rushed topside to find him trying to drive away Yves, Luc, and Le-hiro-de-biere.

"Leave them alone, Rudy. They're the deliverymen," he said.

"These bums?"

"Hey, back off and give them a hand."

Ben pushed past Rudy to meet the three men. He hauled a package off the cart and up the gangway where he handed it to Rudy, who was to take it below. When all the packages were onboard, the three deliverymen remained standing on the dock. Ben asked them to come aboard the ship, drawing twisted looks from Duane and Rudy. They declined. Then he offered them a cold beer. At the mention of the internationally-understood word, Le-hiro led the way.

Ben's three friends sat quietly in their unaccustomed surroundings. Ben performed a number of tasks below in the galley while Duane and Rudy sat with the men to keep an eye on them. The normally talkative Yves didn't initiate conversation and only replied with simple direct answers whenever Rudy or Duane spoke to them. When they finished their second beers, Yves finally decided to ask a question.

"To what part of Tahiti do you sail tomorrow?"

Duane and Rudy both looked intently at Yves, who smiled as he began to sink back in his seat.

Sounding disinterested, Duane replied, "We're going to a little island off Moorea where the water is very shallow and the snorkeling is very good."

"If your guests enjoy the snorkeling, I would suggest a trip down to Tahiti Iti. Inside the reef on the east side the fish are very abundant and no tourists ever go there," Yves said.

Ben returned in time to hear Yves' remark and asked, "Where on the east side?"

"It's hard to say. But the reef opens at the south and in the middle. About halfway between the entrances there is very good snorkeling."

Ben turned to Duane. "There you go. Take the clients down to Tahiti Iti and snorkel someplace new, then circle north so you do the whole island. Catch the sunset as you sail into Moorea, dive at the island the second day, then head back in the evening."

Duane stood and gestured for Yves to show him the location on the chart.

"Sounds good, but I hate to go there for the first time on my own. And how do you know anything about snorkeling down there?" Duane said skeptically.

"Monsieur, I make my living from knowledge of my island. If people want to know anything about Tahiti, good or bad, they can get the answer from me."

"How deep is the water at the reef opening?"

"Five to ten meters. It is a safe anchor."

"Why don't you take Yves with you? He does know a lot," Ben said.

"Take a rag man? I'm not taking him on a sail," Duane said, turning away.

"You don't need to talk like that. I can lend him clothes, and if he shaves he'll be fine. Yves, would you be willing to go out as a guide for two days?"

Yves cocked an eyebrow, and the adrenaline brought on by opportunity made him stand more erect. "Monsieur Beck, Monsieur Capitaine, once you have had Yves for a guide, you will want no other. I accept your offer conditional of an appropriate fee. Shall we say five thousand francs?"

"Three," Duane said.

"That is the exact number I had in mind. May I borrow your razor, Monsieur Beck?"

\*\*\*

The next morning, Ben met the clients and got them situated onboard the ship. He laid out the breakfast trays in the upper salon, prepared a pitcher full of champagne and orange juice, then helped shove off. When he turned to leave he spotted Luc and Le-hiro sitting on the opposite side of the dock and walked to join them. They sat with their eyes downcast in the manner of those left behind.

"Luc, what will you two be doing for the next two days?"

Without looking up, Luc said, "Yves told us to meet him here tomorrow evening."

"Yes, but what will you do until then?"

Luc didn't answer, and Le-hiro had not moved since Ben arrived.

"I have work for you if you are available. It's not too hard, but it will take a while. You'll get food, a place to sleep, and a few francs. Interested?"

Luc remained silent for another second or two, then looked up at Ben and nodded acceptance. When he stood, Le-hiro stood as well and they walked with Ben to the van. He drove them back to Rene's compound and gave them a number of cleanup tasks to perform while he took the van out on a tour. Once they started their work he prepared a plate with bread and cheese for them to eat later. He hid all but two bottles of beer in a box under Maeva's bed. With that done, he left to pick up the tourists for the island tour.

Ben's delivery of local facts and stories had become easier and more relaxed. Some of the tourists asked him questions as if he were a resident. Like Rene, he loved to explain the history of the snails at the pineapple plantation and enjoyed the look on their faces when he smashed one of the creatures on a large rock. At the Market, he said good-bye to the happy shoppers and left for the hospital to take Rene his money.

Maeva stood when he walked into the room; her smile glowed through her tired, lackluster expression. She moved to Ben and placed her arms around him, leaned against his chest, and allowed all of her weight to press against him. He felt like if he moved, she would fall to the floor. Her floral scent still reached deep and aroused his sense of being with her, and the slightly salted musk smell pleased him more because it meant he knew more of her. He placed one arm around her back and placed his other hand on the side of her head to hold her firm against his neck. She stood content; eyes closed, her breathing at a regular, steady pace.

Rene was asleep once again, but this time he had fewer machines connected to him.

"Will you come home with me tonight? You need to rest," he whispered.

"I can't."

"Your father is better. The nurses will take good care of him. He would feel very bad to see you wearing yourself down because of him. Come and sleep in your own bed, have a bath in the stream, and eat a meal from your own kitchen."

"Will you bring me back first thing in the morning?"

"I won't wake you if you're still asleep."

"I have to come back first thing."

"I'll get you here. Say good-bye and let's go."

Ben had forgotten to tell her about Luc and Le-hiro, but she never gave it a second thought when she saw them standing by the fire pit. She knew who they were, and she knew Ben talked with them most days at the café. If he showed no alarm at the sight of them, then she would show no alarm.

After a light meal, Ben made her go to bed and she found sleep in little time. Ben removed the box of beer from under her bed, took it back to the refrigerator, and returned to his two workers.

"You've done good work. Will you stay tomorrow and work until we meet the ship?"

"Oui." they said, nodding strongly.

"Bon. I'll get you food and a beer."

He sat and ate with them, then stayed after dinner and drank a beer with them in front of the fire. He gave them hammocks and pointed out hooks mounted between sets of trees, then left them alone after providing them with one more beer.

Maeva liked to sleep facing out toward the fire. She adjusted her position in the bed without waking as he gently got in behind her so that she slept turned away from him. He snuggled up close behind her and hovered over the side of her face that he could see while resting on his elbow. He looked down at her hair which fell away so that her small circular ear reflected the firelight, as did her smoothly rounded forehead, her softly curved nose, and the soft ellipse of her lips. He bent down and kissed her cheek beside her ear and felt the soft fuzz that graced the side of her face. Then he lay back on his pillow. The kiss caused Maeva to roll toward him, lay her cheek on his chest, and lift her leg and arm to rest over his body. She then quickly returned to her deep sleep.

She awoke early on her own as the sky began to brighten with morning light. She now leaned on her elbow over the sleeping Ben and drew the back of her hand softly down his cheek. He awoke to her smile and moved to kiss her, but she jumped up and pulled on his hand, forcing him to leave the bed as well. She threw him a towel, then wrapped one about her body and led the way out of the hut. Ben stopped for sandals, but she pulled him on before he had placed them on his feet.

"You don't need those. There are no thorns in Tahiti," she said.

She pulled him along through the compound to the road that led into the jungle. A short distance down the road, she turned up a path and walked into the high bamboo. They walked past a clearing where at the far side Ben could see the pack of wild dogs beginning to lie down. He warned Maeva to move deeper into the forest, but this made her laugh. "They won't do anything to us back here. They've been up all night scavenging. They want only to sleep."

Deeper into the trees, Ben could see the valley walls getting higher, and soon he heard the stream. She had told him about the stream, but he had never visited the water. He usually slept when she slipped away for her morning bath.

They approached a wide patch of brush as the sound from the stream increased, but still he could see no water. Maeva entered the patch of brush on a thin path she had worn herself, and he followed its curves through the flowering green. She stopped to unwrap her towel, hung it on a bush, and then stepped down and to the side, disappearing behind the bushes. Ben removed his towel, tossed it over a bush as well, then stepped into the pool of water. She stood naked beside him in water that came up to her knee. She had soap and began to cover herself in foam while Ben bent to feel the water, never taking his eyes off her smooth tanned skin. She moved to him and began to apply soap to his dry skin. The soap pulled at the hair on his chest, so she pushed him into deeper water. She lowered her body then floated over and pressed against his. She felt his state of arousal and said, "I missed you too, Ben Beck." She kissed him, and they both submerged under water and held the kiss as long as they could. They burst to the surface and stood skin-to-skin, wet and eager for each other. They locked eyes and let their hands roam over the other's skin, stopping to explore spots that when touched caused involuntary changes of expression in the other. When they couldn't keep from touching each other more fully, they embraced again, kissing deeply. He lifted her slightly off the bottom, and she wrapped her legs around him as he entered her. She held on tight, her head beside his, her arms outside his shoulders, her hips pulling away then pressing urgently back against him. They both enjoyed the fast, intense climax of the early morning. Quickly, their need of each other's intimate flesh was satisfied.

They returned to the hut and ate breakfast with Luc and Le-hiro. After giving the two men more work to perform, Ben returned Maeva to the hospital, where Rene greeted them angrily. He accused them of abandoning him to the endless interruptions of young doctors and nurses who did not yet fully appreciate the healing qualities of extended sleep. His spirit had returned, and Maeva knew he would make a full recovery.

# Chapter 15

As the *Aurawind* returned, Luc and Le-hiro occupied the same positions on the dock where they had been when the ship departed. Yves threw a line to Ben. Ben secured the bow, then ran to the stern to wait for Yves to get in place to throw a second line. Rudy stood leaning against the salon table and watched him run.

Their passengers stood erect at the bow, arms crossed over their chests waiting for the gangway to be settled in place. Their luggage sat beside them. When Ben greeted them from below, they nodded without saying a word. Once Yves cleared the walkway for passage, they picked up their belongings and left the ship in a hurry. They got to the dock, then turned and marched tight-lipped past the smiling Ben. Ben looked up at Yves and gestured, What's up? with his hands, to which Yves rolled his eyes and tilted his head in Rudy's direction.

Ben took off down the dock and caught up with the quickly departing clients.

"Mr. Gilchrist, is there something wrong?" Ben asked.

"I'll say there's something wrong: that idiot Rudy. He doesn't know a thing about these islands, he doesn't know shit about snorkeling, he can't drive a boat, he provides terrible service, and he couldn't keep his eyes off my wife's tits." Mr. Gilchrist turned and started walking again.

"Wait, Mr. Gilchrist . . . "

The man stopped and stepped back toward Ben. "You ripped us off, that's what you did, you ripped us off."

"Mr. Gilchrist, if that's how you feel, I'll refund your money, and I'll have a talk with Rudy as soon as I get onboard." He stopped to gauge Mr. Gilchrist's reaction, then began again in a stutter, "H-h-how much longer will you be staying at the resort? I'll . . . I'll come visit you later."

"Forget it. If I see anyone from this ship again, I'll kick the hell out of them."

"Please, Mr. Gilchrist, can I give you a ride back to the resort?" Ben pleaded.

"Go to hell," Mr. Gilchrist answered.

Ben watched their backs as they walked down the dock. When they disappeared around a corner, he turned to find Yves and his two waiting companions watching. They lowered their eyes and turned away as he joined them.

"Yves, did you hear all that?"

"I have recently been witness to Monsieur Gilchrist's anger and can hear his raised voice from a great distance. What you experienced moments ago was nothing."

"Was it that bad?"

"Bad comes in many flavors, mon ami, and Monsieur Rudy can leave a very disdainful taste. I did my best to undo the damage he caused, and at one point had soothed the savage breast, but Rudy is a pig. I will never sail on the *Aurawind* again if he is aboard."

Ben stood still and silent, then nodded after a few seconds. "Sorry. Thanks for helping out." Ben turned and walked toward the ship.

When he arrived at the pilothouse, Duane and Rudy exchanged glances and waited for Ben to say something, but his eyes only shifted from one to the other.

Finally Rudy spoke. "It could have gone real good," he said.

"He said you kept staring at his wife."

"She had nice tits, and she marched around topless most of the time. What else could I look at?"

"He's right, nice tits," Duane added.

"Jesus," Ben said, "What happened that he said you didn't know anything about the islands and snorkeling? Why didn't you leave all that stuff up to Yves?"

"I'm not going to let that drunk ruin this business for us. He kept trying to show us up," Rudy said.

"You twerp."

"Fuck you," Rudy said as he came upright from leaning on the table, his chest pressed forward.

Ben looked away. Heat began to envelop his face and neck. He looked to stern and saw the skiff lying upside down with the side of one of the pontoons ripped out and the propeller blades folded over like puppy ears. More heat rose.

"He said you couldn't drive a boat. I guess I can't argue with that."

"Yves told me the wrong way to go. I told him to tell me left or right, but he had to use those boat terms."

"Then you should have let him pilot the skiff." He continued to stare away from Rudy.

"Like I said, I wasn't going to let him ruin anything. I wasn't going to put him in control of any of our equipment." Rudy's chest pressed out farther, and he clenched his fists by his side.

"So like the dumb shit you are, you decided to ruin things yourself." Ben saw the blur of Rudy coming fast toward him. He continued to stare at the skiff as if not noticing, and when Rudy fully committed to his point of attack, Ben leaned toward him, arching the point of his elbow upward to catch Rudy in the throat just to the side of his Adam's apple. Rudy's head stayed at the point of contact. His legs continued forward and swung up off the ground so that he hung momentarily from Ben's elbow with his chin, then he did a free fall, landing on his back and smacking his head on the deck.

Ben got down with him to pin the prone man's arms, making him feel even more helpless. Wide-eyed, his skin reddening on its way to blue, Rudy gagged, choked, and fought for air.

"Don't ever come at me, Rudy. I know you've wanted to, and now you know that you better not." He saw Duane move in the pilothouse. "Stay where you are, Duane," he said without taking his eyes off Rudy.

Duane stopped, but yelled, "He needs help, somebody's got to help him."

"He'll be all right. I didn't hit him that hard." He smiled at Rudy now. "You're a dumb shit, and you did a dumb-shit thing. Accept that and this won't happen again."

Ben stood and walked toward Duane, ignoring Rudy's noises.

"I'm going to see what needs to be done down below. When I'm finished, I'll line up someone to fix the skiff. Get Rudy to do the laundry again. And I told that guy I'd give him his money back, and since you're the captain and you let Rudy fuck things up, you and Rudy are going to pay it. I'll take the money when I go, so have it ready." Ben could feel his voice fluctuate in its delivery. The adrenaline caused little quivers; he relished the tremble of the high.

***

Two weeks later, with Rene still having difficulty getting around, Ben regularly took out vanloads of tourists on island tours. This morning he left the compound early and drove down to the marina for breakfast. When he took the left turn onto the roadway, a speeding car with rusted-off paint came speeding around the corner where Rene had been struck and almost took out the rear end of the van. Ben had been forced to drive on the dirt shoulder on the opposite side of the road because he accelerated to get out of the car's way and overshot the pavement.

"Drunken idiot," he said aloud, once he steered back onto the asphalt. A little farther down the road he spotted the pack of dogs returning to the woods from their night of scrounging. He swerved at them to give them back a little of the scare they had put in him.

He hadn't been back to the *Aurawind* since he'd gone with the boat repairman to pick up the skiff. Although he had no desire to return, he felt some comfort when he saw her still moored at the marina. He walked to his table in the café. When he looked over at the waiter, he saw the man holding a pink message slip up in the air while continuing to read his newspaper. Ben walked to the counter, took the slip from the unmoving hand and ordered coffee and firi firi.

The handwriting belonged to Duane. It said that Carl had a client arriving in two days—not much time to get things arranged. He drank his coffee and ate his sugared pastry. With a few minutes left before he had to begin picking up tourists, he walked out to the ship.

He spotted no one on the upper deck, so he went below. The galley looked clean and ready to go. He looked in the refrigerator and found it empty. He looked in the cupboards and found them empty as well. Okay, he had to buy everything. Next he took a quick look at the dining room and lower salon to find them neat and tidy. *Good*, he thought, then turned and went to Duane's cabin. He knocked lightly on the door and heard some rustling. A second later the door opened and Duane looked out. "Where the fuck have you been? We been trying to get ahold of you for days, man. We got clients coming in four days," he said.

"If the date is right in your note, they'll be here in two."

"The seventeenth, right?"

"Yeah, two days."

"Shit."

Ben said, "I'm tied up today, but I'll be back tonight around five. We'll get it all together. Did the skiff come back?"

"No, you said you were taking care of it."

"Okay. I'll have Yves pick it up and bring it back. Give him a thousand francs and try not to be a prick toward him."

Duane gave him a fuck-you smile, and Ben turned and left.

As he walked toward the gangway to leave, he heard the hatch lid of his berth slide open. He stopped, expecting to see Rudy. But why would Rudy be in his berth, when he had moved into the second cabin at the stern? Instead of Rudy, Miss Malloy emerged from the opening.

"Well . . . well," he said, "Look who popped out."

"I was hoping the footsteps I'd heard were yours. How've you been?"

"Good."

"Great. I hear you don't live with us anymore."

Ben smiled and kept his eyes riveted to hers. "Long story," he said, "I'll tell you about it if you insist."

"I may. I haven't decided yet."

He nodded and looked off toward the dock. "Clients in two days, right?"

"That's right."

"I think this idle time is affecting Duane. He's lost track of what day it is. He thinks we have more time than we do."

"I'll straighten him out."

"I have to go. I'll be back around five. We'll catch up," he said, beginning to slowly back away. "It's good to see you again." He turned and walked off the ship.

***

At the end of the day, when the tour ended at the Papeete Market, he had planned to go straight to the *Aurawind* and begin to organize the trip. One of the tourists had gotten sick during the tour so instead of staying on at the Market, Ben needed to take the tourist back to his resort. Since he would be driving away from the city, he decided to stop back at Rene's to let Maeva know about the upcoming trip.

She didn't worry about him going away for a week's sail, and assured him that she could handle all of the tours in his absence. He wished she could come along as hostess. However since Rene's accident, she wouldn't entertain the thought of leaving her father alone for more than a few hours. He left, saying he would return much later.

Back onboard, Ben learned that the clients had done some research on French Polynesia and had come up with a very interesting suggestion for the trip. They had specified a number of islands and atolls they wished to visit, and planned to leave the ship after a week of sailing. Then they'd stay at a small, secluded resort on an island none of them had heard of. Duane had found it, and all the other specified locations, on his chart. So their course had been established.

Three things remained to be discussed: supplies, equipment and personnel. Ben informed the crew of what had to be done; he assigned tasks to everyone, taking on the majority of them himself, so supplies and equipment were dealt with quickly. Personnel presented a serious obstacle.

"We don't have a cook but we can get by. We don't have a guide that has any local knowledge. Yves—"

"Forget about your drunk friend," Rudy interrupted Ben. "He's not coming back onboard."

"Well, not if you're here," Ben said, turning to Duane. "He said he wouldn't work as our guide again if Rudy stayed on the *Aurawind*. I think we need Yves, and if I'm here I'll use him properly."

Duane looked down at his clenched hands resting on the table. "I'll think about it," he said.

"What?" Rudy said heatedly.

Ben ignored him and said to Duane, "Don't think too long. I have to get him tomorrow."

"What? You're not listening to him, are you?" Rudy said to Duane.

"Cool it, Rudy. I said I'd think about it," Duane said.

"Miss Malloy," Ben turned to address her, "will you be sailing with us?"

"I hadn't planned on it."

"I think you should. I found that having a woman in the crew makes everyone a little more at ease. You saw it for yourself when you brought clients onboard to give them the pitch."

"Sounds nice. I guess I could go along."

"If you do, then we have a problem with where you will berth. Yves would stay with me in my berth, but I wouldn't expect you to share the cabin with Rudy. It would all be much better for everyone if we left Rudy behind."

"You prick," Rudy muttered.

"Food for thought, Duane, food for thought," Ben said.

"What have you got against Rudy?" Duane asked.

"Lots, but mostly I think he's useless." Ben looked at Rudy as he spoke. "Miss Malloy would have stayed in a hotel while we were sailing, so instead of her, now it's Rudy. I'll line up Yves tomorrow. Rudy, looks like you get to sit around and do nothing for a week. Not bad, huh?"

"I guess so," Rudy said. He smiled sweetly and held Ben's stare until Duane asked about the return of the skiff.

"I'll have it back in time," Ben said, then turned to Miss Malloy. "Can we meet for breakfast tomorrow?"

"Sure."

"The café?" he said, tugging his head in the direction of the beach.

Miss Malloy nodded.

"See you then," Ben said, then turned and left the ship.

*** 

Ben awoke to the touch of Maeva's cool hand sliding across his lower abdomen. When he opened his eyes, he saw her serious expression hovering over him against a background tent of mosquito netting. The heady aroma of flowers indicating her presence alerted his nose. She moved her hand, pressing softly with three fingers, her pinkie raised. "It seems you have a man's needs this morning," she said.

Ben smiled as she lifted her leg over his lower body and straddled him, positioned herself, then arched her back at the initial pleasure. She worked her hips against him slowly with her eyes closed, changing her rhythm, sometimes stopping completely to feel and appreciate the immediate sensation of lovemaking's point of contact. Ben watched her move. He ran his hands along her waist down to her hips then up her sides to where he could feel her ribs. He moved them to her breasts and gently ran his palms over the soft skin and the hardened nipples. She pressed forward, trying to feel more pressure, her face serious as if feeling a welcomed pain. She started a slow swaying movement against him. The new rhythm, the new touch sensation, increased her sense of urgency. And as she quickened her movements she opened her eyes and began to smile at Ben. He could feel her change, and he knew that they had both been heightened to a new level when she had opened her eyes. He moved his hands to hold her hips and at this point drifted into the dream state of making love. He didn't know what his hands did then, he didn't know what his legs did, and he didn't know how his face contorted. He only knew Maeva's eyes, how they opened wide and how her smile became harder when their morning climax twisted their bodies, entwining them tighter and deeper into each other, as deep as they could see into each other's eyes.

Soon her arms could feel the weight of her body; weight that she could ignore only seconds earlier. She slipped her palms up the bed, lowering herself onto his chest. Her cheek lay across his collarbone so the tip of her nose touched his chin when he spoke.

"You're so beautiful, Maeva."

"No, not so."

"I don't think I can leave you for a full week."

She chuckled. "You won't ever think of me while you're gone. You'll have American girls in bikinis on your boat showing off their big breasts."

"They could never be as beautiful as you. I won't even look at them."

"Men always look at women. You just try not to, impossible. You go ahead and have fun with the big-breasted Americans."

"What?" Ben craned his neck to look at her face.

"Did you like what we shared in bed this morning?"

"Yes."

"Sharing is good. It's okay to share."

"I don't . . . "

"Don't think about it too hard. Enjoy your trip. I want to share more love with you when you get back."

She got up on her elbow, kissed Ben, then rolled away to grab her pareo and went for her walk to the stream. Ben stared through the off-white netting where she had rolled out and scrunched his face as he thought about her parting words.

# Chapter 16

Yves gestured in wide frantic arcs with his hands and arms while babbling in French faster than anyone could listen even if they understood the language. Brian and Gisela Borwick stood beside him, staring up at the large stone Tiki that had been carved from volcanic rock and moved to this location on the hill overlooking the strip of beach far below. They paid no attention to Yves. They wondered how the ancients could have moved the rock. Their research told them not to bother looking through the meadow for chunks of the material discarded during the carving of the Tikis; they had been carved somewhere else. Very few islands in the South Pacific boasted of having the mysterious Tikis, and Raivavae was the least known of those that did.

Yves had never heard of the ancient stone gods and refused to believe the Borwicks when they told him why they wanted to visit the island. When their climb ended at the edge of the meadow, and the huge sculptures first came into view at the far side, he had turned to look at the clients in amazement and apology. Then, he began to run along the winding path as if unable to wait to see the giants up close.

Halfway to the Tikis, the walking Borwicks caught up to the wheezing and resting Yves. They waited with him while his breathing settled down. Then they finished the trip together.

Ben and Miss Malloy strolled up a few minutes later and stood equally awed by the magnificence of the site. Ben finally noticed the high-speed verbiage Yves spewed forth and turned to ask, "Yves, what are you going on about?"

Yves turned and looked at Ben with his mouth closed shut, his eyes wide, and his arms still flailing in the direction of the carved black stone.

"In-in-in-incredible," he managed to stutter out.

Slowly they split and circled the object in opposite directions, regrouping on the other side.

"How long has it been here?" Ben asked.

"Eight hundred to a thousand years," Brian Borwick answered.

"This trip has been so different from the others. I'm sorry to see it end. I've never thanked the guests for planning a great trip; they usually thank us."

"We've enjoyed it too. It's nice to share something we felt we had to see with people who also appreciate the experience."

"Next port you have on your schedule is Tubuai for a week. You're sure you want to stay in one place that long instead of bouncing around to a few more islands?" Ben asked, smiling.

"I'm tempted, but I'm a bit of a *Bounty* fan. Tubuai is the island Fletcher Christian tried to inhabit first, and I'd like to explore it in some detail. Plus, Gisela found this B&B that sounds right up our alley."

Ben turned to Yves. "Yves, since it's Brian and Gisela's last night, do you think you can cook up something a little special?"

"Every meal I've cooked has been special."

"Yes, I agree, but you know what I mean."

"I'm afraid I do not. I cook to my best ability every time I pick up a sauté pan. What makes you think I will do better or worse this evening?" Yves looked hurt. The guests and the entire crew received an unexpected surprise the first night of sailing when Yves took over in the cooking duties. When Duane asked him why he hadn't cooked the first time they sailed together, he answered in a heated manner that the pig-dog Rudy wouldn't allow him to touch anything in the galley.

"Sorry, Yves. Your cooking has been spectacular. I'm looking forward to tonight's meal," Ben said. The Borwicks and Miss Malloy expressed their agreement, and Yves swaggered as he walked back down the path.

***

The next day on Tubuai, the Borwicks said good-bye and told Ben and Miss Malloy they didn't have to wait with them for their transportation to arrive. After a short, clumsy silence, Ben finally said so long. He and Miss Malloy jumped back in the skiff, leaving their passengers at the Mataura town dock, wishing they could stay and share their adventure a little longer.

"They're an interesting couple. So, how'd you read them, are they going to buy into the *Aurawind*?" Ben asked.

"I think so . . . unfortunately."

"Unfortunately?"

She sat in the front of the craft facing him, but in the beam of his questioning look, she turned away and looked forward.

"Miss Malloy, what do you mean?"

"I'll tell you later."

"Tell me what?"

She turned back deliberately and stared at him hard, then said with finality, "I'll tell you later."

Her clenched jaw and squinting eyes made him realize that later meant later, so he replied with a nod.

Back onboard with no passengers to entertain, their time belonged to them. The Borwicks had stirred up a strong level of curiosity in them, so with little effort they convinced Duane to sail to the uninhabited island of Maria. They chose the island based on its relative closeness to their return course. Maria was only a day's sail, and their enjoyment of the islands in the area that the Borwicks had chosen had been immense. They moored offshore near a small beach and went ashore to find that the island would have a difficult time convincing anyone to start a life in such a place. Low scrubby grass and a stiff breeze shortened their stay.

"We sailed an extra day for this?" Duane said with a cockeyed look on his face.

"I guess the Borwicks knew which islands to go to and which ones to skip," Ben said.

None of them turned for a last look as they set sail toward Tahiti. After dusk they approached the island and decided to spend one more night at sea. They sailed on to the snorkel beach they frequented on Moorea to show it off to Miss Malloy.

At a late hour, they finished the grilled fish that Yves had prepared. When Ben checked on him after the meal, he found him sitting on the forward deck with a bottle of brandy.

"Thanks for your help, Yves," Ben addressed him.

Yves gazed at the horizon, his focus questionable, his smile strong.

"For you, I will sail. For you, I will cook. Always . . . remember that."

"I will. You looking forward to getting home?"

"I'm already home," he said as he patted the brandy bottle.

When Ben returned to the upper salon at the stern, he discovered that Duane had gone to his cabin and Miss Malloy had opened a bottle of wine. He sat beside her and poured himself a glass. When he leaned back in his seat, Miss Malloy leaned toward him and rested her head on his shoulder. They sat that way for a long time. Ben remembered her body against his when she lay beside him in his berth. The warmth, the softness of her flesh, the firmness of the muscle beneath. His body reacted with a natural stirring, and when he acknowledged the stirring, he thought of Maeva. His stirrings belonged to her, or so he thought. Before he had set sail she had told him to have fun with the women on the trip and had indicated that sharing was good. Did she mean he had permission to make love with other women? Did that mean she would make love to other men if she felt the desire to share?

She wasn't the first person to indicate that lovemaking with different partners didn't have to be viewed in a negative light. Rudy had gone on and on about how the Tahitian women had an extremely open and friendly attitude toward men, but he had regarded this as another example of Rudy's crass nature. Then, when Yves saw how he had become attached to Maeva, he had subtly cautioned him, letting him know that the exclusivity between men and women that foreign men preferred had a black-pearl-like quality in Tahiti—much appreciated, but hard to find. Yves then shed more light on the departure of Maeva's mother who wanted to stay with Rene, but couldn't stand the hurt he displayed when she shared her attentions with her male friends. Friends she had no intention of giving up.

Had Maeva adopted her mother's attitude? Should he work to strengthen their relationship in an attempt to win her exclusively, when he would be leaving in a few months, after Carl found a buyer for the ship? Did he feel strongly enough about her to come back after the sale? His mind strained many times to answer these questions during the days of sailing. Now, sipping wine, he sifted through his logic, his feelings, and his questions one more time.

As he did, his stirring intensified. Miss Malloy had twisted toward him. He felt the nuzzling of her nose against his neck, the weight of her breast against his ribs, and the stroke of her hand along his inner thigh. Their physical contact in the past had always thrilled him, and he had always beaten himself up over not giving in to the desire they both displayed, yet prided himself for not taking something he could not confirm that he wanted. She continued to softly run her hand along his leg. He felt the shifting against the fabric of his shorts, and he groaned. He placed his wineglass on the table. As he moved forward, Miss Malloy lay down on the bench seat. She handed him her glass. "Take my clothes off," she said.

Ben took a deep breath and slipped her T-shirt off. She left her arms outstretched over her head while he reached behind her back to untie her bikini top and remove it. He stared at her breasts, then saw his hand cover one of them, saw it glide over the surface. A surge ripped through his body, and his desire to discover all of her flesh, in a slow fashion, vanished in the burn that directed him. He grabbed the bottom of his own shirt and tore it over his head, then reached down to her waist to pull off her pareo and remove her bikini bottoms. His hand ran up inside her thighs. The moist flesh ignited his blood, and he stood to remove his shorts. He moved between her legs. They both paused to make eye contact and confirm their want, then began soft strokes in the light sea breeze on the gently rocking waves. In their excited state it didn't take long to reach the heights, and soon he lay on top of her, a light layer of sweat fusing their bodies together.

Her breathing pressed her tighter against him as he rested his head beside hers. He concentrated on the rise and fall of her chest below him until he became aware of his own lack of oxygen. He lifted his head up to drink cool air and to look at her face. He smiled when he saw her smile of contentment, and he lowered down to softly touch her lips with his.

"That was too fast," he said.

"Come downstairs. We'll go slower."

They stood and pressed against each other's naked bodies. He wrapped his arms around her to satisfy his urge to squeeze her into his chest, and then they allowed their bodies to warm together.

"We'd make a hell of a painting on black velvet right now," he said.

She laughed then reached for her clothing and dressed before going below. Ben checked on Yves and found he had gone into the forward berth. He stared out at the island for a few minutes, letting the breeze clear his thoughts, then walked quietly down the deck, went below, past Duane's cabin, and turned to join Miss Malloy in hers.

She lay on her bed with a sheet pulled down to her waist, exposing her top to Ben. He undressed, and she pulled the sheet away as he lowered himself to lie beside her. Then he began his slow exploration of the body, as he had not been able to accomplish on deck.

Hours later, he awoke to her movement, which he interpreted as her attempting to arouse him again. He quickly felt the desire to make love to her once more, but when he looked into her eyes he saw a different type of interest.

"I'll be leaving the day after tomorrow, and I won't be Miss Malloy anymore."

"What?" Ben said lifting his head. "Why, what's going on?"

Miss Malloy turned on the reading lamp mounted on the headboard and reached into her bag, which sat on the ledge. She retrieved a pamphlet and handed it to Ben. When he read it, he found information regarding an investment opportunity related to a private fleet of yachts. He stopped and looked at Miss Malloy, who stared at him while he read. She said nothing, but pointed at the brochure to get him to read further. He folded out the pages to see pictures of sailing vessels either moored at a dock or at sea with wind-filled canvas. He first thought that the brochure belonged to another group offering private sailing trips, and that they themselves should put together a pamphlet like this one. But then he spotted a picture of the *Aurawind*. He flipped the brochure and looked at the middle page on the backside for contact information, and found a name he didn't know.

"Who are these guys?" He asked as he flipped it back over to look at the pictures to make sure he had seen his ship.

"It's Carl."

"Wow! Carl owns this many yachts?"

Miss Malloy remained silent. When Ben looked at her for an answer, she looked away from his eyes.

"Purrette?"

She looked back at him.

"No, Carl doesn't own any of them."

"Except the *Aurawind?*"

"No, not even the *Aurawind.*"

Ben sat perfectly still, staring at Purrette, hoping things would start clicking together, but his mind stayed blank. Here he sat, on the ship Carl had hired him to sail on. He'd sailed it across the ocean and lived its life for these past months. She held his stare and waited, thinking he would ask her another question. Yet he could only shake his head to indicate he didn't have a clue about what she was trying to tell him.

"I came here for two reasons, Ben. To get the clients situated onboard—and it took some convincing to get Carl to let me come for these ones—and to tell you what I'm about to tell you." She paused to take a deep breath. "Carl is going to send you guys to New Zealand to sell the ship."

"But you said he doesn't own it."

"He doesn't. Now listen."

Ben sat spellbound for the rest of the night while Purrette explained the business Carl had involved him in. Only the *Aurawind* existed; there were no other yachts. Carl used the *Aurawind* to demonstrate a real ship to the potential investors and said the other yachts were either in the process of being sold in shares or had been fully subscribed. The only one they could check out and invest in was the *Aurawind*. He told the investors he would only have ten subscribers per ship, but he sold shares to twenty or more.

"He's made a lot of money so far and now wants to cash in on the sale of the boat, so he's sending you to New Zealand where he has some interested parties. He thinks the deal will close by the time you arrive," she said. "You'll be getting orders to leave Tahiti in a couple of weeks."

"But he doesn't own the ship. How can he sell it?" Ben asked.

"The ship is stolen, Ben. You and Duane stole it the night you sailed to Catalina."

Ben dropped his jaw and stared at her in disbelief, but she kept nodding her head to convince him of the truth.

"No, no . . . I didn't steal it, because I had no idea it was being stolen."

"If all had gone well, then the ship would have been sold, you would have received your money, and you would never have known."

"What went wrong?"

"Me. I told you the truth. Here. Right now. I told you the truth."

"Why?"

She lowered her eyes and pursed her lips as a distant and lost stare came over her face. She raised her hand and placed it over her mouth as if she wanted to hold back any more words. She sat frozen until Ben placed his hand over the hand resting in her lap. Then, she uncovered her mouth. He could see her coming into focus. She lifted her head, then sat more upright and began to speak.

"At eighteen, I got my first job—part-time secretary in Carl's corporate office. He actually is who he says he is, an heir to a toy company. I worked there through a probationary period, then they offered me a full-time job. They offered a better job than the one I had. It turned out that Carl saw me one day and asked for me to become part of the secretarial pool in his offices.

"I met him a few times while working, and he seemed like a nice guy, but he started to make statements about the two of us doing things together. Not like a date really, he wanted to catch a movie or go to the racetrack. No strings attached. I knew he had a wife and kids so I wasn't going to let anything happen. Eventually I did some of the things with him. He was very nice through it all, and I liked him.

"This went on for about a year. The whole time, in the back of my mind, I kept wondering when he was going to try to get more intimate. I kept thinking about what I would tell him to let him know that I couldn't let that happen.

"There was a two-month stretch when he didn't ask me to do anything with him. There had been times when he wouldn't contact me for a week or two because of business or whatever, but it had never been this long, and I knew he wasn't traveling on business because I saw him at work. I figured he got tired of me, and it was over. I understood, even felt relieved. Still, at the same time I enjoyed doing things with the guy; he treated me with a ton of respect.

"Then one night I get a call from him. He's in a hotel near the office, and he wants me to come over. He didn't sound drunk, and to stall I talked to him for a while and eventually told him I didn't think it was a good idea."

She stopped talking. Ben watched her with a stern expression. Her jaw worked up and down, and she swallowed hard. After a few seconds she looked at Ben again and continued.

"So he told me what he had done. He'd left his wife and kids. He'd left them because he wanted to live with me; he said he would get us an apartment so we could be together, and then asked me to come to him at the hotel. I couldn't speak. I knew that if I did, I would have asked him if he was crazy. I felt like yelling 'How could you do that?' at him, 'What made you think I would ever live with you?' But I didn't. I said I was sorry, but things are happening a little too fast, and I need some time to think about it. Then I hung up.

"What followed was a messy divorce. His wife took everything and created a lot of obstacles to prevent him from seeing his kids. He had his job, his salary, and nothing else. I told him I didn't feel good enough about him to live with him.

"I tried to quit my job, but he didn't accept that. He laid a guilt trip on me. He said I had cost him his wife and kids, and if I left my job he'd lose me too. He said that with time I might change my mind, and the only way he could make something of his terrible situation was if I would stay near him at work and let time try to bring us together.

"His work started to suffer, and living on his salary instead of his riches didn't appeal to him. He started looking for other opportunities by using his contacts in the world of the rich, and the next thing I knew he told me he had started an investment company and would be leaving the family business to go out on his own. He also threw a whole new load of guilt my way and said I had to stay with him until he rebuilt his life.

"That's what I've been doing—staying with him. It's been a good run. He left me alone and gradually accepted that I would only be a tool for him, a valuable tool. I am a good assistant, and he made sure I had everything I needed for safety and security. I've traveled and met a lot of interesting people during my time with Carl. Things I wouldn't have done if I'd not stayed with him.

"I probably would have continued, except that he made the mistake of hiring you. He's never hired nice guys before. He usually hires guys like Duane and Rudy who always need money, always spend more than what they have, and aren't too particular about how they make their money.

"But with you they tried something different. They wanted to keep you in the dark, let you work for a year, give you your money, and send you away none the wiser. That changed when Carl started getting nervous about the plan. He thinks someone is suspicious and is digging into what's going on with the yacht investment group. I figured he was overselling it, based on the numbers he would shoot out during his pitches to the investors. Then I figured out that he didn't own the ship and would be pocketing all of the investor's money and the money from selling the *Aurawind*—about two-point-five million, all profit except for the expenses to keep things going for the year, and your fifty grand.

"His intent is to get the money, and then he and I would run away and finally be together. I couldn't believe it, and I couldn't tell him what I really thought. The catch to the whole plan is the sale of the yacht. If he gets away with selling it, he pays you, you go away and we take off.

"If there is somebody investigating us, and they lay a trap for us in New Zealand . . . " She paused, and the muscles in her face sagged the slightest bit, then she said, "They let you take the fall, and we all disappear."

"Holy shit! They're setting me up? How did I not see that? I saw what looked like a brochure in Duane's berth, and Mr. Labrio told me he was buying a share of the *Aurawind*."

Purrette continued, "It's still not that obvious. You don't think like these guys, you're too nice a guy. That's why I came here. You treated me like a respectable person; you tried to find out who I am. The other men in my life only care that I do the job I'm supposed to do, and that's a job that makes them a lot of money. When I needed help, when I needed to be held by a decent man, you let me hold on to you, and you held me like you really cared for me. You're different, Ben. You remember when you last heard a long-lost song you liked, and you even remember when you heard it the time before that.

"I needed to break away from Carl, and I couldn't let people like him and Duane and Rudy ruin a good person like you, so I decided now was the time to split. I had to tell you. I don't know what to tell you to do. You could get your money if you go along with them, but you could also get caught."

Ben flopped back onto the pillow and covered his eyes with his forearm. His chest heaved as he took deep breaths and let them out slowly.

"What am I supposed to do? What will I do without you around to warn me? When do you think you will leave?" he asked.

"Like I said, I can't tell you what to do. But I know you'll make out okay. I'm leaving the day after tomorrow."

"Where are you going to go?"

"It's better if you don't know."

"Do you have money to get away?"

"A little. Carl controls any accounts I've had access to."

***

After docking in Papeete, Ben made sure the ship was tied up and ready to be moored in the marina for some time. He quickly left to be with Maeva. He felt it was best for him to stay as far away as he could possibly get from the ship and the people onboard. He'd never told them about Maeva's father or where the compound was, so he felt sure they couldn't track him down on land.

Being away from them was critical. He wasn't sure what he would do, but he knew if he was near Duane or Rudy he was likely to give away the fact that he now knew what had been going on. Knowing they still thought that he was ignorant of their plan, he knew he would lose his temper when they tried to make out like things were normal, or they dangled his share of the money to motivate him to continue to do what he was expected to do.

A day away helped him cool down and he began to think more clearly. The physical attraction to Miss Malloy was gone, and he felt guilty for giving in to his desire. Finding out that she was part of the con—and even helped to keep him in the dark—angered him, but he harbored feelings of guilt for leaving like he had when Miss Malloy had come to help him. She'd obviously felt regret about the situation she had assisted in putting him in. She'd displayed a desire to change from the person who could mislead another to potential peril, someone she said she cared about. The fact that she was running away from it all with little money to support herself was a clear sign of that intention.

On the day Purrette was to leave for good, Ben drove Rene's van to the marina and went onboard the *Aurawind* to help her with her bags. Duane and Rudy greeted him with their normal silence and remained on deck, letting him do the work of retrieving her pack from the second stateroom, which she had remained in after they docked. While below, he made a quick stop in Duane's cabin.

With Miss Malloy's luggage at the gangway, he went below into his berth, now occupied by Rudy, and retrieved some of his own things that he'd left behind.

They left the ship, and Ben drove Miss Malloy to the airport. When she sat beside him, about to say good-bye, he handed her a package.

"Here. Rudy, Duane, and I each had a little stash of cash that we managed to accumulate. They don't know it, but they've donated theirs to you to help you find a happy place. Now that you're leaving, I really feel like I'm on my own," he said.

"I can't stay now, and I can't take that."

"Take it. I don't know how much it is. I didn't count it, but it will help. Also, here is a phone number. It's a friend of mine back in the States. Call it and leave a message if you need something, or to let me know you're safe. Especially to let me know you're safe. Will you do that?"

"No."

Ben smiled.

"What are you going to do?" she asked him.

"Stay here. But I'm not going back to the ship, even if it means I don't get the payoff I was working for. I don't want their kind of money."

"You're the good guy."

She leaned forward to kiss him good-bye. He hesitated, but met her lips, kissing her without feeling. When they parted, they looked into each other's eyes and both smiled. Ben had to turn away. She left without saying another word.

# Chapter 17

Ben stayed away from the café at the marina, to avoid any contact with Duane or Rudy, and also because he hated that his association with the *Aurawind* had ended. Seeing her sleek lines as she moored weightlessly at the dock and remembering her luxurious appointments made him wish to go back onboard. His new experience as a sailor had been exciting and he wanted to continue to sail the ocean.

He had contacted Yves. They began to meet at a different location in order for Ben to get updates regarding the ship's activities. Two weeks had passed, and the ship remained tied up at the dock. Then one day Yves met Ben on the second level of the Papeete Market, in a patisserie looking down over an ornate white railing onto a small vegetable stand. He handed Ben a note he had received from the waiter at the marina café. Ben read the note, crushed it in his hand, and threw it into his empty coffee bowl.

"They've got their sailing orders. They want me back onboard to leave for New Zealand."

"Will you go?" Yves asked.

"I don't think so. Like you, I've had enough of Rudy. I like it here, so I think I'll stay."

"Bon, I would hate to lose a friend."

"Let me know if they come looking. I don't want to say good-bye."

***

They met each day for the next three days, and each day Yves informed Ben that Duane had come to the café looking for him. That morning, the third day, Yves had watched from a distance as Duane went inside the café and left minutes later. Yves entered the café soon after to see if Duane had left a message, only to be surprised when Duane walked back in and confronted him, making him sit while he asked about Ben's whereabouts. During the questioning, he asked Yves a number of questions related to Rene and his daughter. Yves told him nothing, even though Duane adopted a threatening tone. He ended the interview that morning by telling Yves to let Ben know they were sailing the next night, and that he and Rudy couldn't handle the sailing alone.

Ben shook his head, unmoved by the appeal. He told Yves he had a tour to drive for Rene the next day and suggested they meet at the Market when he finished. He then suggested that Yves stay away from the marina.

Ben and Maeva took the tourists out on tour the next day. They enjoyed working the tours together, and Maeva told him things seemed to go a lot smoother with him there. They joked with each other, and their joking seemed to put their customers in a good mood.

When they ended the tour at the Market, Ben asked her to wait for a few minutes while he ran to find Yves. However, when he went to the patisserie above the vegetable stand, Yves was nowhere to be found. He walked through the lower level of the Market to the wall above the water to see if the *Aurawind* remained at the dock. It did. He was glad and planned to watch her set sail in the evening. He wanted to let Yves know he would return after he drove Maeva back to the compound, but since they didn't connect, he knew he would have to hunt him down later.

When he and Maeva arrived back at the clearing, they found Rene sitting in his chair in front of the fire pit. He greeted them, asked when his dinner would be ready, and then mentioned that two visitors had come looking for Ben.

"A black man and a short white guy?" Ben asked.

"A black man and a short *angry* white man."

"What did they want?"

"You," Rene said.

"How long were they here?"

"Not long."

"Did they leave a message?"

"No."

"Papa," Maeva spoke sternly to her father, "stop making Ben Beck ask the questions and tell him exactly what went on when the men were here."

"What is there to tell? They came and asked for Ben, and I said he wasn't here. They waited for a short time and left without leaving a message. And don't talk to your father in such a way." He turned to Ben. "You see how she treats me like an infant since I came home from l'hopital?"

Ben smiled then went and poured Rene a glass of Pernod, which he delivered before returning to the kitchen to help with the cooking.

After the meal, he took the van to return to the Market and watch his ship leave port without him. He started his turn onto the road, but decided to look again to his right—then slammed on his brakes as a speeding car rounded the corner. He'd had too many close calls in both directions while leaving the compound, and decided he'd have to mount mirrors on the far side of the road as soon as the ship departed. He made his way safely onto the road and rounded the first curve when he saw the pack of wild dogs on the flat shoulder. They recognized the van as the one that always tried to run them down, so they retreated back to the tree line to wait for him to pass.

He parked the van a few blocks inland from the Market and walked along Boulevard Pomare to look out at the marina, hoping that Duane and Rudy hadn't left yet. Night had fallen. Above the glow of the Market he spotted the Southern Cross. Its bright stars shined in contrast to the sky's deep, dark black. Everywhere he looked the light seemed brighter. The neon of Le Marche's sign glittered, the shiny aluminum of the food stands along the street glowed, the smoke cast off by the sizzling meat and seafood made a bright haze. The vivid blues and reds and yellows of the people's clothing stood out as they milled about drinking beer and eating the delicious-smelling food.

He entered the Market and walked among the stands that would be open late into the night. The vendors, who had traveled from their homes to sell their produce and had nowhere to go at night, would stay for days until they sold their entire inventory. They slept in their stalls during their stay. He received smiles from them as he walked by. Laughter erupted. He heard music playing in the distance. He walked toward the water and stood at the wall to look out over the marina. The *Aurawind* had lighted its mast and run a string of lights up the sheets. He thought he would spot Duane in the pilothouse going over his charts, with Rudy running around the deck making ready to heave off, but he saw no movement onboard. On his right, toward the marina, he could see the band he had heard from within the Market.

A noise came from his left where the wall of the Market curved out toward the water. He saw the angled concrete wall of a boat launch. Below it he saw the figures of three men sitting in the shadows. When he left the Market he purchased a bottle of beer from a street vendor, then turned and walked toward the boat launch. At an unlighted street he turned back toward the water. Walking slowly, he listened for voices to see if he had turned down the right street. Total silence surrounded him. Zero visibility caused him to take cautious steps. He didn't want to announce his arrival, so he dropped into a crouch when a bottle smashed loudly on the other side of the wall. He rose slowly to peer over the wall and spotted Le-hiro-de-biere twisting the top from another beer.

Ben now stood and called down to his three friends. Yves, who sat in the sand directly below where he stood at the wall, called back in greeting, then held up his liquor bottle, which reflected a small glint of light as he craned his neck back to look up at Ben. Beside Yves in the dark, crumbled, concrete corner a barely-visible pile of refuse had accumulated with the ebb and flow of the tides. Oil cans, plastic food wrappers, broken bits of Styrofoam, and empty bottles. A few feet away, Ben could see the outline of a large barrel. Le-hiro sat on a black rock that poked above the shallow surface of the bay, his back to water, his feet on the blackened sand. More Styrofoam and plastic floated behind him. A few feet away Luc slept on his side using his shoulder for a pillow, his arm stretched out above his head with his feet being licked by small waves.

"Monsieur Beck, bonsoir. Distillateur allons-nous nous réunir pour observer votre bateau partir du port?"

"You lost me, Yves. I think you better use English."

"Oui, oui. Will we still meet to watch your ship leave the harbor?"

"Yes, I think so. Are you feeling okay?"

"Until now, Monsieur Beck, you have not seen me at my finest. Now, I am quite okay." Yves held up his bottle to show Ben and frowned when he looked at it himself and saw the amber line approaching the thick glass bottom.

Ben lifted his legs over the wall and sat where he could see the beauty of the ship to which he had come to bid farewell. He twisted the top off his beer.

"Will you toast our fine ship adieu with me?" Ben asked.

"Of course." Yves struggled to rise from the sand. He stepped toward the barrel and put his free hand on the rim to steady himself. Then, looking back at Ben, he lifted his bottle. As Ben raised his beer to speak a toast he saw Yves' eyes grow wide and his jaw drop.

Behind Ben, Yves had just seen Rudy step into view. As Rudy approached Ben, he swung hard with a rock he could barely get his fingers around. The arc of his swing brought the rock down hard onto Ben's head, behind his ear. Ben tumbled forward off the wall, unconscious. He fell, a deadweight, and landed with a thump on his forehead and knees, remaining in that position with his haunches up in the air.

The alcohol-induced, slow-motion view of the attack on his friend caused Yves to collapse in shock. He plunked back on the sand, landing in a sitting position, legs straight out in front. Stunned, he watched Rudy, then Duane, hop over the wall to check on Ben.

"He's still breathing," Duane said, his own breathing deep and stressed.

"Then I didn't hit him hard enough," Rudy responded casually.

They both turned their attention to Yves, who had abandoned his bottle as he struggled to get to his feet. Once erect, he charged at Rudy screaming, but he couldn't deliver the blow he had planned. Rudy sidestepped him, but grabbed the front of his shirt as he passed, then tugged hard, spinning the disoriented Yves around to face him. From close range Rudy struck Yves in the forehead with the heel of his hand. Yves dropped back straight-legged to the sand again, then crumpled to one side, out cold.

Seeing Yves go down, Le-hiro stood up from his rock, scaring the other two men when he asked, "Hey, what you doing?"

Rudy walked to the large docile-looking man. When he stood a foot away, he hauled back and swung a blow that landed in Le-hiro's lower abdomen. The big man buckled over in pain, and as his face came down, Rudy lifted his knee with all the force he could muster, making contact squarely on Le-hiro's nose. The sick crunch of breaking bone was followed by the splash of his body going into the water. Rudy watched as he went under for an instant, then saw him emerge to float among the harbor's garbage.

Rudy turned to see Duane rolling Ben over onto his back. Music and the sound of laughter drifted down from the marina. The Market continued to light the night a short distance away. In the dark, by the abandoned boat launch, while black waves shifted the flotsam, Duane ordered Rudy to run back to the ship and return with the skiff.

# Chapter 18

Ben awoke to bright sunlight beaming through the high window of *Aurawind's* main salon. It seared his eyes. He whipped his head to the side, but the painful throb made him suspend his motion. Cymbals crashed at the base of his skull, causing his eyes to rattle in their sockets. A weak groan emitted from his throat. His stomach muscles clenched and twisted him violently, making him retch and roll off the sofa. He tried to move his hands to break his fall, but they were tied behind his back. After a hard impact on his shoulder, he slammed his cheekbone into the teakwood floor, then lay convulsing in dry heaves between the sofa and the fixed table. The crashing inside his skull transformed from subdued to rampant, crackling as if a Geiger counter swung next to his head. His back pressed against the sofa for a few seconds, then he felt suspended and toppling until he felt his shoulder pressed against the table as he rolled with the rise and fall of the ship.

His eyes opened when he heard footfalls on the steps. The crackling in his ears had stopped. Seconds later he felt a kick against the soles of his feet.

"You back among the living?" Rudy said.

Ben could only grunt.

"I guess you are."

Rudy moved around the table to Ben's head and grabbed him by the shoulder. With one hand in Ben's armpit, he lifted and pushed Ben forcefully onto the sofa. His head snapped back. When it rocked forward he began to slump to one side. Nevertheless he wasn't going to go down at the hands of Rudy and managed to support himself on his elbow. His head lolled inches above the leather cushions. He sucked in a deep breath and called upon all his strength to lift his upper body into a sitting position. Sweat began to form at his hairline and on his upper lip.

Rudy withdrew to sit on one of the chairs in the dining room and watch Ben try to clear his mind.

"I hope you feel better than you look, but I doubt it." Rudy smiled as he taunted.

"Get me some water," Ben croaked.

"You'll puke."

"Get it."

"I'm not getting you shit."

Rudy stood up, walked to the galley, and poured himself a glass of water. He drank the whole glass, licked his lips, and left.

Within minutes Duane hurried down the stairs into the salon. He looked at Ben and nodded before going to get water. He returned with a little water in a glass, a towel and a bucket, then sat beside Ben and lifted the glass to Ben's lips. The water soothed his dry tongue, melted the sticky saliva at the back of his throat, and trickled down his esophagus, all the while greatly improving his state of mind. Then it reached his empty stomach and he felt nauseated. He took a few slow, deliberate breaths to ease the queasy feeling.

"I'm going to untie your hands," Duane said. "I didn't know Rudy had tied them."

Once he released Ben's hands, he handed Ben the glass, but numb hands prevented Ben from gripping it.

"I'll leave the water here while I make you some soup. I need you to get into shape in a hurry. We've got some wind, and Rudy's struggling with the sails."

Duane went to the galley and opened a tin of soup and heated it. When he returned Ben held out the empty glass, asking for more water.

"I know you still need some rest. We can manage for a while, but we're getting off course due to poor sailing. Do you want to be moved to your berth, or do you want to stay here?" Duane spoke from near the sink.

"Stay here."

"Okay. You going to try some of that food?"

Ben nodded.

"I gotta get back up top. Get some soup in you."

\*\*\*

The next day, Ben's energy level increased, and the noise in his head had dwindled to a low hiss. He couldn't stay awake very long, but each time he awakened, he felt more like himself. Duane checked on him a number of times, making sure he ate and had plenty of water. Rudy kept his distance. When he woke in the afternoon, he wanted to go topside. He stood stationary for a second to get a feel for the roll of the sea, then made his way up the stairs. The wind blew stiff, and he squinted as he scanned the deck for Duane and Rudy. He spotted Duane forward, checking the jib sheet, and then looked aft to find Rudy sitting in a deck chair watching him.

"Why aren't you doing that?" Ben yelled in order to be heard above the wind.

"I always fuck it up," Rudy yelled back.

Ben felt his energy starting to drain so he sat down on the pilot's stool. Detached from his surroundings, he stared forward wondering if Maeva knew the circumstances behind his departure from Tahiti. He didn't know Duane had come up behind him until he heard him speak.

"Feeling better?"

"Did you tell anyone I was leaving with you?"

Duane's smile disappeared. "Didn't have time. But I'm sure your friend Yves will let everyone know."

"How does he know I've left?"

"You were with him when we found you by the boat ramp."

"You found me?"

"Out like a light with a nasty bump on your head. Your friends were too drunk to help you, so we took you back with us, and then we had to make sail. We tried to get in touch with you before, to tell you we were leaving, but it seemed you weren't interested. We figured we'd bring you along; do you a favor. You get your fifty grand after the sale, and you can go back to Tahiti."

"You think you're doing me a favor? Why'd you have my hands tied if you're doing me a favor?"

"That's Rudy being a prick. He's fuckin' with you, man, 'cause you hit him in the throat that time."

"Bullshit. I know what's going on. You stole the ship. It's not Carl's to sell, and you couldn't leave me behind."

"So, she did tell you. Where is she? Did she steal our money or did you?" Duane dropped every pretense of his friendly attitude.

"Like I'd tell you. And what difference does it make? She's gone, and I want nothing to do with this anymore. I don't care what you do, I don't care if you get caught or get your money. Just drop me off somewhere."

"You'll get off in New Zealand. The sooner you can help around here, the sooner we'll get there, and the sooner you'll get away. But make no mistake, you're going all the way with us."

***

As Ben grew stronger he stayed on deck more and more. After another day, he felt he could take some of the work off of Duane if Rudy could provide even the slightest bit of assistance. When Duane indicated that they needed to jibe, Ben volunteered his and Rudy's service on the jib so Duane could handle things in the pilothouse. The wind remained stiff, and the swell of the sea remained strong. Duane called out the start of the jibe and turned the wheel. When the jib went slack, Ben instructed Rudy to switch the sail to the other side, but as the wind began to fill the canvas, Rudy had too much slack in the line. The canvas snapped outward, snatching the line from Rudy's hand. The knot caught in the pulley for a second, and the sail eased up. Then a gust filled it again, and this time it forced the knot through the pulley. The sail flapped and snapped while the line flipped through the air like a bullwhip. Ben yelled for Rudy to lower the jib, but Rudy stood ignorant. Ben unraveled the halyard from the cleat, dropped the sail, and yelled at Rudy to start hauling it in. When Rudy had the line, he had difficulty untying the knot so they could get it back through the pulley, and Ben had to do the work once again. With things set straight again, Ben raised the jib, caught the wind, and trimmed the sail. His body felt the strain, and his head began to swim with the exhaustion.

He could barely stand and fight for his balance on the romping deck. Without looking at either Duane or Rudy, he went below and rested in his berth.

Hours later, Duane yelled down that another jibe had to be performed. After Ben performed the task, Duane told him that the difference he had made performing the jibes was why he had to replace Rudy completely when it came to handling the sails. Ben handled the sails the rest of the way.

They had less than three days to go. Strong winds had favored them for most of their journey. Once Ben began to feel better, he enjoyed the challenge of the difficult sailing. They had been in this kind of wind before, but it had never been this forceful this long. He stayed forward and handled the sail work, only going behind the pilothouse to go down to the galley for his meals. When he did, Rudy always seemed to show up sniffing around, trying to get him to cook for all of them. Ben refused, each time using the opportunity to remind Rudy of how useless he was.

"Useless? I managed to get you back onboard."

"You got me back onboard?"

"Yeah, I spotted you with those drunks you call friends. Duane wanted to talk you into coming with us to New Zealand, but I didn't give him a chance. I got to you first and tried to crush your skull. I'd like to try again."

"I'd like you to try, too, but I know you won't do it face-to-face. You have to wait for a chance to sneak up from behind so you can take your best shot, a cheap shot."

"Hitting you with that rock was the best cheap shot I ever took."

"Then you must feel really small knowing that the best cheap shot you ever took didn't do the job. You can hurt me, Rudy, but you can't take me out. You're useless." Ben glared at Rudy, waiting to see if he had the nerve to strike, but could see that Rudy knew he had no chance. He put his hand on Rudy's shoulder and moved him to the side, then went back up top.

Duane worked on a coil of line on the port side of the ship. The full moon provided a great deal of light and Ben could see the silver sheen of the clips connecting Duane's harness to the safety lines. Because of the roughness of the seas, Duane had ordered them to wear their safety harnesses whenever they were on deck. After clipping on to the safety lines along the starboard side, Ben walked forward. He stopped beside the mast to look at something that caught his eye. When he began to move again, he heard a swishing noise and turned toward it. He saw the pole coming for his head and ducked while lifting his arm. The pole struck just above his elbow, but the angle of his arm caused it to glance off after running the length of his forearm. He stood upright as Rudy swung the pole back in the other direction. It came back slower. Ben grabbed its end, twisted, and jerked it out of Rudy's hands. He spotted Duane coming at him from behind and turned to point the gaff pole in Duane's face. When he did, Rudy took a step closer so Ben flipped the pole around to stop Rudy's advance.

"Okay. Put it down, Ben!" Duane yelled as he removed his own harness. "What the hell's got into you, Rudy?"

Ben stood looking from Rudy to Duane, then with one hand released the clips of his safety harness. Moonlight gleamed off the end of the pole he held. The waves rose black behind Rudy; spray made white by the moonlight blew off their crests. Rudy knew he couldn't get to Ben without Duane's help from behind. He shouted at Duane, egging him on. "We have to get to him, Duane. We have to get to him at the same time."

Ben held the gaff hook pointed at Rudy, but swayed a little toward Duane to keep him at a safe distance.

"Duane, we have to dump him before we reach Auckland anyway. We're just going to do it a little bit earlier. We both have to hit him at the same time."

"We still need him," Duane yelled back.

"He won't do anything we ask now."

Duane hesitated, and then moved a little closer. Ben flinched in his direction. When Ben turned back to see if Rudy had moved, he seemed closer too.

"On three, Duane. Ready?"

Ben knew that he couldn't afford to have Duane on his back— his size and strength made him more dangerous than Rudy. If they both came at him at the same time, he had to be prepared to take on Duane first.

"Ready, Duane?" Rudy called again.

Duane hadn't taken his eyes from Ben the whole time, and he didn't take them off of him now. He nodded slightly, his nerves on edge. They all three staggered at times trying to maintain their balance.

Rudy yelled out, "One!" but he didn't make it to two. Duane's nerves got the best of him. He charged at Ben early. His movement surprised Rudy, causing him to react an instant late.

Ben reacted late as well. He swung the gaff hook hard to catch up with the charging Duane. Rudy moved within the arc of the hook. Without knowing it, Ben struck Rudy as Duane crashed into him. The hook caught Rudy at the corner of his eye then tore upward, ripping the skin through his eyebrow, up his forehead, and deep into his scalp. The blow stopped his forward motion, and he bent over in pain, covering his eye with his hands. Blood flowed into his eye, and he instinctively turned opposite to the direction from which he had been struck. He couldn't see and he turned too far. In his haste he tripped over the safety line and toppled overboard.

Ben and Duane crashed to the deck, and their noise muffled the sound Rudy made as he hit the water. He dropped below the surface and felt a new sting in his wound. He opened his good eye and saw a blue-black world with a creamy white haze above. The full moon guided him to the surface. He stroked hard and broke through, sucking loudly for air. In his next breath he felt the sting return to his face as blood poured back into his eye. He sucked in more air as a wave swamped him, filling his mouth with water. He kicked hard to gain the surface and managed to come back up and cough out the water. His lungs forced him to suck for air to breathe again, but they made bubble sounds and caused him to cough even more. The sting and the salt taste in his mouth started his first hint of panic. He coughed again, this time harder, trying to clear his throat in an attempt to get air. He rose on a wave, and then dropped into the trough as the crest of another wave poured down on top of him. He went under. He closed his eyes. He stroked against the weight of the water. He had to see; ignoring the sting, he opened his eyes. The light seemed farther away. In his panic he started to churn the water with his arms and legs; he reached with both as if to climb a ladder. Again he made it to the surface, this time completely exhausted. He lie back to float, to rest, to survive, but his legs kept sinking. He felt himself ready to go under again. He thrashed the surface to keep his head above the water. His wound meant nothing now. His arms tired, he thought he'd go under for a second to rest, then kick back up and try to float again. He took a deep breath and allowed himself to drop below the surface. He sank for a few seconds. It got darker, and his instincts said to start making his way back up. His lungs started to pull at his chest, screaming out for air.

Again he flailed his arms and legs trying to get closer to the surface, and he thought he made some progress. His lungs pulled harder, and he fought to hold the air that currently filled them, but he could hold it no longer, and he released it in a stream of loud bubbles. His lungs pulled hard, but he closed his mouth. The sound of his grunts to keep it closed filled his ears. His lungs pulled once more, and he thought his ribs would collapse. The water became even darker; suddenly it slammed him with cold, causing every muscle in his body to constrict. He gasped, sucking in liquid. It reached his lungs and he gagged, flushing it outward, choking on the icy seawater. Involuntarily he drew in and again filled his lungs, but this time he couldn't push it out. His panic caused him to flail once again, but it lasted only seconds before he gave in. Then he drank the cold and salty sea to fill his lungs and abdomen, to sink faster and deeper, to end the exhausting fight for life in a sea where moonlight no longer existed.

Ben's forearm hurt as he clutched Duane's shoulder, trying to pin him to the deck. Duane squirmed, trying to scramble to his feet, all the while yelling something Ben couldn't understand. He swung at Duane's head with his other arm, but connected on the other man's collarbone. Duane turned his back to Ben, got his feet under himself, and tried to sprint away, but Ben got his arms around his hips and tackled him. Duane tried to turn and face Ben while attempting to loosen Ben's grip on his body. He got his hands on Ben's face and pushed, bending Ben's torso backward until Ben's arms snapped open and released him. He sidestepped Ben and tried to get to the starboard side. Ben caught his leg and tripped him. Holding one of Duane's legs, Ben dodged the other leg as it whipped and kicked at him in an attempt to break his grip. Ben wondered why he fought Duane's efforts to flee. Duane should be attacking, not trying to get away. He also wondered why Rudy hadn't jumped on him from behind.

"Wait, wait. Rudy's gone!" Duane yelled.

"What?"

"Rudy's gone." Duane pointed starboard. "Over the side."

Ben released Duane's foot and they both moved to starboard. Duane began to call out Rudy's name. Before long he stopped calling and ran to the pilothouse to snap on the spotlight. After a quick scan, he yelled for Ben to take over while he tried to figure out their position and mark it on the chart.

"Okay, we gotta go back," Duane said, "How long do you think it took from when we started fighting until we stopped to look over the side?"

"Minute, maybe two."

"And we've been another two or three since then. The wind's pushing him toward us, but pushing us harder. We have to backtrack a bit, and it's going to take at least twenty minutes to get back to a point where he may be now. Go forward and prepare to turn."

They turned and tacked their way back to the point where Duane wanted to start the search. He then sailed in lines that crossed their previous course every hundred meters. When they passed the point to which they felt Rudy could have drifted, they turned, tacked back, and sailed the lines again.

As they searched, Ben manned the spotlight while Duane watched the wave tops hoping to spot Rudy's profile. Because it was night, Duane considered them lucky to have the full moon.

They finished their second pass, then turned again to go back and start over. When the sun came up they went back again, allowing for drift, and sailed the lines once more. They soon realized they weren't going to find him. Ben stood by the mast looking back at Duane, who kept his eyes on the chart. When he lifted his head, he looked at Ben and said, "He's gone."

Ben stood silent for a moment while the words sunk in. "What do we do?" he asked.

"Go to Auckland . . . sell the ship."

"Shouldn't we call for help?"

"I don't think so. We don't need to rub elbows with any coastguard or cops."

"Forget about getting caught! We can't just go about our business, for Christ's sake. Rudy drowned out there."

"You killed him, Ben. You want the authorities to know you killed him?"

"I didn't try to hit him."

"But you did. You knocked him overboard. It was no accident."

"You fucking creep."

Duane rose from his seat when he saw Ben approaching and backed out of the pilothouse, circling it in the same direction as Ben to stay away from him.

"Think about it, Ben. You kill me like you killed Rudy and you're not going to be able to sail yourself out of here. I can handle the ship on my own, but you can't. Think about it."

Ben stopped. He took several deep breaths, his shoulders rising high each time. Then he moved forward and took his position for handling the sail.

*** 

He stayed forward for the next two days and only spoke to Duane to confirm the completion of his tasks. They spotted land the second day and at dusk sailed into New Zealand's Tamaki River on a southeasterly course. When they passed Sandy Point, they headed due south then turned southwest, hugging the shoreline as they passed the marina at Half Moon Bay. They sailed on. When it began to get dark they turned and sailed back to the north. As they came even with the marina on their return trip, Duane dropped the mainsail and instructed Ben to drop the jib. Ben felt the engines power up as he stored the sail, and then he felt a slight lurch forward as Duane put the engines into gear.

The *Aurawind* entered the marina with the engines running, in the dark of night with the running lights on. Duane pulled up to a clear stretch of dock far away from the marina's main building. Ben jumped over the side and secured the bow, then ran to the stern and secured a line there as well. When he came back onboard, Duane had already gone below. When Duane came back up on deck, he carried a small, overstuffed canvas bag.

"I have to let Carl know we've arrived. You stay here and I'll be back later," Duane said, trying to walk past Ben.

Ben stood in front of him, blocking the gangway. "I'm going with you," he said.

"No, somebody has to stay here in case the marina master comes by."

"I'm going with you."

Duane stared at Ben for a second, then stepped back and told Ben to hurry and get his belongings.

Ben went below and grabbed a small nylon carry bag in which he placed his shaving kit and a change of clothes. He glanced around his berth quickly, partly to see if he was leaving anything important behind, partly because he thought it would be his last look. He grabbed his alarm clock and tossed it into the bag, then moved to the ladder and began to climb out. As soon as his head poked out from the hatch Duane hit him with the short bat they used to kill fish. Ben fell back down the ladder and landed in a heap on the floor. He lifted his head. He heard the hatch closing above him, and he heard footsteps run away, leaving him in silence. He spotted the chair by the desk and crawled to it. He pushed up, straightening his arms. He managed to get one elbow onto the seat of the chair, but the exertion caused his head to swim, and he collapsed, smashing his chin on the chair's seat as he fell.

# Chapter 19

"Ahoy, skipper," a short, stocky man hailed from the end of the gangway. A morning gust lifted the end of his brown tie, flipping it over, pushing it to the side, and raising it to flap against the gold-embroidered patch sewn to the shoulder of his shirt. He stood with his head cocked to one side, shifting his eyes along the length of the ship. One of his well-worn brown boots rested on the gangway, the other on the dock. He rested one of his hands on the aluminum railing, the other on the handgun holstered on the belt. The belt disappeared under the even roundness of his girth. Round, except for a flat disk-shaped trampoline made by the cloth of his shirt stretched over his navel.

Below, Ben heard the faint, muffled voice coming from far away. He opened his eyes, but they remained filled with darkness.

"Ahoy. Permission to come aboard." The voice called again. Ben heard it, but couldn't register the words. He closed his eyes and passed out once more.

The stocky man walked cautiously up the gangway and walked aft to the pilothouse. He called below from the top of the stairs, but heard no return answer. Next, he turned and walked past the salon to the very stern of the ship and found the skiff secured in its proper place. He smoothed his wind-blown tie, held it in place momentarily, then let it go while he reached back and scratched his neck. Walking forward to leave, he spotted the forward hatch and stepped over to get a closer look. A small bat wedged the door closed. He removed it and tested to see if the hatch was locked, but it slid open easily. Looking below in the dark, he could see Ben's white sneakers and thought them to be left behind, but then he noticed the feet in them. He got down on his knees, stuck his head inside the opening, and called out. No reaction from Ben. The man pulled away and began to climb down the ladder, managing to squeeze his bulk through the tight fit of the hatch. He got down on the floor and put his fingers on Ben's neck. While he searched for a pulse, he noticed the blood caked on the back of Ben's head. Bending in for a closer look, he began to feel strong blips from a neck vein. He shook Ben lightly and spoke, trying to get Ben's attention. At first Ben moved with the man's hand. Suddenly he resisted the movements and emitted a groan.

The stocky man shook him again.

"Hey, who are you, mate?" The stocky man asked.

Ben opened his eyes and seemed to think about the answer. He stared long at the floor then slowly turned in the direction of the annoying hand. His eyes were glassy; they began to close once more, but again, the damned shake from the hand.

"Who are you?" Ben threw back at the stocky man as his eyes drooped closed.

The man shook him to keep him awake.

This time Ben got angry. "Quit shaking me, and I asked who the fuck are you?"

The stocky man removed his hand and pulled upright to a kneeling position.

"Marine Police. I have some questions for you."

"Oh . . . Okay." Ben's eyes closed.

The policeman lifted Ben and placed him on one of the beds. He went into the head and brought back a damp cloth to place on Ben's forehead. Ben's eyes popped open at the touch of the cold cloth, and when the policeman offered him a drink he gladly took it. After a few minutes he became coherent and managed to keep his eyes open.

"Your ship came in two days ago. You been down here the whole time?" The policeman asked.

"I guess. I remember tying down, but that's about it. Where's Duane?"

"Who's he?"

"The captain. Isn't he here?"

"There's been no one spotted onboard since you arrived. The marina staff didn't see you come in. You mind if I look around while you have a rest?"

"Go ahead."

The policeman went straight to the engine room and wrote down the serial numbers of each engine. He opened a floor hatch providing access to the keel beam and wrote down the serial number he found etched there. He looked in the various cabins, but found nothing of interest until he found bullets for a handgun in Duane's desk. He pocketed the bullets and returned to Ben.

"I guess we better get that head looked at, mate. Do you think you can climb the ladder?"

Ben rolled on his side and pushed himself up to a sitting position where he remained, eyes closed, taking a few slow breaths. His head felt clearer. He managed to get his feet under him and started up the ladder. When he stood near the top he sat on the deck, pulled his legs out, then spun on his haunches to clear the way for the policeman.

"You seem to be moving okay, but there's blood in your eyeballs. I'll take you to a clinic, and we'll see if you need to go to a hospital. But before we leave, I have to tell you that you're under arrest for boat theft."

***

Gray paint. The hospital walls had gray paint. Paint he stared at for three days. The football games on the television he tried to watch had crazy rules so he couldn't follow the action, and although the words spoken on the other television shows were English, they were used to form a language he didn't understand. When the doctors told him his head wounds presented no danger, detective Oren Palwin took him into custody and locked him in a room at the police station, a room covered with gray paint. The same gray paint used in the hospital, but this time he had no television, and both the bed and the treatment were less hospitable.

Detective Palwin listened to his story without reacting during the long narrative. When it ended, he said it might take a few days to verify Ben's story, but he would try to get it done in a jiff. Ben nodded, then waited. Every other day or so, the detective would return to ask a quick question about some aspect of the story. Ben would fill in the details, the detective would nod, Ben would ask if they'd confirmed his story, and Detective Palwin would shake his head negatively. Ben's headaches weakened and became less frequent, but the current batch of headaches weren't related to the blow he'd taken to the head—they were from boredom and frustration.

Day after day, question after question, nothing ever changed.

One morning after Ben had eaten his breakfast, the guard unlocked his cell and asked him to follow him. He found himself alone in a room with a table, bolted to the wall, and four chairs. The change of scenery generated a little curiosity, and instead of sitting with his eyes focused on one spot on a gray wall, he searched every inch of every surface in the room. The variety held his interest for a long time, so he didn't mind waiting. A loud click came from the door as the lock was released. He turned and watched the door open. Detective Palwin entered, followed by two other stern-looking men. The two new men were introduced: Gordon Anderson from the insurance company of the true owner of the ship, and Joel Santos of the FBI. Ben lifted his eyebrows at the introduction of Santos.

"Ben," Detective Palwin started, "We think you're a bloody liar."

The room became very cold for Ben, yet heat wafted up from his collar.

"These two gentlemen want to hear your story from the beginning, so let's start in Idaho, and let's go with the truth this time."

"I told you the truth," Ben said.

"Tell it to us again, Mr. Beck." Agent Santos smiled and spoke with a patient tone while Mr. Anderson kept his eyes from making contact with Ben's.

Ben began his story. During its telling they interrupted him to tell him they had confirmed a number of the facts he had outlined. They had found the ad in his local newspaper, confirmed that Carl had been at the hotel in Coeur d'Alene, confirmed with his friend that he accepted a job to go sailing for a year. Later they confirmed his timing by indicating they had found the record of the room reservations in Las Vegas, but after that, they said, things didn't add up.

When Ben finished his story, Santos looked at Anderson and said, "I'm still not convinced. How about you?"

"Convinced of what?" Ben asked.

All three men ignored him. Gordon Anderson shrugged.

Santos turned to Ben. "Have you ever heard of or met a man named Paul Miller?"

"No."

"Craig Savin?"

"No."

"Randy Foster?"

"No."

Santos opened his briefcase and pulled out a folder. He opened it so that Ben couldn't see inside and flipped through a few pieces of paper before he extracted a photograph. He placed it in front of Ben. Ben looked at it for a second, then looked up at Detective Santos, but said nothing.

"Do you know this man?" Santos asked.

"It's Rudy, Rudy Fletcher. You didn't know that? Who did you think it was?"

Santos leaned forward and looked Ben straight in the eyes and held his stare for a number of seconds, then made a note on a pad of paper in the folder.

"This is the man who drove with you from Idaho to Las Vegas?"

"Yes."

"And then he joined you in Catalina and again in Honolulu?"

"Yes."

"And he stayed with you for about six months in Tahiti?"

"Yes."

"But he didn't sail with you to Auckland?"

Ben hesitated, then said, "Correct."

"It will help you a lot if you can tell us where this Rudy Fletcher is now. Do you know where he went when he left Tahiti?"

Ben hesitated again, then shook his head no.

Detective Santos pursed his lips and twisted them to one side while he thought about this information. Both Anderson and Detective Palwin displayed no interest.

Santos turned to Palwin and said, "We're going to need Mr. Beck's fingerprints." Palwin made a note.

Santos then produced pictures of Carl, Duane, and Miss Malloy, but didn't show the level of interest in them the way he had been interested in Rudy.

"Now," Detective Santos said, "You said you didn't know anything about the boat being stolen until Miss Malloy told you about it in Tahiti, correct?"

"Yes."

"We have nothing but your word on that, and right now your word isn't very convincing. Unless you give us something to prove you were in the dark the whole time, it looks like you're going to be spending some time in jail. You need to lead us to one of these people. Because if you don't, you're all we got, and if you're all we got, then we're going to throw the book at you real hard. And I have to tell you that the company you kept isn't working in your favor. We knew the man you called Rudy Fletcher had an association with Carl Claymont, but we didn't know he was involved in this boat business. If you help us locate him, you'd be doing yourself a big favor."

Ben swallowed hard, and the detective didn't miss his reaction.

"I don't know where he is," Ben said.

"What about Miss Malloy, do you know how we can find her?"

"I said good-bye to her outside the airport in Tahiti. She didn't want me to see which airline she was taking, and I wanted to help her get away from Carl. I gave her some money, but didn't try to find out where she was headed."

"Why didn't this Rudy sail with you to Auckland?"

"Don't know, and I never asked when he didn't drive with us to Huntington Beach or when he didn't sail with us to Honolulu. It seemed Carl had other plans for him from time to time."

"So how did he leave?"

"Don't know."

Detective Santos smiled, then looked at the others before saying, "We've got some things to check into. We may be back to talk to you in a day or so. If you think of something to help us out, then you better let us know. Right now, you're in hot water up to your chin."

Ben felt the bottom drop out of his stomach.

***

A perfect blue sky spread over the Santa Barbara hills. A soft breeze roamed through the canyons, helping to keep everyone lounging at poolside comfortable. Standing at the front entrance, the FBI agent rang the bell a number of times without receiving a response from inside. He heard voices when he checked at the side of the long ranch-style bungalow, so he went back to the door, held his finger on the bell, and listened to the continuous sound of chimes inside the house. Finally the door was pulled open.

"Is this the Labrio residence? I'm looking for a Mark Labrio," he said.

Admitted to the house, he sat on a soft suede sofa while waiting for Mr. Labrio. When Mark arrived, he offered the detective a drink and sat down to answer his questions. The agent asked a few questions related to the *Aurawind* investment, then asked if Mrs. Labrio could join them. A few minutes later Janice appeared, offered him a drink, refreshed her own, and sat on the arm of the overstuffed suede chair that her husband occupied.

The detective showed them a picture of Ben, a mug shot faxed to him from Auckland. Ben looked pale, stoned, tired, and dirty.

"That's him," Mrs. Labrio stated, "but he's seen better days. He has wonderful green eyes."

They talked about the times they had spent with Ben in Catalina and then for the week in Hawaii.

"Did you ever ask him about the yacht?" the detective asked.

"In Catalina I asked a lot of questions about the yacht, but when we were onboard I spent my time with the captain and Carl. They answered all my questions," he answered.

"And Ben kept pouring me those generous glasses of champagne," Mrs. Labrio added with a smile.

Mark Labrio looked at her with a cocked eyebrow, then turned back to the detective. "In Hawaii, I asked him if he thought I should invest in the ship. He looked at me, clearly not understanding what I meant. I had to explain to him my intention to buy a share of the yacht, and then I had to explain how the shares worked. He didn't understand the business end of the investment at all."

"God, Hawaii made me sick," Mrs. Labrio commented then bloated out her cheeks as if she would throw up.

"I'm sorry to hear that, Mrs. Labrio. Well, I won't bother you any longer." With that the detective stood and left.

\*\*\*

Two days later Detective Santos opened the door to the gray-painted room, lifted his leg over the chair, and sat down to face Ben, who waited across the plain wooden table. Ben sat up straight, hands resting on the table, one fist inside the other open hand like a schoolboy during roll call. Neither man spoke, as seconds ran by while they held each other's stare. Finally, Santos said, "Anderson, the insurance guy, might be going soft on you, but I need to know something. The other three, Carl, Duane and the girl, I'm not too concerned about them. Eventually we'll run into them, but the guy you call Rudy, I want him. You spent a lot of time with him; maybe even did a little crime with him. You're the guy who saw him last as far as we're concerned, so help us out, and we'll work something out on the charges. Where is Rudy Fletcher?"

They continued to maintain eye contact while Santos spoke. Ben's brain did laps trying to figure out what to tell the detective. He could tell him what he knew; he could tell him where he had seen Rudy last and under what conditions and set the detective's mind at ease. Or, he could continue to protect himself from potentially more serious charges by pleading ignorance. If he told the truth, it would be his word against no one, until they found Duane, but then they might not trust him because he had lied in the first place. If he continued on the ignorance track, they would continue to look for Rudy. Then if they did find Duane, like they said they would, they would come looking for him. He could also tell them his reason for not telling the truth right from the start, that Duane told him to keep his mouth shut about the boat theft or he would accuse Ben of deliberately killing Rudy.

After his mental revolutions, he responded that he didn't know Rudy's whereabouts.

Santos slapped the table, causing Ben to lean away. With squinted eyes he began spitting out a series of fast questions: "Why was his stuff still in the second cabin? Wouldn't he take his razor if he were leaving the ship for good? Is he supposed to meet you here and pick up his gear when he arrives? Come on, Ben, things don't add up. You know more than you're telling me. Where is Rudy Fletcher?" Spit sprayed from Santos' mouth.

Ben began to feel a craving to physically put Santos in his place for trying to intimidate him, but something about Santos' manner didn't jibe. Santos didn't turn red, didn't hit the table in spontaneous anger. He raised his voice deliberately, not instinctively. He only squinted with his eyes. He didn't seethe.

"I told you . . . I don't know where he is. And if I was in on it, why did they have to knock me out and lock me in my cabin? Would they do that to someone that was part of their plan?" Ben said calmly.

"Yes, if they stopped trusting him or wanted him to be the fall guy." Santos sat and watched Ben's reaction for a short time, then stood and left the room without saying another word.

The next morning, like every morning, Ben's breakfast tray included a small plastic cup filled with a brownish paste. Every morning he ignored it. None of the meals, no matter what time of day, filled him; so after two weeks he felt hungry enough to try the paste. He asked the guard what to do with it and the guard only replied, "You're supposed to eat it, mate." Ben looked at it, scrunching his face, smelled it, then jerked his head back. He scooped a little onto the end of the wooden tongue depressor that served as his butter knife and spread it onto the corner of his toast. He took a deep breath, exhaled loudly, then bit the corner of the toast off and began to chew. After the substance made its way around his mouth, he jumped toward the toilet in his cell and spit the mash into the bowl. He rinsed his mouth at the sink, then sipped his orange juice to cleanse his palate. He turned to the guard and said, "You're wrong. You're not supposed to eat that stuff, you're supposed to flush it."

That afternoon Detective Palwin came to visit.

"You're a right lucky wally, I'd say," he began, "The insurance company isn't going to press charges."

"Really?" Ben said with a wide smile, not believing what he had heard.

"Yeah, they're satisfied with the return of the ship. They don't want to spend any more time on it than they have to. I heard the owner isn't at all happy. He hadn't used the ship for a while and hadn't planned to. Would just as well have had the money. Besides, they talked to those people you mentioned, some investors or something."

"The Labrios?"

"I don't know, didn't pay much attention to the name. They figured you may not have known you were actually stealing the ship, based on your comments; so the insurance guy said to hell with it, didn't want to get involved."

"So I can go?"

"No," Palwin said, "just because the insurance company and the owner don't want to press charges doesn't mean you get to go scot-free. The city of Auckland, the country of New Zealand—and if I had my way, the whole of the Southern Hemisphere—doesn't want you here. You're being deported. You'll be transferred to the lockup at Immigration Services where you'll stay till they put you on a plane.

"You steal a boat, get an all-expenses-paid trip to the tropics, all your meals, and then get free transportation home. It's like you won the grand prize."

At first Ben took this as a slap in the face, then realized he had no way to get back to Tahiti on his own.

"Where do they deport me to?"

"Your home country, fastest possible way."

"I want to be deported to Tahiti. Have them send me there."

"Not likely. In fact . . . no chance at all." Palwin seemed to enjoy shooting down Ben's hopes.

"Can I make a phone call?"

"Local calls only."

Ben flopped back on the cell bed and stared at the ceiling. He felt the coarse blanket against the skin of his arm. He didn't need to answer any more questions. Palwin only intended to make him feel hopeless with his responses. He ignored the detective until he left, but when he heard the door lock behind Palwin he shot up and took two quick strides to the door and gripped the bars. He called to Palwin.

"Hey, what about the *Aurawind*? What are they going to do with the ship?"

Palwin turned and stared at Ben for a second, then turned to walk away.

"Palwin, the ship?" Ben called again.

"Who the fuck cares?" Palwin called back. "Go ask the owner."

# Chapter 20

The fifteen-hour flight evaporated the year that Ben had invested in sailing to a new life. The people at LAX moved like they had important things waiting for them. Signs pointed out where the gates were, where the toilets were, where the telephones were. Ben moved to the telephone and called Tim Leweski back in Coeur d'Alene. Tim's surprise at receiving the call was obvious. Not wanting to provide Tim with a detailed explanation of his recent exploits, but feeling he had to give him something, he summarized. He told him he'd sailed the South Pacific, been in jail, gotten himself deported from a friendly country, arrived in Los Angeles only a few hours earlier, and just got released from Immigration. The abbreviated version made Tim want to know everything that had gone on. Ben agreed to tell him later, but for now he needed some cash to make a few arrangements. He told Tim five hundred dollars ought to do it, knowing it would be tight. Tim wired the money to a cash facility in the airport.

Before leaving Auckland, he had convinced an immigration agent to let him make an international phone call. He called the café at the marina in Papeete. The waiter answered, spoke French, and had no idea who Ben was or what he was talking about. When Ben spoke of his morning ritual of buying coffee for his three friends, the sudden recognition stunned the waiter; he forgot he had always spoken French to Ben, and carried on the remainder of the conversation in English.

First Ben asked if Yves was nearby. The waiter said he was not and hadn't been for a long while. Then he asked if the waiter knew Rene Argent. He did not. Ben then asked the waiter to do him a favor. He asked him to find Yves and tell him Ben had called and would call back in a couple of days at the same time. Would he please have Yves available to take the call? The waiter agreed.

Ben found a cheap motel and slept for a long time. When he woke up, he couldn't remember exactly what time he had made his first call to Tahiti and, with the confusion of the international dateline, couldn't figure out if one or two days had passed. Still he didn't intend to let calendar math cause him to miss contacting Yves. He dialed the operator, and the operator put his call through. He heard the strange sound as the phone rang in the café. The waiter answered after the first ring, and Ben heard excitement in his voice as he reminded him who he was. Then he heard disappointment when the waiter said it had only been one day and that his friend would be at the café the next day, but three hours earlier. Ben said he would call back and said good-bye.

After the call he picked up the yellow pages and looked up marinas. When he found a concentration of marinas located in the same area south of Long Beach, he made a list of addresses. Then he went to shave and take a shower. He didn't want to look bedraggled when he asked the marina operators for information. He'd learned from Carl that he made a good first impression, so why not take advantage of it?

During the flight he'd had plenty of time to put together an initial plan to get himself back to Tahiti, and the marinas played an important part in the plan.

He left his room to grab a taxi. He visited a few marinas concentrated in one area and was received with interest. The people in the marinas understood his request, and said for him to keep in touch. He decided to move to a second area and had another cab drop him near the dock in the parking lot of a marina in the new area that was a little farther away. The lot's asphalt had grayed. The white stripes marking the parking spots were cut with thin lines of black tar. Tufts of grass grew out of the tar as they divided the lot into a series of irregular rectangles. In spots he saw the clear, green and brown gemstone remainders of broken bottles. A rusted barrel dented by a number of meetings with car bumpers lay sideways by a twisted chain-link gate that had the swing knocked out of it. Ben felt disheartened at the rundown setting until he looked past the gate and down the dock to see a forest of yachts, good-sized expensive yachts, tied up to a maze of floating walkways. He walked down to a flat barge, with structures built on top, floating at the end of the main walk. The barge consisted of a long roof on blue support poles over two large white counters with wood-patterned plastic laminate tops. There was no enclosure, but at one end stood a wall of refrigeration units. Some held ice, some sodas, some bait. On the far side a series of fuel pumps lined the barge. A considerable distance separated them. There were openings in the counters on the far side, none on the shore side where Ben stood waiting to talk to the man ringing up a sale for another customer behind the counter. The man was shorter than Ben, older, with long black hair. Ben noticed his hands, black with a lifetime of grease. Thin brown skin over tightly strung muscle made his thin wiry forearms. When he finished he turned to Ben, looked at him from top to bottom to top, then jerked his chin up, to get Ben to talk.

"Name's Ben Beck. A guy at another marina said you might know of some crew requests coming up soon. Is that right?" Ben asked.

"Happens ever so often. Can't think of any right now."

"How often do you get requests?"

"Lots, sometimes. Sometimes not for months. Never happens a ship's looking for a crew at the time a crew's looking for a ship. You care where it's going?"

"I want to get back to Tahiti."

"Back? You been and left . . . now you want to go back."

"Yeah, I sailed there before. I want to do it again."

"We get some those ever so often. You just goin' to do the trip there, you comin' back?"

"No, one-way."

"We get some. . . . Usually need a flight back. You'd save somebody some money if you stayed. Sailed before, right? Okay, leave your name and a number where I can get ahold of ya."

Ben asked the man his name and where the nearest motel could be found. Stew Bishop told him about a place two blocks back of the waterfront that rented by the week, and Ben set out to find it. He paid for the first week and moved in. That night he called Tim Leweski and provided him with a detailed report of his travels thus far.

He did okay with the story until he spent a good deal of time describing his life while he lived at the compound with Maeva and Rene. When he mentioned how he had left without leaving word with them, he got very quiet. Tim had to prod him a little to get him to talk about the rest of the trip. Ben told him everything, except he left out any reference of Rudy being onboard the *Aurawind* when they left Tahiti. After he hung up, he sat and thought about Maeva and how much he wanted to get back to her. He needed to get the plan for his return in motion, but decided he would allow himself one night of inertia for some soul searching.

Maeva held the foremost spot in his mind. Her attitude—or should he say the Tahitian attitude, as he believed it to be—toward the man-woman relationship made him uneasy. By going back to French Polynesia, he would be choosing to commit his entire life to a newly developing feeling for a woman who might, like her mother, shift her own feelings to another man. How would he handle such a shift? Become Rene? What if it had already happened? She hasn't heard a word from him in over five weeks. Six months together, and then he disappears. He could hardly blame her if she had already moved on. The time they did share together seemed very committed, very comfortable. However with her comment about allowing him to enjoy the women on the last trip, how committed could she be? Did he feel strongly enough about her to travel halfway around the world with low prospects for love or work and give up a chance to start over in his own country? In the end it came down to one question: Would he want to live in Tahiti and try to have a life if Maeva didn't want him anymore? He had thought about getting back to her from the first moment he woke up on the *Aurawind*. Now he had to determine if he should.

The next day, he made contacts in a few other marinas and found no trips available to his desired destination. He talked with most of the marinas in the area, but didn't have the resources to check out places farther away.

He checked the time and found a payphone so he could call the café in Tahiti. He hung around outside a convenience store for about a half-hour waiting for the agreed-upon time and then pulled out a roll of quarters. The strange burping ring of the phone system in Tahiti sounded through the wires, and then the waiter answered the phone in English.

"El-low."

Ben identified himself, and the excited waiter rattled off a quick sentence in French. Ben didn't understand a word, but the voice sounded angry. When he heard the phone hit the countertop, he thought he had been ditched. Still he waited. Soon he could hear two voices yammering heatedly in French, and then Yves came on the line.

He greeted Ben in a mix of both languages, and Ben could hear a tremor in his voice. Yves asked question after question about what had happened to Ben and explained that he feared Ben had been killed and dropped into the ocean by Rudy. After hearing Ben's story, he asked when Ben would return. Ben answered, soon, he hoped, then asked if he had talked to Rene and Maeva. Yves said he had informed them of his expected call and that they asked him to report back to them after the conversation.

"Good. Please tell them I'm making my way back, but it may take a few weeks. I'll call in a week at this same time. Will you ask Maeva to come to the café with you?"

"Oui." Yves responded.

"I'll leave a message with the waiter if anything else comes up."

"Tres bon. Ah. . . . There is one more thing. The night Rudy took you away it seems he attacked our friend Le-hiro-de-biere," Yves said sadly.

"Is he alright?" Ben asked.

"No. He's gone."

"Gone? You mean . . . "

There was silence. Then Yves said, "In a week then. Au revoir."

It took a while for the shock of Le-hiro being victim to Rudy's rage to recede. At least Ben knew Rudy would never be able to harm his friends again, and now they all knew that he hadn't deliberately left them and that he intended to come back.

Now he had to find a way to sustain himself in his current surroundings until he could find a ship to Tahiti. He knew the money from Tim wouldn't last too long and that he needed to find a source of income. He checked with a few businesses in the area and found some places that said to come back in a few days.

After a day or two, he'd had enough of the job hunt and decided to make the rounds of the marinas again to see if any trips had come up. He walked down the main dock and spotted Stew Bishop back by the refrigeration units, scooping anchovies out of a holding tank into a large plastic tub. Ben moved to that end of the counter and waited to be noticed, but Stew continued to scoop the little fish.

"Stew? I'm Ben Beck. I stopped to see you a few days ago," he said.

"I remember." He didn't look up. A few anchovies had jumped from the net and flipped about rapidly on the deck. Ben could hear a slight thump-smack noise as they burned up their energy struggling to get back into water. Some made it into the holding tank only to come right back out for bait duty in Stew's next scoop.

"Have you had any crew requests for Tahiti?"

"Kinda. I didn't think it suited so I didn't call."

"Didn't suit?"

"Want'd their yacht in Hawaii. Might go on to Tahiti after a month or so. Didn't think that suited."

Ben walked past the end of the counter and looked out at the open water over one of the gas pumps. He sucked on his teeth for a while, then confirmed to Stew that indeed he didn't want that kind of trip.

"I didn't think so. You still stayin' at the Sleeper's Lodge?" Stew asked.

Ben nodded without looking at him, thinking Stew had looked up from his work when he asked his question.

"I asked you's still staying at that motel I tol' you about," Stew said with a tone of impatience.

"Sorry. Yes I am, but I can't stay there too much longer unless I find some work. You know anybody that needs a laborer?"

"What kind of work you do?"

"Anything I guess. . . . Grunt work."

"Scrub waterlines?"

"Don't know what that is, but probably."

"I get lots of requests to scrub that greasy black smudge off the hulls of these yachts. People leave them sitting in that marine filth too long and then want 'em cleaned up before they go out. You do that?"

"I suppose. How do you do it?"

Stew explained the process of getting in a dinghy and using an acrylic scrub pad to clean around the yacht's waterline. Said he'd pay fifteen dollars for each boat he cleaned and that he had enough requests to keep Ben busy for a while if he wanted. Ben would rather clean hulls than get rejected asking for work, so he started right away. In two days he had enough money to pay for another week at the motel, and it didn't look like Stew's list of requests had gotten any shorter, but within a week Ben had done all of the hulls that needed cleaning. Stew told him he didn't want to lose him if any more requests came in and started getting him to do a number of other odd jobs around the marina. Although Stew wouldn't show it, he liked having Ben around. Every dirty job that Ben performed meant one less for him.

A few days later Ben took an afternoon off to check around with the other marinas he had contacted regarding crew assignments. When he stopped at one down the road a couple of miles, he found the manager. When the manager spotted him, he showed him a big smile and commented that Ben must have been reading his mind, since he was about to call him. One of the patrons of the marina decided to enter a race to Tahiti. Yachts from Los Angeles left a week before yachts from Honolulu and they all met in Papeete. The man was late in deciding to enter the race, so they would be leaving in less than a week. The man's young son would also be on the trip, and the son's age meant he wouldn't be much help with the sailing. The sail would take three weeks, and they planned to stay a while once they arrived. The man might leave the yacht in Tahiti to return at some later date to do some additional sailing in the region and would therefore fly back home. He had offered to provide Ben with a ticket for a return flight. Ben jumped at the trip and asked to call the man right away. When he talked to the yacht owner, he explained his intention to stay in Tahiti, and the man asked him to join him.

Thrilled to have a trip to get back, Ben rushed to Stew's marina to give him the news. Stew had a yacht gassing up at one of the pumps. When Ben came around to the waterside of the barge, hooting about his good news, Stew shot him a cold look and said, "I'll be with you in a minute." He finished filling the tanks and went to the register and posted the sale to the owner's account. When he finished he turned to Ben.

"Got some good news, did ya?"

Ben told him about what had happened at the other marina. Stew congratulated him with restricted enthusiasm, then went about his business. The next day Stew didn't have much to say to Ben. He would give him a job to do, then leave him to do it without any friendly chitchat.

# Chapter 21

At night Stew locked the gas pumps and put what little inventory he had on hand into the cupboards and locked them up too. The refrigeration units weighed a ton and weren't likely to be stolen. And if someone wanted to steal the bait, then let them. The only things he really needed to keep safe were his cash register, his customer account books, and the telephone; so every night he unplugged them, strapped them to his little chrome dolly, and dragged them out to heave them into the trunk of his car. Every morning he pulled them out of the trunk, wheeled them back down the dock, and plugged them in again.

This morning he didn't make it halfway down the dock when he heard footsteps coming up behind him. He stopped and looked back at two men, a large one with black hair and a nice smile, and a black man with a bandage on the side of his head, the result of meeting a flying ashtray. They walked up beside him.

"Good morning," the man with the black hair greeted him.

"Can I help you?' Stew asked, hooding his eyebrows and pushing his jaw forward.

"I wanted to ask you a couple of questions," Carl beamed his smile.

"You a cop?"

"No, I'm not a cop."

"You comin' to check out a yacht?"

"No, no yacht."

"You intendin' to anchor a yacht here?"

"Nope."

"Then you got no questions I can answer." Stew turned and began walking to the barge.

Carl's smile disappeared as he looked over at Duane's expressionless gaze. They took off after Stew again. When they caught up, Stew had gone around to the waterside of the counter and had wheeled his dolly inside. He undid the straps and returned his business machines to their places while Carl asked him about Ben. Stew gave them short answers containing no information, but they didn't seem to mind. They asked questions for a while, then walked down the dock a short distance and waited. Stew unlocked the cupboards and the gas pumps. While he was checking the refrigeration units, the phone rang. When he arrived to answer it, he saw Carl and Duane arrive at the other side of the counter. They stood and watched as Stew picked up the phone.

"Stew here." Stew said loudly then listened for a while.

"Collect call? No I won't accept charges on a collect call." He paused to listen again and said, "No, he wants to talk to me, he can use his own dime." He listened for a few more seconds, then hung up the phone. He turned and looked at Carl. "That was him. Used to live two blocks over that way in a motel, and now he's calling collect. I 'magine he's not coming in."

Carl and Duane looked at each other, then shrugged and began walking down the dock toward the parking lot.

A few miles away, Ben stood in the lobby of a coffee shop staring at the receiver of a payphone. *What the hell?* he thought.

Ben spent the morning sitting in a booth near the kitchen. After the previous night's confrontation with Carl and Duane, his nerves were on edge. The restless sleep in the vacant lot had provided no rest, and his back ached from leaning against the wall. With his back to the wall of the coffee shop, he kept his eyes on the double doors of the front entrance. When the lunch hour approached, he left to spend the afternoon sitting in the vacant lot again. He grew impatient. A few more days of waiting and he would set sail for Tahiti. He was so close to getting away. Why did Carl and Duane have to show up?

Late in the afternoon, he returned to the coffee shop to use the payphone. He called Stew again. This time Stew let him know about the two men who had been asking questions about him.

"I guess I can't show my face around the barge again," Ben said, "I hate to ask you for it, but I need the pay you owe me. Can you meet me somewhere?"

"Sure." Stew didn't ask him why the men were looking for him, but did tell him about a bar located in the back of a large parking lot adjacent to a nearby mall and told Ben he would meet him there after he closed up. Ben went straight to the bar and waited.

At the end of the day, Stew wheeled his dolly out to his car, then drove to the mall to make his daily bank deposit. Once he concluded his business, he walked out the mall entrance side of the bank instead of the parking lot entrance he had come in. He walked down the mall to the far end and exited the mall onto a small street that he crossed to enter a multilevel parking garage. On the other side of the garage, an access road and six-foot cinder-block fence separated the garage from the bar where Ben waited. Stew went through an opening in the fence, came out beside the bar's trash bin, and walked through a back entrance to get to the taproom. Ben sat at a small round table on a brown vinyl bench that ran the length of the wall. Black metal-framed chairs with red vinyl seats sat in front of each table. The walls were dark, the lights were low, and the cool air-conditioning felt good. Ben had a fresh mug of draught, and as the bartender placed another one on the table, he said, "Hey, Stew." Stew grunted.

"Don't tell me nothing," he said, then waited for Ben to understand and acknowledge. "You goin' to be okay?"

"I just need to survive here for a few more days."

"Phone me. I'll let you know if they come back. I think they're gone though."

"I hope so," Ben said.

Stew lifted his glass and downed its contents. He put the glass back on the table and smiled, enjoying the carbonation burn. "Here's your money. Call me before you set sail, let me know you got away . . . " Stew paused for a second. "And good luck." He stood and departed through the back of the bar.

The day before departure Ben bought himself a few things, and that night took a cheap motel room to wash off the vacant lot. The shower felt good. When he finished, he called Stew. The day of their previous meeting, after Stew had left him in the bar, he had picked up his money and counted it. Stew had slipped him a little extra. Ben called Stew, wanting to give it back, but Stew refused. Ben wanted to thank him and convinced him to meet at the bar for a drink before he left for good.

Ben arrived first and sat at a table near the back of the bar. He hadn't waited long when Stew arrived. A waiter dropped a glass of beer in front of him.

As Ben lifted his glass to Stew, he saw Carl and Duane approaching. Carl grabbed a free chair from the nearest table while Duane lifted the back of Stew's chair and said, "Over there, buddy."

Stew slipped across to sit beside Ben.

Ben smiled silently at both men for a moment, then turned to Duane and asked, "How's your ear? You're taking good care of it, I hope."

"It burns a little," Duane replied.

"Ben, I'm inclined to believe that you really didn't know anything about the money, so I'm not going to bother you about that. But I need you to tell me how to find Miss Malloy. Will you help me?" Carl said.

"No."

"Ben, you're all I've got."

"And I've got nothing for you."

Carl leaned back in his chair. He crossed his arms over his chest as he tried to stare Ben down. Ben cocked his head a little to one side; as he did, he saw someone familiar come through the front door. He watched for an instant, then looked away from the man so they didn't make eye contact. He leaned to the side, attempting to keep Carl between himself and the figure who took a seat at the far end of the bar. Ben couldn't get a clean look at the man, but the size and posture of the figure plucked at his memory.

Carl uncrossed his arms and leaned forward to press his face close to Ben's and began to hiss words from between tightly drawn lips. "Now you listen to me, Ben. I'm not going to be nice if you don't give me what I need. If I walk out without knowing where she is, I'm going to send someone back to deal with you. You understand?"

As he spoke, Ben's memory flashed the identity of the new arrival. He hadn't really heard what Carl had said, so he didn't respond to Carl's anger. Instead he shrunk in his seat and said, "Oh shit."

Carl looked at him as if his words had had the desired effect, until Ben gathered himself and spoke. "Here's what I'm going to do for you. I'm going to give you a head start," he said.

Carl and Duane both sat up higher and compressed their eyebrows, then leaned in a little closer, placing their elbows back on the table.

"You're going to give us a head start?" Carl asked.

"Yep. And when I tell you why, you're going to need it and you're going to want it."

"Pretty ballsy, Ben. I understand you got that way near the end of the trip. But let's cut out all this crap. Tell me where she is and you'll live. If I get nothing from you, you're going to get a lot of pain from me. You're the problem now, Ben. A problem I'm going to be glad to get rid of."

"Well, how's this for some crap? That guy sitting at the bar," Ben continued, "he's the FBI agent that interviewed me in Auckland. If he's been watching me, it's because he wants to get to you. And now he's got you."

Ben stopped to let them think about this fact. Carl and Duane didn't attempt to look around and confirm what Ben had said. Instead they sat silently going over their options if Ben wasn't bluffing and the agent was actually there.

"There's a way out of this if you're interested," Ben said, interrupting their thoughts.

"What have you got?" Carl asked.

"First, I want to tell you once more that I don't know how to find Miss Malloy. I asked where she was going, and she didn't want me to know. Second, I had no idea she took your money. And third, I want you to fuck off and leave me alone. I'm tired of your bullshit. I don't think he knows who you are yet, but I can bring him up to speed really quickly if you like. What do you say?"

"Shoot."

"I'm going to go over to the agent, and I'm going to tell him who you are. He doesn't want you two. But he's got a sore spot on his ass for Rudy and thinks you guys will hand him over. I didn't tell him where Rudy ended up, and I'd like to keep it that way. So you see, I want you to get away. Do you want me to tell you how to get out of here?" He waited for both men to nod, then continued. "Down the hall beside Stew, you get to a rear door. It comes out by the trash. There's an opening in the fence back there. Across the street from the opening is the parking structure for the mall. Go through there, get into the mall, and get lost.

"I told this agent in Auckland that I would help him as much as I could, and I'm going to keep my word. In about ten minutes. If he recognized you guys, he'd have grabbed you by now. So when I say go, slip out the back."

Ben watched Agent Santos. When the bartender went over to talk to him, Ben gave Carl the word. He and Duane moved quickly toward the hall as Ben slid into Carl's chair and motioned for Stew to cross over into Duane's.

"If the agent comes over here I might not be able to give them their full ten minutes," Ben said.

"Don't try to explain nothing to me," Stew said, "You still think you'll set out tomorrow?"

Ben looked at Stew and paused before saying, "The trip got scrapped. The guy called and said his wife had second thoughts about letting the kid make the trip, so I might not go back now. Might go back to Idaho or something." Duane had lied to the harbormaster in Catalina and to the commodore in Honolulu, so Ben thought he might as well try to confuse Stew with the same technique.

They sipped their beers, speaking infrequently. Every second that passed without Agent Santos coming to the table, Ben considered a huge reward. When his nerves could stand it no longer, he turned to Stew. "Thanks for your help. Do me one last favor and wait here for another half hour after I leave." Stew nodded, and Ben stood and walked over to look down the hallway to the rear door. He rocked back and forth, looking concerned, then turned and hurried toward Santos. Before he got to him he called out, "Santos, that was them! They took off."

Santos spun around in his seat. "I know it was them, I'm waiting for the other guy. Where did they go?"

"They went to the can down that hall, but they didn't come back. I was waiting for you to come and get them."

"Shit." Santos opened his jacket lapel and spoke into it briefly. He told Ben to wait in the bar, then ran down the hall toward the rear exit. He went out the back door slowly and looked both ways. He saw the back cinder-block fence and turned to his right to see another fence running off at a right angle. He walked toward it and slowly looked around the corner along the building and saw the front parking lot of the bar. He turned the other way and went back along the back fence behind the trash bin to the opening. To his left, two agents approached on either side of the street. Santos pointed to the entrance of the mall's parking lot and crossed the street where they began a search among the hundreds of cars. When they spotted the mall on the other side, Santos sent the other two agents in for a quick look and went back to get Ben.

Ben hadn't wasted any time after Santos went out the back. As soon as he disappeared, Ben walked out the front door and kept going straight to the far end of the parking lot, where he turned left into a residential subdivision.

Roughly ten minutes earlier, Carl and Duane had left by the rear door and they, like Santos, first turned to their right. When they got to the end of the building and looked down to the right and saw the parking lot, they didn't turn back and go to the opening in the fence; they climbed the fence in front of them and landed in someone's backyard. They walked to the front of the house and disappeared down the street.

Thirty minutes later, Stew finished his second glass of beer. Instead of going out the back like he normally did, he decided not to go the way the agent had gone and walked out the front door. He then took a long walk around the mall to get to his car, which he had left in front of his bank. The next morning when he arrived at work, Agent Santos met him at his car. They had a long talk, but Stew had nothing helpful to say.

# Chapter 22

It took no time at all for Ben to get used to being at sea again. His captain, Allan Martin, didn't have to explain much to him after giving him a tour of the forty-six-foot yacht *Breeze Rider*. The night watch schedule had been set, and Ben was up every four hours to write down the course and check the sails. During the day Allan's son, Toby, followed Ben around asking questions. Allan appreciated the time Ben took to explain to the boy the setting of sails and the reason for jibing and why sails were set to starboard or to port. With each little lesson, Ben also talked about the wind—which direction it came from and how it was caught by the sails. Then he gave Toby the sailing term for the heading the ship was on based on the wind factors. Ben hoped he would be able to ask Toby to describe the headings by the end of the sail to Tahiti.

After a week, Ben asked Allan to teach him what was going on in the pilothouse. He told Allan that someday he wanted to own a yacht, but even before that happened he would like to be able to at least pilot a yacht with some confidence. On Ben's last ship the captain had stated quite clearly that if he should become sick or incapacitated in any way, Ben would not be able to handle the ship on his own. Ben didn't want to feel that helpless at sea ever again.

At the mention of his last ship, Allan asked him about his time and responsibilities aboard the *Aurawind*. Ben knew he had nothing to hide, except for the end of Rudy, so he began to tell the story of his journey from Coeur d'Alene to Auckland.

Between the storytelling and the sailing education, he kept busy during the day. The only time he had to himself was during the night when he had to get up and take the course readings.

In the early mornings, after he noted the readings in the log, he would sit by himself in the blue-black dark of the sea before sunrise to listen to the wind race across the sails and to think about what awaited him in Papeete. Seeing Maeva again caused him the most concern. He wanted her to understand that he had no control over his departure from the island and that he never meant to leave her. He hoped she would believe the fact that he wanted to be with her always, that being away from her made him realize the truth of his feelings toward her. He also hoped that she felt the same.

Yet he acknowledged that he had no sign that she felt the same way. She hadn't come to the phone when she knew he would be calling, and he never had a chance to call Papeete again after telling Yves he was making his way back to the island.

Ben's intention to have the ability to take control of the pilothouse helped somewhat to keep him from getting bogged down in the what-ifs of his return to Papeete. His gathering of information for the purpose of sailing a ship required full concentration. He needed that skill to enhance the opportunity in Tahiti. He had to be able to sail a yacht, even if coastal sailing was all he ever did. Allan asked Ben why he took such keen interest in helming a ship. When Ben told him of his plans to get back in the sail-tour business once they were back in Tahiti, Allan asked about the business opportunity. Ben explained his relationship with Rene Argent and his network of resorts feeding him tourists to take out on one-day sailing trips. He hoped the network hadn't dried up because of his unexplained absence. Allan hummed a slight interest.

For the remainder of the sail, Ben became Allan's devout student. Toby pouted at the loss of someone to hang out with because Ben spent his time reading charts and sitting in the chair behind the wheel. On the occasions when his duties required that he make adjustments to the sails, he found Toby right on his tail, eager to help and loaded with questions. Ben could tell Toby missed the sailing lessons, so he tried to spend more time teaching the boy about the duties of a deckhand.

At meals, Allan became Ben's student, learning about how Ben planned the daytrips he had offered on the *Aurawind*. He wanted to know which locations Ben went to and what activities were available at each site. Ben told him about the small nearby islands with the excellent snorkeling and picnicking that Maeva had suggested, and also told him about Yves' cooking skills and his fountain of local information.

After hearing about what Ben had in place for the venture, Allan suggested they should go on one of the daytrips once they were in Tahiti. If it turned out to be as interesting and straightforward as Ben made it out to be, then he might be interested in becoming a partner. Of course, he would want to talk with Rene and some of the resorts to make sure that the venture Ben had described wasn't imaginary. After all, Ben had just spent a few days explaining a grand scheme involving the theft of a yacht. If his story panned out, and the resorts were still willing to be part of Ben's day-sailing venture, then Allan was truly interested.

The last week of the sail seemed to Ben as if it would never end. The navigation was set, and there were few course corrections, which meant there weren't too many things about sailing that Allan could teach him. The wind remained constant, so the sails remained in place and no adjustments were necessary. Ben didn't even have much opportunity to teach Toby any more about the art of catching the wind. They seemed becalmed, even while maintaining a steady pace.

With more time on his hands than he wanted, Ben continued to grind on what he could expect when he arrived back at the island. Would anyone trust him again? He feared the arrival; he feared receiving the worst possible reaction to his return, and refused to think about his situation if Maeva rejected him. At the same time, he wanted to get it over with. Once he knew where he stood, he could begin to build from there. And no matter how bad his reception could be, anything was better than being chased by Carl and Duane. He was—he hoped—done with those two forever.

When they tied up in Papeete, Ben took Allan and Toby to the café first, so they could get something to eat that wasn't cooked onboard. The Frenchman in the café greeted them in French and hugged Ben, kissing him on both cheeks. He had them sit, and brought wine and bread for them while he cooked them a special dinner. He tried to stay in French while he talked to Ben, but he was so eager to answer Ben's questions that he slipped into English often.

"Has Maeva been by lately?" he asked first.

"Oui, monsieur. Today she came."

"Was she here looking for me?"

"Oui. Why else would she come?"

"And Yves?"

"The same."

"It seems your friends really want to see you again." Allan said. "You can relax a bit."

Ben's smile was uncontrollable. "Yeah, I guess. It's getting dark, or I'd ride out to see her and Rene. Maybe she'll be back tomorrow with the van and we can go out to their place so you can meet Rene."

"You sure you don't want to find a way to get there tonight? We'll stay onboard. You can come get us in the morning."

Ben nodded and said, "Ten o'clock?"

Ben remembered to check the headlight on the scooter before heading out to see Maeva. As he approached the compound, he spotted the glint of eyeballs in the ditch. He twisted the throttle to full, tucked his legs in tight to the cycle's frame, and bent low with his chin almost on the handlebars. The dogs began their barking, and he saw the flash of teeth while he concentrated on keeping the bike moving straight ahead. He passed the scruffy animals without incident and slowed as he approached the turn into Rene's place.

\*\*\*

The car dealership's slowest days always happened on Mondays. Tim Leweski liked to give his salesmen a break; he scheduled a sales meeting during the lunch hour so they could take their time coming in after a busy weekend. During the meeting, he reviewed the weekend's sales, announced sales targets for the coming week, and pumped the group up to hit the phones. He wanted them to call all their prospects to see if they were still interested in buying a car and to tell them that a few new cars in the model they were interested in had just arrived on the lot. After the meeting, they flooded out and poured into the sales room where they told jokes until someone suggested that they grab something to eat before the evening rush.

Tim returned to his office where he removed his sports coat and hung it on the coat rack behind his desk. He took a cardigan from one of the hooks and put it on while standing at the window, looking out at the fifty or so vehicles angle-parked in straight rows. He watched the lot jockeys brush the snow or scrape the ice that had accumulated during the morning snow flurry.

Before Tim had buttoned up his sweater, big thick flakes of snow the size of dimes began to descend from the fuzzy gray sky to land on the recently cleared sedans. Gradually, each of the lot jockeys looked skyward and cursed. The newest worker continued with his scraping until the others yelled and told him to forget it. Slowly they began to wander back to the service and body shop.

Tim returned to his desk. He checked the lights on his telephone to see if the sales calls were in progress. Only one had a yellow light, his private line.

"This is Tim," he said.

"Tim, it's Ben."

Tim sat in his overstuffed burgundy leather chair and caught up with his friend. They contrasted the weather, discussed mutual friends, and asked about loved ones for a few minutes. Ben asked if Tim had received the money he had sent, and when it seemed like all topics for discussion had been exhausted, Ben asked Tim about what he really wanted to know.

"Did you get any calls about me from a strange woman?"

"Yes, a few months ago. She was very brief. After she asked if I was a friend of yours, she said to tell you she was okay and hung up. What's that all about?"

"She's the one I told you about that worked for Carl, the one that ran away. I asked her to leave word with you to let me know she got away safely."

"Well, that's all she said. You still not going to tell me where you are?"

"Best if I don't, but it shouldn't be too hard to figure out."

"Yeah. Well, I won't put too much thought into it. No one else has come around looking for you."

"Good. I better go. Later."

Ben hung up the payphone at the orientation center of the pineapple plantation and turned when one of his tourists asked him about the large snails crawling everywhere. He explained their origin, picked one up and smashed it against the rock to the horror of the tourist.

Clear blue sky stood above the rich green hills of the mountain. A slight breeze lifted Maeva's hair and twirled it as she stood in a group of colorless tourists. The white Tahitian tiara stuck behind her ear, her wide, white smile evident as she spouted local history. Ben caught her eye and pointed toward the van, and she asked the tourists to board so they could continue the trip.

With the tourists back in their seats, Ben stood at the front of the van and asked if they had enjoyed the trip so far. He received a favorable response.

"Next stop is the Chinese bakery where we're going to sample the best baguette in the world. Most of the French nationals that taste this bread say it's better that the bread they eat in France. Their opinion may be a little embellished due to the beautiful tropical surroundings. I've never been to France so I've never tasted the French baguette. Maybe it is as good as in Tahiti, but I doubt it."

The slight laugh led him into his newly created sales pitch. He started by confirming that they said they had enjoyed their tour so far, then asked if they had enjoyed traveling around the island with Maeva and himself by land. Indeed they had. He then conjectured that they would probably enjoy sailing around the island with Maeva, himself, and captain Yves aboard the *Breeze Rider*, a fully-equipped forty-six-foot sailboat designed to deliver an exciting tour and the most exotic views of Tahiti from the sea.

# Other Novels by Mitch Davies

## A Wind In Montana

Enjoy the ride through High School with Rory and Victoria. They see changes coming so they begin to make decisions for themselves. First Rory drops out of the school band and basketball programs, alienating his teachers, in order to pursue a prestigious chemistry scholarship. Then they start a relationship and Victoria begins to consider alternatives to the music career she is being groomed for.

## The Inn of Fallen Leaves

Chobei is a disillusioned samurai who, after being forced by his clan to perform atrocities, works as a yojimbo and handyman for a second-tier inn along the Nakasendo Highway. Akiyama is a samurai who wants to maintain the honor of remaining loyal to a clan that no longer wants him. A beautiful woman, Miyo, is attached to one man, but coveted by the other.

Information regarding books by Mitch Davies is available at -

www.pensmithbooks.com